BENDY®

FADE TO BLACK

AN ORIGINAL NOVEL BY
ADRIENNE KRESS
SCHOLASTIC INC.

All rights reserved. Published by Scholastic Inc., *Publishers since 1920.* SCHOLASTIC and associated logos are trademarks and/or registered trademarks of Scholastic Inc.

The publisher does not have any control over and does not assume any responsibility for author or third-party websites or their content.

No part of this publication may be reproduced, stored in a retrieval system, or transmitted in any form or by any means, electronic, mechanical, photocopying, recording, or otherwise, without written permission of the publisher. For information regarding permission, write to Scholastic Inc., Attention: Permissions Department, 557 Broadway, New York, NY 10012.

This book is a work of fiction. Names, characters, places, and incidents are either the product of the author's imagination or are used fictitiously, and any resemblance to actual persons, living or dead, business establishments, events, or locales is entirely coincidental.

ISBN 978-1-338-88905-5

10 9 8 7 6 5 4 3 2   23 24 25 26 27

Printed in the U.S.A.   40

First printing 2023

Book design by Jeff Shake

To all the Bendy fans, old and new.
To people who like to tell scary stories in the dark.
And to the incurable optimists.
—A. K.

Every ending is a beginning. And every beginning finds its end. And so the cycle continues. On and on. A loop on repeat. Drawing itself into itself. Further and further into the shadows. Until you are completely consumed.

It's best not to fight it.

Or maybe that's a lie.

Maybe that's what they want you to think.

The darkness.

And the ink.

PROLOGUE

If you were to walk down Broadway in January 1953, on a day when the snow is falling but the wind blows so fiercely that everything flies at you sideways, where snowdrifts are flattened and cars emerge from the white, like monsters in the dark—if you were to walk down Broadway on a day like that, you would have entirely walked into the chaos without realizing it until it was too late. You might have walked into one of the large hulking men in heavy overcoats and muffs on their ears, or flat caps on their heads because they'd lived in the city long enough and "didn't need no protection." Scarves around their throats, up to their mouths, damp on the inside from breathing heavily.

"Of course it had to storm today," one would say and another would grunt and agree. Then a large steel door would burst open. One of those doors you don't even notice are there until you do. Then you might actually look around you. Look up at the building in front of you. You'd see boarded-up windows. An abandoned warehouse, you might think, right here in the middle of Broadway? Right under your nose?

You might think: *What else goes on in this city that I don't know about, right under my nose?*

"Can I help you?" you might offer as two more large men emerge from the dark inside, carrying large boxes and wheeling heavy crates. You'd notice then that the boxes are stamped with the word "Gent." You might wonder if that was short for "Gentleman," maybe they belonged to an old suit factory. The men would ignore you of course, because they have everything under control. Even as they huff and puff and complain, they know what they're doing.

One of them steps to the side after heaving his end of a crate into a large moving van. He places his hands on his lower back and stretches, the scarf slips around his mouth, the snow finds his mustache quickly.

You don't know why you're so curious. You don't know why it matters. But you might try to make small talk. Even though you have places to go to, and things to do.

"What's all this? Why in a snowstorm?" you'll call out over the wind.

"Has to be done fast. Has to be done now," says the man with the mustache.

"What is all this?" Because the boxes are all such different sizes and shapes and make no sense to you, and again, because something compels you to ask. You might rub your hands together a bit, trying to warm them up.

"Your guess is as good as mine, kid." But then he'll decide he doesn't want to go back to work right away so he'll say, "Some strange things in there, experiments looks like. You probably don't want to know."

What a surprising answer, something you had not anticipated. The building looks so dreary, no hint of life or strange goings-on. "Where are you taking it all?"

"To the Kismet Production Studios, other side of the city. For TV, you know. TV is going to be the next big thing, mark my words," he replies, brushing the snow that has accumulated on his mustache.

You'll nod because you already think it is *the* big thing, nothing next about it. He won't see it though. Through the snow, the wind, even just turning to look at someone is a struggle.

"Harvey, what do you think 'under the radar' means!"

"Oh yeah, sorry." He might look at you now and mime locking his lips, then say, "Forget I said anything."

"Harvey, get over here." And then some choice profane words in the style of all New Yorkers. It doesn't bother you because you are also a New Yorker.

If on this day you were to do all this, you may have been

part of a very small slice of history. Something that only a choice few ever really knew anything about, and those who did have long forgotten. You would have seen a massive crate, large enough to hold a car, which is the only thing you could think to compare it to, be craned over, held by large heavy chains, watch it creak in the wind as Harvey trudges his way over to help steady its descent from a window up high.

You'd have seen the word "fragile" in large, black, inky letters along each side beneath the word "Gent" again.

You'd have felt the wind pick up speed.

If on this day you had been there. To witness both the beginning of a thing and the end.

But of course you weren't.

And you never saw it.

And the truck, once loaded, drives off into the snow, disappearing into the flurries. And there is a stillness next to the building.

And then from deep within the walls a sound like an echo of something. Like a roar or a scream.

Or maybe it's just the wind.

From an old journal found in Joey Drew's Greenwich Village apartment in 1972, dated New Year's Day 1953.

~~The Illusion of Living Second Edition~~

~~PART VII~~

~~The End Is The Beginning~~

~~The end of Joey Drew Studios was part of a well-laid plan. The studio closed in 1948. Now you may feel some level of sorrow for me, old Joey. You might concern yourself that I was heartbroken. But~~

Sometimes when I'm asleep I dream I'm in Bendy's world. The walls around me cartoonishly pulled high into the sky, warped and mangled, drawn by hand. And the ink seeps between the cracks in the planks of wood. I dream I'm walking down a hallway, the floor covered in ink, like the shallows of an infinite bay. He calls out to me. They all call out to me. And I wonder if I am truly dreaming or if I've slipped into another world. A world more real than what we call real.

I wake up. I am in my bed.

My studio is gone.

But I am not.

I am here.

And dreams never die. They just shift and squeeze themselves through different cracks. Until they find you again. Consume you again. I will wait until they do. I can be patient.

I'm not frightened.

I've never been scared of the ink.

~~No one will read this no one will read this no one will read this no one will read this~~

1

I have always been an incurable

optimist. That's what my parents called me at least. It made it sound like I had a disease. In fact, the first time Mother ever told me this, I genuinely panicked. I was very little, and I didn't know what "optimist" meant. I just knew it was a big word, and big words frightened me. I figured that big words were invented to hide the truth, because if you wanted to just say something, there were a lot of little words that worked. Of course now that I'm almost officially an adult I feel differently. Big words are marvelous and exist to be even more precise in our communicating.

But when I was little, well, I thought my mother was telling me that I was going to die.

I cried so hard I could barely breathe as she held me close, desperately trying to explain that being an optimist was a positive thing.

"An optimist sees the good in the world. They are happy and positive."

Still more sobbing.

"Don't you see, Rosebud, you bring us such joy!"

"I. Don't. Understand," I said between heaving sobs. Snot flowed out of my tiny nose. I remember that very well. The grotesque has always fascinated me, even as I evidently went through life as if skipping through a meadow. At least according to my mother's perception of it all.

Mother's hand released her tight grip on my heaving back. Even so young, I understood she was trying a different tactic with me. "Not everyone sees the world like you." Her warm hand slowly started stroking my hair. I almost instantly felt calmer, even as I clung to her knee with my sharp little nails digging into her leg.

"I don't see the world as anything!" I insisted, feeling desperate, but my breathing became more regular.

"Rose, we all have our own little ways of looking at the world. Some people see only bad things. They see dangers and grumpy people."

"I see dangerous things! I always look both ways before crossing the street."

"Of course you do because you're a good girl." A heavy sigh as my poor mother tried to explain the concept of internal bias to a six-year-old. "It's like this: You know how yesterday it rained?"

"Yes, I know that."

"But we still dressed you up in your raincoat and boots and went to the park and played?"

"Of course I remember. It was only yesterday."

"Well, was it a good day?"

Five-year-old me rolled her eyes very hard at that, which was tough because my face was smushed into her leg. "Of course. We jumped in puddles." Puddle jumping was amazing;

Mother understood I felt that way. What she didn't understand was why it was amazing. Sure, the splashing was the best part. But I liked how the world was all upside down in puddles, how it wasn't quite like a reflection in a mirror so it looked kind of like another world was inside there. I always thought that if you jumped hard enough you could jump right into a whole other world, the same as ours but a little different. Mother didn't know that part. She wouldn't have understood anyway. It was my own private little secret make-believe.

"Well, you see some people might have thought yesterday was a bad day because it rained. Because it was gloomy and not sunny outside."

"They would have?"

I pulled my face away and looked up at Mother. She was very pretty, and her halo of curls always made me feel warm inside. "Yes," replied Mother. She smiled that soft smile back. It was a special kind of smile, only for me. And for Ollie. Though Ollie wasn't around yet. So I thought at the time it was a secret thing between mother and daughter. But it turned into a secret thing between mother and daughter and son. Which, of course, I was perfectly happy with. Especially since Ollie and I had our own secret looks between us.

"They don't like puddles?" This was a hard concept for me to grasp.

Mother let loose a small laugh and sat us both down on the settee. She held me in her lap, her arms wrapped around my waist, mine around her neck as I stared at her intently.

"Some people can only see the disappointments, the bad things in the world. But you see the good."

"Because the good is there," I explained.

"Exactly," she replied. She pulled me in close so I could feel her warmth and smell her perfume.

I thought about it all, about seeing the good in things and being an optimist. I thought it was funny: If I saw good in everything, then why had being called a word I didn't understand fill me with fear? Shouldn't I have thought it was exciting? Me, the incurable optimist? Maybe I was more complicated than Mother understood. I decided it had to be that. I also really liked the word "complicated." It sounded complicated in and of itself.

"I still don't understand," I explained, though not able to articulate my doubts. "All I said was that Father would be home safe and sound soon."

"I know." She squeezed me tighter.

"That isn't being an optimist. That is just the truth." Now she squeezed me so tight it kind of hurt a little.

"I know, Rosebud, I know."

And then it was Mother's turn to cry.

2

"I got the job!" I burst into the foyer and I think I did expect that all three of them would be standing, waiting with bated breath for me to return from the city, but it was empty. As it always was. It made sense—who spends their free time in hallways after all? But I heard my mother's "Yay!" from the kitchen and I followed the sound to find her and Ollie together making banana bread. Or at least she was. Ollie was just covered in a mess of ingredients. If there was one thing I knew about the kid, he liked to sneak a taste.

"The TV job?" asked Ollie. He was a boy obsessed. Even though we couldn't afford our own television, Ollie just thought it was the keenest thing. Your own little movie theater right in your front room. And his friend Pete had one. We all knew that. We all went to the big party to unveil it and watched *The Jack Benny Program* together, piled into their tiny sitting room. Kids on the ground in a heap, parents on the sofa, a few kitchen chairs, or leaning against the archway into the room.

I ran over to give his hair a tussle and a safe, ingredient-free hug. Not easy—he was really covered head to toe. How on earth did he do that? "You proud of me, little guy?" I asked.

"I'm always proud of you, but yes, this makes me extra proud. I'm going to go tell Pete." Ollie was up on his feet but Mother had him by the shoulders almost instantly.

"Not until after we finish. We don't leave a task halfway through."

Ollie nodded and sat back down. He was such an amenable kid. He wasn't like the other seven-year-olds on the street, boisterous and trying to jump on the back of the milk truck. He played outside, he had his friends, but his energy was very contained. A small orbit around just him. Though he did get very competitive when we played marbles; with that it was every boy or girl for themselves.

"Why don't you go tell your father. He's in the living room."

I nodded and smiled; I was already planning to. But her tone of voice said more than her words. I knew it well. Father was having a bad day. A puddle day, child me might have called it. Even now, nearly eight years after his return, he had these days. They were fewer, and he was able to work now and spend whole weeks in our world with us. But he still had these kinds of days. Telling him my good news would hopefully break him out of it.

You see, Father had thankfully not died in the war. That was the good news. That was all that had mattered to me when he came home. It hadn't bothered me that he looked skinnier than when he'd left because, at ten years old, I had lived almost double my life by the time he returned, and who he had been before was a faint memory to me. Almost like a dream.

A dream.

While my father lived in a waking nightmare.

That was the bad news.

The older men in the neighborhood called it "shell shock" and Mother said it was "combat fatigue." Neither was a term I had heard before, but I knew a lot more words now, at nine, and I was excited to learn some more. But these words did not make me feel good even with my optimistic outlook. I tried, I really did. I told Mother that the important thing was that he was home, and that he was still good at hugs. That we were a whole family again.

But as the months went by, Father retreated further and further into himself. He was becoming a shadow even as Mother grew bigger and bigger because of Ollie. Mother was round and rosy, but her hair was thinner. And while she smiled and played with me still, I saw her expression darken every time I caught her in a quiet alone moment. When she thought no one was looking. Sitting in the shadows, like a darkness had passed over her.

Darkness played with our family a lot in those first few years after Father returned. There was love and kindness there, but my parents would dip into those shadows. Mother and Father could be taking Ollie for a walk in the pram, and I could be running beside them with my jump rope, the sun could be out, not a cloud in the sky, but still the darkness would find them. I saw it fill them up, like pouring water into a glass, higher and higher, to the very top, spilling over. I desperately wanted to brighten them up, but how could you shine a light inside a person?

As a child I had called them puddles. I always liked playing in puddles when I was very young. Splashing around. The idea of them being portals to other fantastical worlds. But, the older I got, the more I came to realize what puddles actually were:

dark and murky water, where your reflection looked back up at you from below, grotesque and brown, and if you jumped too hard it got water in your boots. Made your feet squishy. And so, at eleven years old, I said it one afternoon. When Mother disappeared inside herself again, it was like she'd fallen into darkness, into a puddle. It felt right, it felt accurate. "Are you in your puddle again?" I'd asked as I saw my mother seep into her faraway thoughts.

And Mother, who had always appreciated my cleverness with words, gave me her soft smile. The smile just for me and Ollie. So I said it again the next time, and the next. And each time for a moment she'd step out of the puddle, dry, crisp, clean and reach out for me. And sometimes she'd stay a while. But other times she'd slip back quickly, and I'd have to take baby Ollie onto the stoop and we'd play in the sunshine. Where it was safe.

The problem was that on the outside Father looked healthy. Father looked well. He came back entirely intact on the outside. He could do chores, he could fix a leak or shingle, he could pick up Ollie. I know that some of my friends were mad at me because of that. Because their fathers had not come back with all their limbs. And when Father came back, he came back entirely. But he hadn't really and you couldn't explain. You could try, and try I did. But how do you explain puddles to someone? How do you explain his screams in the night to your friend whose father woke up because of real pain?

No, those were unkind thoughts to think. Father *was* in real pain. He would never pretend that kind of thing. Father had always been a quiet, warm soul, never complained about anything as far as I could recall, though I had been so young when he left. But memories of him—not clear, precise pictures like a movie, more like a feeling or when you smell something that reminds you of something good but you can't quite place it—those memories hinted at who he had been before for me. Even in the puddles he'd reach out to hold my hand or give me a wink. He tried so hard to pull his head up to the surface. So his screams had to be very real. The pain had to be real.

"The doctors say that sometimes your father can't tell what is real from what isn't," Mother had explained. Of course she had tried to explain it because she didn't believe in keeping secrets.

"Like when you wake up from a nightmare and forget where you are even though you're in your bed in your room," I said. It wasn't a question, I understood what she meant. I was relating.

Mother nodded.

"He thinks he's still in the war," I said.

"Sometimes. But he also knows he's home, with the people who love him. And we just need to keep reminding him of that."

I was very good at taking instructions. I was always the top of my class, the first to answer a question, and the one assigned to lunch duty the most often. I was responsible. And I could remind Father that I loved him.

At age eleven, with Ollie not yet even one, I took my duties incredibly seriously, but I was excited by them as well. I knew we just had to work hard to keep Father here with us and not in the puddles so that one day he would leave them completely. And then Mother would too.

Ollie was truly my primary concern. Little Ollie with his chubby cheeks and impossible hands that didn't really work except when they held on to your finger so tight, like he would never let go. Little Ollie, who grew every single day and reached out for me every time I was in the room. I was his person, and he was mine.

Our age difference was actually very normal for so many on our street. So many babies popped up all of a sudden when the war ended, and so many only children like myself suddenly had these important new big sister or big brother responsibilities. I didn't care when Ollie cried in the night. Maybe it was because I knew his cry was pure and there was an easy solution, unlike when I heard my father cry out. Or maybe it was because of that connection: When he hurt, I hurt. And I was going to fix it. I solved all the problems.

Maybe that's also part of being an optimist: When you believe that things will work out okay, then you can look easily for the solutions. Because there are always solutions.

You just have to find them.

Even if they are hidden in the dark.

Or deep inside the puddles.

The living room was inky black, the curtains drawn, the lights off. A thin beam of light managed to sneak in between the two heavy pieces of fabric Mother had draped across the windows. They were normally pretty, a pale green with large pink roses on them. They matched the fabric of the sofa and the wingback chair that Father was sitting in, his eyes closed. There was something unsettling about the dark room in the brightness of the day. Something that sent little prickles up my spine. I quickly shook them off.

I could make myself small and quiet. I'd learned how to do it many years ago. I knew how to creep through the house from my room to the kitchen and back without making a sound. How to close a door without a creak. To gently rock Ollie's cries to content gurgles when he was a baby. I knew how not to startle with my quietness, which is a whole other lesson. It's one thing to pretend to be invisible, but to do it without scaring anyone? That's quite something else. You don't want to sneak up on anyone, you don't want to startle them, you don't want them to lash out at you from within their nightmare.

You want to wake them gently.

So I made myself quiet and small and entered the room. Then as I crossed the carpet toward Father, I made a small sound. It doesn't matter what the sound is, a footstep a little heavier on the ground than the others, a ruffling of your petticoat under your skirt. Or in this case a quiet private clearing of the throat. Not one to gain attention, just something meant just for you. Except of course it was meant for him.

His eyes opened.

I continued my journey as his head turned to see me. He came out of the puddle and smiled.

"Rosebud," he said, his voice strained and tired like someone who has just woken up after a night's sleep. "So, do we have good news?"

I nodded and leaned against the arm of the chair. "I got the job."

"Well, I would have been surprised if you hadn't. They clearly have good taste." He took my hand in his and gave it a squeeze. I squeezed back.

"Clearly," I replied.

"And I'll bet Ollie is excited. Big sister and the big city. Big dreams." He looked tired, so very tired. It was something strange that I had observed that the more my father slept, the more tired he was. When he was deep in the puddles, he was exhausted. The world he was living in inside his own mind drained him far more than the real one.

"He is. He is also covered in flour."

Father laughed. "These are two very expected Ollie things."

We paused. Together. Holding hands.

"When do you start?"

"Monday. They want me as soon as possible."

Father closed his eyes again. "That's wonderful," he said. But he was already slipping under and away from me. Still I held his hand. Because it was warm. And that was all I needed to remind me that even if it felt like he was gone, he was still right here.

It was important to remember things like that.

That really the puddles were just a metaphor.

That none of it was real.

3

By Monday Father was much better and we were able to draw back the curtains in the morning, letting the sun flood the living room. He even joined me on my walk to the subway stop since he had to go to Mr. Powers's place to clean his eaves and it was on the way.

Then I was on my own, and it was thrilling. It's a funny thing growing up on the edge of a massive city; you do get used to it always being there, looming in the distance. And you love the special occasions: Christmas at Rockefeller Plaza, window shopping on Fifth Avenue. But you also take it for granted, and there can be months that go by before you venture across the bridge or through a tunnel. Brooklyn was very much its own little city, even if it was just a borough. Little communities can sometimes seem far more tangible and real than a large, overwhelming city full of tall towers and busy strangers. But I'd always loved Manhattan. It might have been my optimistic nature, but the sounds and activity excited me. I saw possibility around every corner, even if they revealed small dead-end alleys, but oh the secrets in those alleys!

I had always wanted to work in the city as a kid. I hadn't much cared what I did, but I knew I wanted to experience it.

While many of my friends worked for their family businesses or toward getting engaged and settling down, I was rather steadfast. I'm certain Mother had always been disappointed I'd never had a long-term beau. The boys I'd dated had been fun but oh so local. I wasn't interested in dating someone I had also seen every day at school. And I certainly didn't want to spend the rest of my life in Brooklyn.

It was silly, but Manhattan could have been Timbuktu for all my neighbors thought. Even though I was still living at home, and even though there were plenty of dads who went into the city for work every day, for some reason everyone had had an opinion on my voyage. Make sure to wear two layers of socks, it's colder in the city. Make sure to bring my own lunch, the city is expensive. Make sure not to talk to anyone I didn't know.

The city is dangerous.

So I sat on the train as we barreled into the deep burrowed blackness, bundled up in my winter coat and hat and mitts. Two pairs of socks on. My brown paper lunch bag in my lap to make sure the bottom didn't get soggy from the wet on the ground. I made eye contact with a man, probably in his forties, hat on head, collar turned up, scarf tight around his neck. I couldn't help but smile at him. I was excited. And besides, I always smiled at people. I couldn't help it! Now, I was no small-town girl—I knew you left people alone on the bus, on the subway, but I just wasn't good at hiding my feelings. And my feelings generally were those of excitement, *especially* when I was on a bus or a subway. He squinted at me, suspicious, and turned to look out the window into the black tunnel.

Fair.

Half an hour later I was climbing up out onto the street. My squinting friend actually got off at the same stop as well, and he gave me a kind of resentful salute as we parted ways, touching the brim of his hat at me with a scowl. A polite kind of grump.

I had the address on a scrap of paper in my purse and even though I had it memorized, the butterflies in my stomach insisted I double-check. I definitely didn't want to go into the wrong tower; my cheeks burned at the thought. There, I saw it! A large number in brass attached to a new, gleaming building. I made my way over as quickly as I could. A man accidentally held the door open for me as I dashed through before he could exit, and I quickly went up to the security man behind the desk.

"Mr. Papadimitriou?" I asked. I wanted to declare it, inform him, let him know that I was now a working professional seeking another working professional. But no, it came out as a question. A squeak.

For his part, the security man just nodded and picked up a phone. "There's a girl here. Name's . . ." He held the receiver to his chest and looked at me expectantly.

"Rose!"

He waited.

I waited.

He put the receiver back against his ear. "She says her name is Rose. Just Rose. Right. I will."

"Rose Sorenson," I said, making the connection only after he had hung up the phone, and he nodded. He was tolerant.

"Someone will be down to get you. You can wait over there." But he didn't point anywhere, so I took a few steps to the side, and then a few more when a woman started to speak with the security guard. And I found myself accidentally behind a large fern. I could have stepped in front of it of course, but for some reason I decided to stick to my completely accidental decision and stand there.

I took the time to observe the other men and women walking with great purpose in and out of the lobby. They clearly had reasons behind their comings and goings but, from my strange little observation fern, they came across almost more like background characters in a movie, those people who walk along the street as you follow the main character doing something important. Who fill out the space. Who walk just off frame, turn around, and walk back again.

Not that I was casting myself as the main character in this scenario, mind you; no, definitely not. It was just a thought, a fleeting thing. Something to occupy my mind while waiting. Until the man with all the bluster stormed past.

He stepped off the elevator, no coat, no hat, wearing a very well-tailored tweed vest and trousers, a sharp white shirt, and a cravat at his throat. He was older, gray in his hair and mustache, but there was no sign of old age in his manner. He was lively and full of energy. He fascinated me and I wondered where he was going. He couldn't be arriving, as he came from within the building, but was he leaving? With no coat and no hat, he couldn't be heading outside. Was he the one coming to get me? That would make sense. That would be a reason for someone to enter the lobby without outdoor clothing. He paced back and forth, muttering to himself, and I didn't feel entirely comfortable going up to him like that.

Then he looked right at me.

I felt the impulse to duck but I didn't. I just looked back, feeling rather sheepish now in my awkward situation. He squinted at me, but not the same way as the man on the bus, rather in the way that some people do to focus their vision on something very particular. He moved toward me and, as he did, looked around, puzzled perhaps by my presence and wondering if anyone else had noticed the girl behind the fern.

When he arrived on the other side, he gently pushed down one of the large leaves, a curtain revealing my embarrassment. And still, I didn't move or even just step to the side.

"What the devil are you doing?" he asked. He didn't sound angry; in fact, he sounded amused.

"Oh well, I'm just waiting." I said it as an obvious answer, as one does, when one waits behind ferns in lobbies.

"Intriguing. For anyone in particular?" The man leaned in. He was enjoying the conspiracy, all his fraught energy from a moment ago had dissipated, and I had become his sole focus of attention. It didn't feel strange, though it was intense. It felt fun, like a game. And warm, like seeing a relative you really liked after many years apart.

"Mr. Papadimitriou, I think, or someone who works for him. I'm the new girl. Are you . . . him?"

"Ha!" He pointed at me and then did a little flourish with the finger as if a poof of smoke was about to appear after a magician's trick. "No, I'm not. But you work in production?"

I nodded. Why was he as excited about this fact as I was?

"Well, I'll tell you, kid, so do I, so do I." He grinned; it was a bright, cheerful thing. Which in turn made me think him working there too was a bright cheerful thing.

"How wonderful! Are you the one who was sent to get me?" I asked. I still hadn't stepped around the fern. We were talking through the gap exposed by him holding down the large leaf. Somehow it all felt very normal now.

"I was not, no. No, I was not. But I'll tell you what, I will be now. Let me take you upstairs to reception. How does that sound?"

"It sounds great!" I said.

Finally, I found a reason to leave the fern, and I walked around to the man with a grin on my face.

"Ha! It has legs!"

I laughed at that. "It does!" I did a little spin. I was positively giddy. But it was just so nice to meet someone who was so effortlessly warm and kind. Who didn't need me to help bring him out from the shadows. Who quite literally, in fact, did that for me. I couldn't remember the last time anyone had tried to bring me out of myself. I suppose when you are a generally happy person, people don't think they ever need to do that. But it was nice to have someone notice you behind a fern. And care.

"And a name, I assume?" he asked.

"I'm Rose. Rose Sorenson." I extended my hand. My first official professional handshake. I hadn't even had a handshake at my interview so this felt very grown-up.

"Well, hello, Rose. It is an absolute pleasure. My name is Joey," he said. He took my hand warmly in his and we did a mighty fine shake. A quality shake if I do say so. "Joey Drew."

4

We got into the elevator with

two other men and a woman wearing a very flowery perfume. The interior of the lift was brown and paneled with mirrored strips lining the tops and the bottoms. As the doors closed, I could see our reflections. I stood the same height as the woman, so I felt very much like I fit in. Even as the brown paper bag in my hand might have signaled otherwise. Fine, it seemed people didn't bring their lunches to work, or if they did it wasn't in paper bags, but that was just the sort of thing I was going to learn. Why, I hadn't even arrived at the office yet and I was collecting all manner of professional hints.

For example, I learned that having a conversation in an elevator is not always favorable when others are sharing it with you.

"Mr. Drew, earlier downstairs . . ." I said. And he raised his finger just so in that way that explained to me I should stop. So, I did. I was pretty good with cues. I had been reading far more subtle ones ever since Father returned. I could read a pointed finger with ease.

On the third floor the men stepped out, and then on the fifth the woman did. At that point I spoke again.

"Mr. Drew . . ."

"Please, call me Joey," he said. There it was. I had officially made my first work friend.

"Joey, I just wanted to say thank you again for being so kind to me. I noticed downstairs you seemed deep in thought about something. I hope I didn't interrupt any plans or anything." I tried to sound as businesslike as possible, the way people talked in offices in movies. I was used to being around grocers and teachers and men who worked in the trades, but people who worked in towers, I was less used to their way of speaking. I worried they wouldn't take kindly to mine.

"Ha!" Joey said the word as he laughed it, which in turn made me laugh. "You can't ever worry about interrupting my plans, kid. Ol' Joey is always making plans."

I nodded and laughed with him as the doors opened, even as I was unsatisfied by the answer. I suppose that's what you get when you don't ask things outright. I wanted to know what he was thinking about so intently with all the pacing and energy. I wanted to know so much more about him. But I had asked in the wrong way. I wondered if I'd ever get a chance to ask again.

"I believe this is your stop," he said as the doors started to close again.

"Is it? Thank you!" I quickly dashed between them and looked back just in time to see Joey give me a wink before they closed completely.

I felt a little twinge of melancholy but, as was my tendency, it was immediately replaced with hope. After all, we worked in the same building; surely we'd run into each other again.

The probability was high. I gave a little nod at my matte gold reflection in the elevator doors and turned on my heel to the reception desk. I marched up with all due confidence.

The secretary was on the phone. Though she couldn't have been any older than twenty-five, there was an almost world-weary quality to her, which more than conveyed that, unlike me, this was most certainly not her first day on the job. She looked exhausted and, as she saw me approach, gave me that "in a moment" finger in the same way Joey had. In this case it was less apologetic and more annoyed. But that was okay. It sounded like one of those impossible phone calls. The person on the other end was clearly ranting, not letting the secretary get any word larger than a "yes" to slip into the conversation. I gave her a reassuring smile, and she did seem to notice that with the slightest of nods, and seeing as there were no ferns to hide behind to wait, I took a polite step back and clasped my hands and my paper bag behind my back.

The room was smaller than I'd anticipated. And messier too. Though there was a small couch and a chair against the wall for visitors, and a pile of magazines neatly stacked on a coffee table. Perhaps, after that initial assessment, I realized it wasn't the room that was messy, it was the secretary's desk that was. And to give the poor woman credit, it didn't seem like there was much she could do about it. It was a small desk to fit into a small space. She had a phone on it, she had a typewriter. But both were dwarfed by the stacks and stacks of bound paper, just everywhere, even down by the side on the floor. I surreptitiously read the text on the top sheet of paper closest to me. "The Long Dance." Oh! Oh of course, oh how delightful. I knew I was grinning ear to ear, and the secretary gave me a funny look as she managed an "I understand" before the monologue on the other end of the line continued.

They were scripts! They were piles and piles of scripts. I wanted to go through all of them, read them all. I didn't care if they were good or bad, I'd never read a TV script before. It was all too thrilling.

Finally she clicked the handle of the phone onto its holder and looked at me. Her expression worn, her face drawn. She was the personification of a heavy sigh. She was quite pretty nonetheless, with immaculate makeup and lipstick to match her auburn hair. She wore a gray dress with buttons that ran all the way down the front, stylish but practical. I made a mental note to seek out something like it for myself when I had earned enough eventually.

"Wow, that person sounded exhausting," I said. I was good at this sort of thing. This careful tiptoeing around a person not wholly present or happy.

She nodded and brightened a little with a small eye roll. "He has called three times in the last two weeks. I think he thinks each time he's speaking with someone new, but no. It's always me."

"How tedious," I replied and I shook my head just to demonstrate how tedious I truly found it.

"It is. We aren't even accepting unsolicited work right now, and look." She gestured at the piles around her. "Everything opened is from just last week. This pile . . ." Another gesture now at a stack of thick manila envelopes piled to the other side of the desk that I hadn't even noticed yet. "This is from today."

"That's a lot."

"And then they call, just to follow up. Or show up in person even. They don't take no for an answer. I think someone wrote a piece for *The New Yorker* recently or *Life* magazine about gumption." She laughed a little and so did I. "Anyway, none of it is your concern. What was your name again?"

"I'm Rose Sorenson. I was hired as the new office production assistant." I was very proud to say it out loud.

"Oh." The secretary laughed again. "Well, then, all of it *is* your concern, I suppose. I take it back. Rose, lovely to meet you. I'm Gladys."

"Lovely to meet you too!" I replied.

She stood and stretched out her neck as if she'd been sitting for hours, even though it was first thing and I wasn't late. I wondered how early she arrived to work. I wondered if she'd been there all night, which was a fanciful thing to think.

"Let me take you to your desk, and we'll see if Stephen, or Papa D, is interested in meeting you." I nodded. I was a bundle of excitement. "Please don't take that personally. Papa D rarely is interested in meeting anyone."

I hadn't even thought to be offended. I wondered if my expression had given off something I hadn't intended. "Oh, of course! Men are very busy people," I said.

Now the secretary gave me a strange glance. "Well, so are women."

I had slipped up again, somehow. "Oh yes, women too. I didn't mean to imply otherwise. You look like you are a very busy person yourself," I said with a smile.

The strange look intensified.

"Not to say that you look . . . I mean to say just with the phone call and all the scripts." I stopped talking and took in a breath. "I am getting all muddled, aren't I? Saying all the wrong things."

We were standing at the door behind her desk, Gladys's hand hovering over the handle. She shook her head and her face relaxed somewhat. "It's alright. First-day jitters. I had them too."

I nodded. "I'm glad you understand."

We shared a smile and then she opened the door. We were immediately overwhelmed by a wave of noise and energy. A tall man, no jacket, just shirt and tie, marched by so quickly, it felt like we were going to be run down by a car crossing the street. The traffic was thin but fast; anyone we encountered walking down the hallway deeply engrossed in something that had nothing to do with the present moment and the act of walking from one place to another.

I felt like I'd stepped into another world; the bustle had been kept well at bay by Gladys. That all this energy and all these people were just a door away was thrilling and strangely terrifying. I thought of all the buildings in Manhattan. The ones for business, the ones for living. I thought about all those people. Stacked on top of one another. Teetering. In the sky. All of us together on a tiny island. What kind of magic was that?

We arrived at a frosted glass door, the name "S. Papadimitriou" in black letters written across it. Gladys gave me a look, a "well, here we go" kind of thing, and then knocked, not breaking eye contact with me.

"What?" It wasn't an angry question, it was a demand: Be quick about it.

"Stephen, I have the new PA with me."

"Well, good for you!"

I laughed a little quiet laugh at that response.

Gladys shook her head. "I think you should meet her. She needs to be assigned."

There was a heavy frustrated sigh and a pause. "Yes, fine, show her in. The new PA."

Gladys gave me a nod, an "Are you ready?," and I nodded back, "Oh yes, I am!" Was I ever. I was certain that all this madness and rushing and stressful everything of the office by some point might potentially wear me down like it seemed to do to everyone who worked here, but right now it was exhilarating. Oh, to have stressful, important, timely things going on! To have deadlines, and last-minute rushes! To have a purpose! I still hadn't entirely determined what mine would be yet, but until I did, my purpose was to find that purpose and I was terribly excited at the prospect.

She opened the door to a small corner office. The blinds were down, and it was filled with artificial light and smoke. A harried man in his forties, full head of hair slicked back with a streak of silver running through it, a thick mustache and muttonchops, sat hunched over a stack of paperwork. His cigarette was slowly burning away, untouched in an ashtray filled almost to the brim. A single line of smoke curled toward the ceiling.

"At least let some light in, Stephen," said Gladys, sighing and walking right past the barrier of the desk to the blinds behind him. I had a strange feeling then as she opened them, letting the harsh daylight filter into an already harsh environment, a slight panic. My heart jumped into my throat and I felt my pulse quicken. I wanted to reach my arm out and tell her to stop.

But I remembered then that this was not Father, this was not our living room, and there wasn't any danger of provoking the puddles. I took in a surreptitious deep breath to calm myself.

For his part Mr. Papadimitriou, or Stephen, or Papa D, just squinted and grunted, but he didn't turn away from his work or even make any sign of protest. Gladys reached over his shoulder and stamped out the cigarette as she picked up the ashtray. "I'll clean this. Now, Papa D, this is Rose. She's our new PA." She bent closer to his ear and hissed, "Be nice!"

Mr. Papadimitriou harrumphed but, once again, didn't argue. Gladys marched back to the door and gave me a satisfied nod. Then as she closed it behind her, she added, "Good luck."

With that, we were alone. And only then did I start to feel a little awkward. There was another chair in the room, but it was covered in papers. It seemed to be a general running theme about this office: the woeful lack of storage space.

"Would you like me to file those?" I asked. It felt like a simple, easy, day-one task for the new girl, and something that would be helpful to him too.

Mr. Papadimitriou looked up at me then, for the first time, then over at the pile, then back. "Why on earth would I want you to do that? No, of course not. Just sit and be quiet for a moment."

That was easier said than done. So I stood as respectfully as I could, holding my lunch in front of me, politely, waiting as the man scribbled hurriedly on the paper in front of him, and then suddenly grabbed it with a white hot fury and crumpled it into a ball in his hands, throwing it against the wall with an effortful anguished roar.

"Are you sure I can't help you with anything?" I asked.

He looked at me, stared me down. Finally he leaned back in his chair and reached for the cigarette in its ashtray. Finding the whole thing missing, he clenched his hand into a fist.

"What's your name?" he barked.

"Rose."

"Well, Rose, let's get this out of the way. Just call me Papa D. I hate it, but they all think it's very clever, and you know how creative types are: Clever is the point for them. So just call me that. Don't call me 'mister,' I hate that more. Don't call me 'Stephen.' That's just when Gladys wants to make sure I don't bite her head off. Got it?"

"Yes, sir," I replied. Already a fun nickname for an ornery boss! This day was going wonderfully well. I had to try very hard to hide my giddiness.

Papa D appraised me further, not in a strange way, more like an alien landing on earth and stepping out of its flying saucer and seeing humans for the first time kind of way. "How old are you? You look like a child."

"I'm almost eighteen."

"Shouldn't you be in school?"

"I skipped a year." I didn't want to explain the whole story. Usually people just assumed I was very smart and, since that was a nice thing to have people assume about me, I didn't correct them. What they didn't know was when Father was away at war, Mother didn't like the idea of being all alone so she taught me from home until he got back. But when he got back, everything was so fraught that she made a mistake about which grade I should be in. I never minded it. I didn't know any better, I was just happy to be at a real-life school. I'd even venture to say that even though I was a year younger than everyone, I rather did excel.

"Oh fantastic, just fantastic." Papa D laughed now. "They send me children," he said to the wall. "Fantastic." He turned back to me. "So tell me, Rose, what do you know about the television business?"

"Not very much, if I'm honest." I laughed.

"Is that a packed lunch?" Papa D pointed at the paper bag clutched between my two hands.

"Yes."

He shook his head; he looked almost dumbstruck. "Right. Well, as you can see, we are running on fumes here. I'm the producer who oversees the daily running of this studio. If you don't know what that means, you're an idiot and I'm not going to waste my breath explaining anything to an idiot."

"Of course not, sir. What a waste of time," I replied.

Papa D started at that, just a little reaction, almost approving, but I didn't know him well enough yet to know for certain. I'd figure him out soon enough. I wasn't worried.

"Yes. So." He found his train of thought again. "We have half a dozen shows we run from this office. Four are currently on air. We're in preproduction on the other two. You're a PA for all of them. But mostly you'll be working out of this office. You are the grunt. You are a cog in a machine. You do not have opinions, you do not have suggestions, you do what you're told, and you do it fast. Got it?"

"Got it!" I replied. It all seemed very straightforward.

"Can you make coffee?" he asked.

"Yes, sir."

"Good, or you'd be fired. Okay, well, your presence fills me with an existential dread, you personify everything that is wrong with humanity, and your eagerness to please makes me want to vomit."

I nodded.

"Gladys will set you up with a desk out with the teaming masses. Don't make small talk with anyone, please, and when you go on your lunch break, for god's sake, hide yourself and your bag. It's too awful to look at."

"Of course, sir." I squeezed the bag a little tighter in my hands and it crinkled a little too loudly. Papa D visibly flinched.

"Get out, just leave. I'm done." He shifted in his seat and hunched over the paperwork once more.

It didn't feel right, just turning around and leaving, so I did what I'd heard people did when they visited with the brand-new Queen of England. I walked backward away from him toward the door, bumping into it softly. I was a little off in my remembering its exact location. Papa D sighed hard at the sound and it spurred me to faster action. I turned and whipped open the door, closing it hastily behind me.

What a rush!

I couldn't help but smile now, all alone, in the hall.

"Ain't nothing to smile about, newbie," said a young man practically flying past me and down the hall.

I didn't even have time to consider his personal philosophy, as Gladys suddenly materialized on my other side and whisked me away to the "bullpen," as she called it, a suddenly wide-open part of the office filled with a dozen or so desks and people. People everywhere. The din was exhilarating and surprising. Where had they all been this whole time? I was in love with everything. The surprises around every corner, and even my little desk in the middle of it all. I quickly hid my lunch bag under it and sat with my hands folded on its top.

And waited.

Was I supposed to be proactive? I wanted to be, but surely being so went against Papa D's strict instructions. I was to follow orders, not seek them out. But oh, I thought, as a stout, panicked, older man in a wrinkled suit rushed past me, papers falling out of his arms, how I just wanted to offer a comforting hand to everyone in this office. They all seemed ready to burst, as if a tap on the shoulder would cause them to explode in a puff of white smoke.

I could help.

I was hired to help.

"Here," grunted Gladys. She dropped a stack of packages on my desk, unopened screenplays in their manila envelopes. "Go through these. Toss the ones that are no good. The rest I'll go through and decide who gets them."

I nodded. "How do I know a script is 'no good'?" I asked, reaching over for the first envelope.

Gladys smoothed her hair and gave a nod to a gentleman across the room who was waving intensely at her. "Trust me, you'll know."

I didn't find that answer particularly reassuring but I also knew I had pushed it far enough with my initial question. Just do, Rose! Just do! I had faith in myself that I'd figure it out.

Turned out, it really wasn't a complicated ask at all.

How could some of these people even look at themselves in the mirror knowing they had sent such poorly formatted and punctuated work? I was hardly someone who could distinguish myself by my good taste, especially good taste in art, but at the very least I had graduated from high school. I could read words on a page. Which seemed, in some cases, to be more than what the actual writers who put those words on the page could do.

Then there were the cover letters that accompanied the scripts. Many were just reflections of their general lack of writing abilities, but there was one that was honest-to-goodness threatening. More like a ransom letter than a query. I put it to the side for Gladys to show to Papa D. I didn't want anyone to get hurt. But when she came to collect the four acceptable, at least to me, scripts, she just laughed at my concern. "Is it from Hemlock Moore?" she asked, glancing over the title pages of the screenplays in her arms.

"Why, yes," I said, quite shocked.

"Oh, we get something from him at least once a month. He targets all the studios. We think it's just some game for him. We don't even know if that's his real name. Probably not." She gave me a small smile. "You were very quick with this. Since no one else here will say it, I'm impressed."

I felt that wonderful warm fuzzy feeling you get when you've been complimented for a job well done. "Thank you."

"Well, break for lunch. We'll see you back here in half an hour." She turned on her heel, leaving me surrounded with the discarded innards of manila envelopes, these poor little screenplays destined for the trash heap. I didn't feel nearly as sad as I thought I was going to dropping them into the garbage.

Lunch was a tricky matter. I wasn't entirely sure where I could hide per Papa D's instructions, so ultimately I made the decision to head downstairs and find a spot somewhere outside where I wouldn't be noticed. There was a little park around the corner and an available bench, and even though it was a little difficult eating my sandwich with my mitts on, I did it quite successfully. I was feeling downright proud of my abilities and returned to the office refreshed, full, and content.

"Where the devil have you been?" Papa D exploded out of his office just as I passed the door, making me jump.

"Lunch!" I exclaimed back, not really thinking just reacting.

"Where? The moon? We couldn't find you anywhere!" He was glaring down at me and yet I wasn't afraid. He was an intense man, but I found him strangely lovable. It was just the feeling I had about him. I could tell there was a kindness somewhere in there. Buried. Deep down. Very deep down.

"I went to this little park around the corner," I replied.

"Outside? It's thirty degrees out there!"

"I know." He glared harder. "I wanted to make sure no one saw me eating my lunch. I thought that would be the safest."

At that Papa D rolled his eyes and huffed hard. "Obviously I was speaking in hyperbole. My god, what kind of a monster do you think I am?"

"Oh, I don't think you're a monster at all," I said with a smile. That seemed to catch him a little off guard, and he took a small step back toward the office and looked at me with suspicion.

"I didn't say I wasn't a monster, I'm just not completely monstrous."

"I understand." We stared at each other then. "Was there something you needed?" There had to be, obviously.

"Was there something I needed," he replied under his breath. "Go down to seven. Joey Drew is looking for you."

"Joey Drew?" I asked. I hadn't expected that, and I immediately had butterflies.

"*The Joey Drew Show*; it's new, it's for kids. I don't care for it. They film on seven and he asked for you. He needs an extra PA today."

"*The Joey Drew Show*?" He had his own show. I hadn't realized how important the man was.

"Good god, woman, what do you want from me? It's a show about his Bendy cartoons. It's what it sounds like. Why am I explaining any of this to you?! Just get on with it already!" He stormed into his office, slamming the door behind him.

I stood there in shock, the butterflies now a tornado and my face getting hot. Not because of his dramatic exit but because I finally understood and I couldn't quite wrap my head around it: Joey Drew was the man behind the Bendy cartoons. Joey Drew. The man in the foyer. The one I rode the elevator with. The one who had requested that I be his PA for today. Joey Drew was the creator of Bendy. And Alice Angel. Oh, and Boris! Who could forget darling Boris. I might have been young when the cartoons played before movies on the big screen, but the memories you have from when you were a young child are the ones that last a lifetime.

I had never met a famous person before, let alone a person who had been so important to my early life. I wanted to blush now, thinking about standing behind the fern and meeting Joey Drew himself, but I just couldn't feel shame. I was too overwhelmed with the excitement of it all.

What an amazing day this had been! And it was only just after lunch.

The elevator doors opened

onto a messy foyer with no receptionist desk. It was a room filled with boxes that had been kicked to the side to make a path to the door in the back of the wall. It was propped open with a brick and beyond it I could see a hallway stretching back toward the end of the building, fluorescent lights lining the ceiling and making my eyes ache almost immediately. One was flickering and made a small buzzing sound. It was an oddly empty floor. I was already so used to the frantic buzzing about of people that the silence that greeted me made me almost uneasy. I stared at the light, on off on off. For a moment I felt the urge to turn and make my way back upstairs. But I quickly shook that feeling out of my body and with great determination walked down the hall with purpose to the door marked "Studio 7."

I pushed it open.

I entered into a black void. For a moment I felt as if I'd step deep into the blackness, that it would rise up around my ankles and slowly drag me down. But I landed sturdily, my feet very much on solid ground. And as my eyes quickly adjusted, I could see shadows in the dark and hear the harried but hardworking voices of crew members calling out instructions to one another. In the distance there was a pool of light highlighting a set. I squinted at it. It looked like an artist's table in a corner office somewhere. It even had a window and behind that window a backdrop of the New York skyline. It wasn't made to look realistic like most sets I'd seen on television. Instead it was drawn in black-and-white, like a sketch on a piece of paper or a cartoon strip. Every outline was rendered in a thick black, even the knots in the wood. None of the lines were perfectly straight, not for the table, the floor, not even for the window itself. It was all very whimsical and so charming. I found myself drawn to it and walked toward it in a haze. I suddenly tripped on a cable snaking across the floor. I caught myself before falling on my face, but I did let out a little squeak, which drew all eyes to me.

Now that I was closer to the light, I could see more than just black void. I could actually see the members of the crew running about, setting up lights, and talking intently to one another. I could see the cameramen, two of them, each with his own giant camera, so huge they dwarfed me easily. I had never seen a camera that huge before. I had never seen a cameraman for that matter either. The one closest to me gave me a wink, and I smiled back.

"You okay there?" he asked.

"Oh yes, there's just so much to be aware of on the floor. It's positively a jungle."

"Hey, we've all done it. They'll tangle you up when you least suspect it!"

"There she is!" I saw Joey emerge from the shadows into the light of the set. It was such a strange thing to see, a real man in full color standing in a black-and-white sketch. It made me love the idea even more. He grinned at me and waved. "Well, now we can get started. Our team is complete!"

I knew it was just flattery, but darn it all, it worked. I felt rather special, I had to admit. And all those strange feelings of dread from earlier slipped off me as easily as removing a coat after a long day.

"Come, come. Look at this. Look at all this!" He held out his hand to me, and I reached out from the shadows to take it. He pulled me into the light.

It was blinding. It was hot. It was disorienting. I was taken aback by the sudden change from the cozy magical feeling in observing the scene to this unpleasant reality of standing in it. But as my eyes adjusted, I was able to take in the set more closely.

"So, you see how it'll go. They film me talking about the show we're about to watch. And I sit here, at my artist's desk, like back in the studio. Like the good old days when we all just rolled up our sleeves and pitched in. So here we are, back at the old Joey Drew Studios, though of course it didn't look quite like this. Fun, isn't it?"

"Very fun," I said. Everything was a little too hot still, but my hands were cold. I clasped them together behind my back.

"You must look at this, look! They even have some of the original drawings here on the table and also over here, on the wall." He was a tour guide, and I was his audience of one. I looked at the drawing on the table, Bendy as a cowboy. It was very cute and sparked childhood memories for me. It made me smile thinking of all the kids who'd be introduced to the beloved character for the first time thanks to this show. I felt that strange pang that only comes from nostalgia, that sour sweetness.

I walked around behind the table to where Joey was pointing and looked at the other drawings tacked up on the wall. Now that I was up close, I could see they had even drawn cartoon nails pretending to hold them in place. More Bendy. Some Alice Angel; she'd always been my favorite. A Boris the Wolf. Even the Butcher Gang! I never liked them; they always spooked me a bit. And they were so mean to our little devil darling.

"It's great," I said, turning to Joey. He didn't say anything, just kept smiling at me, anticipating something. More compliments maybe? I was still feeling all over the place, not quite grounded. I quickly rushed to find more to say. "I like the set. I like that it's like your old studio and looks like you've stepped into a drawing. Though, I do wish I could have seen it for real."

Joey sighed wistfully. "Oh, Rose, I wish you could have too. I really do. It was something else. You'd never have wanted to leave. It was the kind of place that just sucks you in, you know?"

"Absolutely." But I didn't know. Not really. I knew that places could be very interesting, but I did also generally like leaving them and going home and seeing my family. Otherwise, it was what, a jail? But that was a silly comparison.

I clapped my hands together in an efficient sort of way. "What can I do for you, boss?"

He laughed at that, though I was learning he laughed at just about everything. "I'll tell you, a cup of coffee would work a treat."

"That I can do," I said. I turned to look into the dark void, all the more dark for the bright lights in my eyes. I actually didn't really know where the coffee was. I turned back to Joey and, as I did, said, "Actually, do you know where I would find some?" But he had already left. There one minute and gone the next, like a ghost. But no, again, silly thought. I looked and could see him in the shadows to the side, talking animatedly to a woman holding a clipboard. I had the strangest sensation then. Like a child who had been walking with their parent down a street and then lost them in the crowd. Suddenly alone. And a little . . . abandoned.

It didn't feel particularly nice, so I shook my head and focused on the task ahead of me. Coffee. I would make Joey the best cup of coffee he'd ever had. The desire to impress my new boss was strong. There was something about his presence that simply demanded respect and I certainly wasn't the only one who felt it. Looking around the set, it seemed to me that everyone was exceedingly aware of Joey's presence. They didn't look at him, or call over to him, or really acknowledge him in any way, but every action felt like a performance for an audience of one. Even the kind but gruff cameraman was sitting a little taller in his seat.

So I too stood a little taller, raised my chin just so, and marched back toward the doors through which I'd entered into the studio. I would find the coffee. I would make the coffee. There would be coffee.

And it would be good.

Once in the hall I felt utterly lost again. The emptiness astonished my senses once more, and I was struck just how soundproof this studio must be. If you never went through that entrance, you might never even know it existed. But I shook that feeling off and walked with great purpose to the left. As

I turned the corner, the lights were out along this part of the hallway, illuminating a pathway into shadow, and with a very certain gut response of "Nope," I turned on my heel and made my way right instead.

Now here is the problem with a square. I figured out quite quickly as I made it to the end of the hall and turned right— as I went along with no people, no occupied offices, and, most certainly, no coffee anywhere to be seen—that I was in short order about to reconnect with that dark, unpleasant hallway. I had a few choices. Namely two. Namely, go back into the studio or keep going.

I wasn't truly afraid of the dark. I certainly wouldn't panic in a blackout or walking down a city street at night. But I did have what you might call an unease with it since Father's return. When the lights went out, when the house went still. That kind of darkness was when the unpredictable things happened. The cries at night, the wails. The sounds of pain, and then Mother's voice a ghostly whisper in the air. Sometimes the sound of things breaking. And crying. It was hard to fall back asleep after being woken up by those sounds. It was hard to mind your business even when Mother would catch you peering into the hall and sternly order you back to bed.

It was hard to then try to fall asleep, desperate to, just to escape the night so that it would be morning and we would all be a happy family again, the darkness behind the eyelids of a desperate need. Just fall asleep. Just fall asleep.

It was a weight that stayed with you.

Though of course darkness in the day was no better. Darkness during the day was a signal that Father had disappeared once again into himself. You didn't have to even look for him. You just had to see a dark doorway from around the corner and you knew.

Darkness as a signal. As a warning.

So I do think I could be forgiven for finding the looming darkness of the hallway with the broken lights discomforting. For feeling that familiar prickle up my spine, and the hairs alert on the back of my neck. But I had a job to do, and in the real world sometimes you find yourself faced with your irrational fears. And in this case, it was truly that. Darkness wasn't the cause of any of these issues. It simply did what it did best, magnified everything in the mind's eye.

And I knew even with the darkness that I was in a hallway. And I knew that this wasn't even that dark because there was a lingering light from the two hallways that ran perpendicular to it. So I knew. And so I told myself.

It's just a hallway with a few burnt bulbs.

I took in a deep breath and pushed my feelings down with my hands in front of me.

Then I walked into the darkness.

I could hear my footsteps clearer now than in the other hallways, my senses heightened. I flinched as I opened the doors to offices, anticipating some kind of scare. I squinted into the darkened rooms. And, sure as ever, was greeted again by a great nothingness. A lack of coffee. The anti-coffee as it were. I became a little more relaxed. A little less nervous.

And then I opened the door to 705.

I say opened, but really I had to wrench it quite hard. At the time it just seemed sticky, but I do wonder now if it had been locked, or at least an attempt had been made to keep people out. Still, if a girl my size could get it open, it hadn't exactly been a quality attempt.

When I stumbled into the room I was greeted with a pleasant surprise: some light. Not a great deal, just that from a single table lamp, like a banker's lamp with a green glass lampshade and a brass stand. It stood on a large drafting table in the corner, covered in papers. But it lit the entire office well enough that I could see the space clearly. Or at least perhaps my eyes were so used to the dark by now that I was impressively good at seeing even with this small amount of light. I felt very much like a superhero. I had x-ray vision! Well, not that good.

I laughed to myself, feeling a sense of ease for the first time again, and even though there was definitely no hint of any kind of coffee-making device, I wandered deeper into the room out of sheer curiosity.

In the center of the room was a giant table. It didn't even feel like a table but like a piece of architecture, a sturdy large block on which was splayed wires and tools and some unspooled film reels in a kind of messy pile. I leaned in and, as my eyes focused on a pair of pliers next to a tiny hammer, I noticed the surface of the block. It was covered with scratches from pencils pressing through paper too hard, and spilled ink, like someone had been writing something with too much enthusiasm. It was a mess of creativity and there were blueprints with some kind of technological specs on it. I had no idea what any of it meant, but it felt exciting and full of something else. A drive, a creative energy, a forward momentum. I had the wonderful feeling that whoever was working here was on the precipice of a discovery. Like Franklin in the rainstorm before lightning struck his kite.

I stood upright and cracked my neck and turned to my left. I was facing a bank of televisions sitting on a thick shelf running along the left wall. They were all off and I wasn't going to touch anything, but I was drawn to them. I loved to look at them and we never really got to investigate Pete's TV up close. It was always on and ready for us when we got there. I reached out and touched one of the glass screen surfaces. It was cold and smooth. I danced my fingers along the surface of the next and then the next, walking down the small aisle between table and television bank. I continued to make my way around the office toward the table, past a corkboard with Bendy himself drawn on paper in a variety of poses. An Alice. Two Borises. And some backgrounds like backdrops for a play. It was very similar in some ways to the set in the studio, but it was messier, and the pages covered one another, and I could see half an arm here, an ear there.

I finally arrived at the drafting table. Another set of blueprints, these ones neat and tidy and deliberate. It wasn't a finished product either, just a large circle really, and it looked like someone was in the middle of working on it. I couldn't read it for anything but I wanted to try, so I reached for the stool to pull it in and sit on. Something clanged to the floor as I did and I felt my heart drop into my stomach in an instant. I bent over quickly and my hands found a pair of glasses. My heart dropped further. I picked them up and held them up close to the lamp to examine them. A wave of relief washed over me. They were intact, unbroken. Thank goodness. I might be a proper working stiff now, but I could hardly afford to replace a pair of broken glasses, not in my first week of work.

"Are they okay?"

"Yes, they are, they're . . ." I stopped mid-sentence when I realized, too late, I'd been caught. I closed my eyes slowly and then opened them again. There was nothing to be said or done in this situation. I was firmly standing there with my hand in the proverbial cookie jar. So I turned and smiled at the figure leaning against the doorway.

"They're what?" he asked as he stepped into the room. I was blocking the light from the table, but even then I could see him a little. He was just slightly taller than me and just slightly older. His jacket had been discarded and his sleeves were rolled up to the elbow. His vest had a chain that led to the pocket and I wondered if it was attached to one of those classic old pocket watches. "They're what?"

I looked at his face. A little gaunt. But not unattractive. He wore glasses.

The glasses.

"They're fine," I sputtered.

He walked over and looked at me closely. I found myself holding my breath, staring back at him, not daring to twitch even a muscle. Then he reached his hand out, and I instinctively placed the glasses in it.

"Move," he said, and he pushed past me to the drafting table. He bent over the glasses and looked at them closely.

"They're fine, I promise. They're fine." *Please be fine.* I clenched my fists. *Oh please be fine.*

"You shouldn't be in here," he said.

That much was true. But also it didn't seem wholly fair. After all: "You shouldn't leave glasses on your stool. Anyone could have sat on them or something."

He didn't turn. He just kept his attention on the glasses. The perfectly fine, not broken glasses. "No one is supposed to be in here so it shouldn't matter where I leave them."

"And yet the girl makes a point." Oh no. A third voice.

A third voice that just made my throat shut tight and my face get hot.

It made us both spin almost instantly.

"We really shouldn't be leaving such things just laissez-faire, now, should we, Evan?"

"No, Mister Drew, you're right. It was a true lapse of judgment." Evan had gone so quickly to fawning I would have laughed if I hadn't been utterly aware of my own particular lapse of judgment in this entire situation.

"To put it mildly." Joey turned his attention to me. He fixed me with a look I'd not seen before from him. Not that I knew him particularly well, but it struck me as a particularly shocking experience. It was like looking down the barrel of a gun. He was aiming right for me. And it felt dangerous. And I felt all the more ashamed because of it. "Rose, where's my coffee?"

"I don't know."

Joey didn't break eye contact.

"What are you doing in here?"

"I was looking for it."

"It."

"The coffee. I was trying to find the coffee. I know I shouldn't be in here." I felt my eyes stinging. *Don't cry, don't cry.*

"Others have fired men for being half as nosy. You had a very simple task." That look, that uncompromising stare.

"I'm sorry." I could barely say it; it came out in a whispered quiver.

There was a pause so quiet I could hear my own breathing.

"Where's the coffee, Rose?"

"I'll keep looking, sir," I said. I wanted to walk past him but I was caught in his gaze. I couldn't look away either. Maybe Evan would do something.

But Evan didn't do anything.

"Good idea," said Joey finally, and he stepped slightly to the side, indicating I should leave past him. I didn't need any further encouragement and did.

I rushed down the hall and sped toward the light, and when I turned the corner, I leaned against the nearest closed door and closed my eyes again. I could feel heat rise up in my throat and burn behind my eyes. No, no, I was not going to cry. I refused.

I took in a couple deep breaths. Just find the coffee. Find the stupid coffee.

But I couldn't, I couldn't. I was too filled with shame and that look, that piercing look. It had cut to a core that felt ready to explode.

I had failed. I had disappointed him.

And I knew, I just knew, I was fired.

6

I didn't want to upset Father,
and Mother didn't have the time to deal with another disappointment in her family. I stood in the dark outside our front door for a moment and took in a deep breath. I would smile. I would allow the smile to inform my feelings and I was certain that if I just smiled long enough, I might actually start to feel happy again. It had worked very well in the past. And even if it didn't, well, the thought that I was sparing my parents the humiliation of having a nosy, impudent daughter who gets fired her first week at work, her first *day* at work, at least for tonight, at least for a brief moment . . . Well, that alone would be very much something that would make me feel good.

This is what I told myself.

In the dark.

On the stoop.

In the cold.

It's what I told myself as Mother served us dinner as we sat at our small kitchen table. It's what I told myself as I answered all their questions about my first day. It's what I told myself when, after two hours of playing Chutes and Ladders with Ollie, I felt it was finally late enough for me to turn in.

But the moment I was alone, well, there was nothing I could say now to myself to feel better. I sat there in the dark, that dark that pries open our minds and reveals our worst thoughts, that dark that makes it hard to breathe. I told myself it would be okay, there were many other jobs out there, even if they weren't at television studios. Even if it meant I wouldn't get to meet inspiring creative genius types like Joey Drew in elevators. Thinking his name made my stomach clench and I fell back, lying on the bed. I felt the tears well in my eyes but I was determined. I wouldn't cry. I saw Joey's face in my mind's eye. That glare. That disappointment.

No! It was just the darkness; it was just lies. It was my mind pulling me toward the puddles. Even though it wasn't, not really. It had all happened. But it wasn't happening now. I was just reliving the moment over and over again. Living in the past. In a loop. This was exactly the trouble: It might have been real once but right now I was in my bedroom, at home, far away from the studio and Joey Drew. The moment I was existing in was a mundane Monday evening. The puddles wouldn't take me.

I stood in a rush and went to turn on the light. When I did, I screamed, heart beating hard in my chest. A small figure in the doorway, still and ghostlike, was just staring at me. Instantly I covered my mouth but it was too late, I heard my mother's footsteps on the stairs. And I saw tears start to form in Ollie's eyes, his bottom lip quivering.

"Ollie! You scared the dickens out of me! What were you doing?" I crouched down and held him by his arms. "It's okay, little man, it's okay. You just startled me!"

"What is it, what's happening?" My mother arrived out of breath with wild eyes. The guilt consumed me. No loud noises, no roughhousing inside, and certainly no screams. Not ever. The rules had been burned into my soul since Father had returned. I was usually so good at following them. I felt a deep well of shame.

"I'm so sorry." I looked from her to Ollie, silently crying, his whole little body shaking and tears rolling down his perfect chubby cheeks. Even he knew not to wail. I grabbed him tight, held him so close. I felt his little heart racing. "It's okay, Ollie, it's okay." I looked up at Mother. "I'm sorry. He was standing in the hall in the dark. He scared me."

"Rose, you know better than that." Mother glanced over her shoulder to the stairs.

"I know, I know." I buried my face in Ollie's soft hair, smelling his shampoo.

"It's okay, Rose, I'm okay," he said softly, muffled in my torso.

I pulled away and looked at him, his blotchy, wet red face. Why was he such a good kid? "I'm sorry, Ollie," I said again.

"I'm sorry," he said back. "I just wanted a story." I noticed then his caveman book, clutched in his little hand.

"That's an old one," I said. "I thought you liked chapter books better now."

Ollie nodded. "But this one is your favorite, and you seemed sad."

I glanced at Mother, who furrowed her eyebrows. "Rose isn't sad, Ollie," she said. "She's tired. She had a long day working a grown-up job. That's all. Isn't that right, Rose?" It was a pointed question, but there was her usual softness to it. It made me feel all the more guilty. What a horrible, shameful day. I felt, suddenly, extremely tired.

"Mother's right," I said. "It was a very full day and very exciting. That makes me extra sleepy now. But I love that you wanted to read my favorite."

Mother reached down and placed a gentle hand on Ollie's back between his shoulder blades. "Come, why don't you get all set in bed, and I'll read you some of The Famous Five?" Ollie smiled at her but looked back at me.

"Is that okay, Rose?"

"It's better than okay. That's one of my favorites too!"

"Go to bed, Ollie," said Mother. "I'll be there in a moment. I just need to talk with your sister."

"Okay." He turned and walked off with purpose into the dark. I watched him. I still felt so terrible.

"Rose," said Mother.

"Yes?" I just stared into the black void. It reminded me of the studio. I remembered that strange feeling of dread and then quickly pushed it to the side.

"Rose, stand up. Let's go sit on the bed."

Oh yes, I was still crouching. I stood and nodded, and we walked over to my bed, then sat on the edge, side by side, our feet dangling just a bit.

"Why are you sad?" she asked, placing her hand over mine.

I felt a lump in my throat. "I'm not."

"Ollie sees people, just like you. You can hide yourself from me and your father, but you can't hide from him. What happened? Was it at work?" I hated the concerned look in her eyes. This was the last thing I wanted.

"No, it's fine. I really am just tired."

"Rose." Where did mothers learn the art of saying your name in just such a way that everything comes crashing down and you are left utterly defenseless?

"I think I'm going to be fired." I pulled my hand out from under hers and covered my face with both palms. I wasn't going to cry, but if I did, I didn't want her to see. And I certainly didn't want to see her disappointment.

"Oh, Rosebud, why would you think that?"

"There's a man there, he's very important, and I was snooping where I shouldn't have been." Oh no, no. I felt wetness on my hands. It wasn't working.

"Did he tell you that you were fired?" I felt her hand in my hair now, gently stroking it. It was comforting but also it made me feel even worse.

"Not exactly, but he said others had been fired for less. And more importantly I'm a nobody. I'm a grunt, a cog in a machine."

"What a thing to say!"

"No, it's my job, that's the point. I'm not supposed to go into places I'm not invited. I feel so terrible."

"Did you break anything?"

"It's not like that, Mother."

"I'm just trying to understand. Were there private documents? Banking information?"

"No, it was a room for inventing things, I think. Like a scientific lab."

"How odd," Mother replied.

I lowered my hands and looked at her. "You aren't mad at me?"

Mother smiled. "Of course not. It doesn't sound like you did anything all that terrible to me, but if you are fired, well, it will be a lesson learned for the next job. That's how most things work. We are constantly learning and growing."

"Well, if learning means realizing that you're a snoop . . ."

Mother laughed and shook her head. "Maybe that is a good lesson to learn. But curiosity is a lovely thing, and something I've always encouraged in you."

I flopped onto my back on the bed. I felt just so tired and frustrated with myself. "Yes, but curiosity did kill the cat."

"And satisfaction brought it back," replied Mother.

I looked at her. She looked even more angelic than usual, the light in the ceiling above her forming a perfect halo around her head. "What's that?"

"The end of the quote. 'Curiosity killed the cat but satisfaction brought it back.'"

"I didn't know there was a second part," I said.

"Your old mother does know some things that maybe you don't. It's not easy—you are my brilliant girl after all." She lay down next to me so we were both now staring at the plaster ceiling, lying there side by side. I could feel her warmth next to me and it made me feel a little better. A little less lost.

"What does it mean?"

"What do you think it means?"

Here we go, another lesson. She never quite ever stopped being my teacher, even when she finally sent me to school.

I sighed. "It means that curiosity can get you into trouble, like, for example, get you fired."

"For example."

"But the possibility of discovering something new is worth it." I wasn't entirely certain I believed that.

I glanced to my side and looked at Mother. She nodded. "There is no reward without risk."

"Maybe," I said. I sighed again. "But . . ." I stopped. I was thinking too many negative thoughts; it was so unlike me.

"But what, Rosebud?"

I sighed and looked at the ceiling again. "But maybe sometimes it's just risk."

The next day dawned bright

and sparkly. Even the frozen air felt refreshing and sharp as I sighed heavily and stepped into the frustratingly glorious sunshine. It was as if nature herself was mocking me and my situation, showing me how little she cared about my dread. That the world kept on spinning even as mine was falling apart.

Mother had given me an extra-tight squeeze this morning and slipped a piece of chocolate from her very special collection into my paper bag lunch. I hadn't had the heart to tell her how much grief that paper bag had cost me yesterday. Oh, I didn't fit in at all, did I? In the working world. Well, the good news was I wasn't going to be a part of it much longer.

When I stepped off the train and made my way to the studio, I could feel the dread build up in my throat. I had loved the look of the tower when I'd seen it yesterday, but now it was a looming thing. A looming tower of doom.

I managed to make it upstairs and mercifully Gladys wasn't at her desk when I entered the office, so the inevitable was postponed. I walked quickly down the hall, practically running by Papa D's office, terrified he'd jump out and grab me, and made it to my desk, where I was able to quickly stash the infamous paper bag lunch before taking my coat, mitts, and hat off. And sitting. Hard. Almost a little too hard.

There was a fresh stack of manila envelopes on my desk. If they were planning on firing me, they clearly wanted me to get some of the busywork out of the way first. And besides, I was grateful for the distraction. I reached for the first one, and it clanged as I placed it in front of me and something brown seeped through at the bottom. I certainly was not going to open that. I tossed it immediately. Well. This was easy.

Okay, I could do this. I wanted to do this. I would put all my attention and energy into this one task and shut my mind off from everything else. It was the only way I was going to make it until the inevitable thing happened. I only hoped no one would ask me to get them coffee. That would probably make me burst into tears.

I had already made my way through half the pile when:

"Papa D wants to see you." Gladys had a way of just materializing out of the ether, but she so absolutely terrified me with her sudden appearance this time that I let out an actual yelp. In any other office, possibly a few heads would have turned, but everyone just kept on with their usual chaos and I just sat there trying to force my heart to return to some semblance of a regular rhythm. "What on earth is wrong with you?" she asked.

"I'm sorry, I was . . . I was deep in thought." Not puddle deep, but deep enough, anticipating the inevitable, which, I realized only then, this probably was. The walk to the gallows, not even a last meal.

"Well, stop that. You aren't paid to think. Come on, it'll only get worse the longer he has to wait for you."

It'll only get worse. Oh dear. I wanted to think the best as I rose, but I was only human after all. One could be generally positive but still see the writing on the wall. Still know that your own actions had caused a very direct response.

People were fired all the time.

But I so hoped I wasn't.

"Sit," barked Papa D. But of course there was nowhere to sit, so I didn't. I just bent a little at the knees and then stood upright again, almost as if I had just curtsied. I heard the door close behind me, like the sound of the rope tightening as the trapdoor was about to be let out from under me. I dropped my chin to my chest and tried to stop my lower lip from shaking.

"Right, so, for some reason . . . wait, why are you doing that? Stop it, stop it this moment!"

I quickly raised my chin and looked at him.

"Good. What's wrong with you, girl?"

I shook my head and felt a stammer burn up into my throat. "I'm sorry, I just, I know I'm being fired . . ."

"What did you do?" asked Papa D, leaning forward. I didn't say anything then. I was too confused to. "What did you do?" This time his voice was severe, a warning.

"I . . . am I not being fired?"

"What is happening in this office; why is everyone insane? No, you aren't. You're being moved."

Oh. Oh, that made sense too. Hide me away, away from everyone and everything, in the corner with the dunce cap where I belong. I wasn't generally one for self-pity, but it felt more like fact than self-flagellation. It was the least I deserved.

"I see."

"Do you? Do you know what a hassle this is for me, all that work to bring in someone new, the job posting, the résumés, the tedious cover letters, and now because some big shot needs a new assistant I have to start all over with a new girl?"

"I'm so sorry," I said. Without meaning to, there was a little quiver in my throat, sadness manifesting as something tangible. And I felt it too. I felt terrible for everyone that my own bad behaviors had resulted in so much grief for everyone involved.

"Yes, well," said Papa D, noticing the change in tone and looking suddenly distinctly uncomfortable, "it's not really that much to bear. Now, come on, girl, you're fine. It's a promotion. Don't go blubbering because you'll miss me of all people. That's insane, and I don't do well with crazy people with crazy people."

"A promotion?" The quiver wouldn't go away, but the feelings inside were now all a mess and that general positive feeling that kept me going was pushing back upward, desperate to see what was going on.

"Yes. Sheesh. Joey Drew wants you as his assistant. Guess you did something right. God knows what it was."

Well, now I was flummoxed. The sadness had flown the coop and the positivity was happy in the sunshine, but my confusion was still there standing in its underwear. Exposed and wary.

"Joey?" I asked carefully.

"Joey Drew. The cartoon man. They're shooting his show on seven. Dear god, woman, you were there just yesterday." Papa D shook his head at me. "This has been one of the worst conversations I've ever had. Get out of my office and head to seven."

I nodded. "Thank you, Papa D. This is wonderful."

"It's not. Now get out."

I nodded again. I felt like a toy with a spring for a neck—I couldn't stop bouncing my head around. Even as I walked down the hall to my desk, my head was kind of just floating around like that. What on earth was happening? Was this some strange extra punishment? No, that made no sense. Papa D himself had called it a promotion. And working directly with Joey? Why, that was like a dream come true.

I wondered if it came with a raise.

I should have asked.

I collected my things and made my way down the hall and through the door into the reception.

"Were you fired?" asked Gladys, looking appropriately upset on my behalf.

"I was promoted!" I was now positively, glowingly happy.

Gladys was shocked. She didn't smile, instead she narrowed her eyes. "What do you mean promoted?"

"I'm going to be Joey Drew's assistant." I grinned so widely I could feel my face stretch.

"The cartoon man?" Her expression did not warm, nor did it return to normal. In fact, it only got more scrunched.

"Yes," I replied. "Is something wrong? You shouldn't worry about me, I'm excited. I mean, I'll miss you of course and Papa D."

She waved off the compliment with her hand. "No, it's fine. I just—" She stopped. "No, it's fine."

"But it's not fine. I want you to tell me, Gladys. I trust you!"

She laughed a little at that. "Why on earth for? We barely know each other."

"I have a gut instinct about people, that's all," I replied.

She shook her head. "Well then, you'd know better than me, wouldn't you?"

"About what?"

"About your new boss."

"What about him?"

Gladys sighed, and I realized I was overwhelming her. I backed away from her desk to give her some breathing room. "I just would like to know if there's anything I should . . . know," I said, softer now, calmer now.

"There's nothing. He strikes me as odd, and that's that. Call it *my* gut instinct, but I've never prided myself on having a particularly savvy one, so I wouldn't listen to me."

I nodded, all spring neck again, though more dazed than giddy. "Well," I said, "I guess we shall see." That was all there really was to it ultimately. To get to know the man and find out for myself.

Gladys smiled at me, either comforted or trying to comfort me. I wasn't entirely sure which. "Yes," she said, "we shall see."

8

I met Joey in the studio. The work lights were on overhead and the large black cavernous space had shrunk considerably in size to be not much larger than a high school gymnasium. The space no longer seemed infinite or intimidating. It was just a space. The set for his show seemed smaller too in the light, far less magical. The cameras, however, seemed to have grown in size. They reminded me of dinosaurs from one of Ollie's cavemen picture books. I still somehow managed to trip on a cable, even though I could see them easily. I was nervous and focused on the man himself, sitting in the director's chair off to one side of the set. He was reading something intently.

"Uh, Joey?" I said quietly, trying not to spook him since he hadn't seemed to notice my entrance.

The man looked up and smiled. It was comforting to see, especially after our encounter yesterday. To see him look happy to see me made me feel so at peace.

"There she is!" he said. He put the papers on a stool beside him and stood up, extending his hand. We shook. I was getting better at handshakes. "I'm thrilled you took me up on my offer."

"I didn't have much of a choice," I said with a laugh. His expression wavered then and I realized how I'd sounded. "I mean, of course, I'm thrilled you wanted me as your assistant. I don't really get to choose where I'm promoted to, but if I could, this would have been exactly it. So, it worked out really well!"

Joey laughed at that. "Of course, of course. We all have free will, but some of us have more of it than others."

What an odd thing to say, I thought, as he gestured for me to follow him. And I did. As we stepped out of the studio, I said, "I wanted to say . . . that is." I stopped. I hadn't actually prepared an apology because I hadn't thought I'd get the opportunity to make one. But it was something I felt was incredibly important for me to do now at the beginning of our official working relationship.

"Yes?" he asked. We turned down the hall.

There was nothing more than to just say it. "I just wanted to say, I'm sorry."

Joey stopped walking and turned to look at me. I had to stop too. It was harder for me to look at him though. I felt such shame, but I willed myself to do it. I met his eyes. They were concerned. He reached out and placed a firm hand on my shoulder. "Rose, whatever are you talking about?"

I had to look down, I just had to. I couldn't face him. "I'm sorry I was in that office. I'm sorry about snooping. I was curious and I promise I wasn't going to do anything, but I shouldn't have been there without permission and I feel so terrible about that." My throat was tight.

Joey put his other hand on my other shoulder and said, "Rose, look at me." Easier said than done. "I mean it, Rose, look at me." I took in a deep breath and raised my eyes. His kind concern met mine. "I'm not upset, and I don't even think you did anything wrong. By George, I respect that kind of gumption, don't you see? A curious mind, why that's a marvelous thing. And not something everyone has, I can tell you, no sir. Why, so many out there are happy just to follow orders and keep their heads down. And I'll tell you, I can't stand those people." He smiled then and I couldn't help but laugh a little. "There you go, you get it." He released my shoulders. "You and I are of a different breed, Rose. Knew it the moment I met you in the foyer by the fern."

"Oh gosh, that stupid fern," I said. I felt myself blushing.

"Why do you think I want you to be my assistant? It's because of your curiosity and your go-get-'em nature. You're just the kind of gal a boss needs at his side. So don't you dare apologize for actually having some feelings and drive."

I nodded. I felt so warm inside, like I was glowing, literally beaming and lighting the whole hallway. "I promise I won't again."

"Good, very good." He looked at me for a moment then; he didn't say anything. "Did you find it interesting?"

"Find what interesting?"

"The lab, everything inside."

I nodded. "Yes, I didn't understand any of it, but it all looked so fascinating. Like some real scientific minds were working."

I didn't think Joey's smile could get any brighter but it did. He started walking again and I did a little skip to catch up. We turned down that dark hallway and that's when it all clicked. We were heading back to the lab. I felt such a thrill then; things were making so much sense now, especially after hearing Joey's words. My curiosity had not killed the cat. Those qualities in myself that I knew others could find tiresome, he admired. I felt seen for the first time in a long time. Even more so than with my family. I was always seeing them. I was always coming to them, making sure Mother had what she needed, making sure Ollie was entertained and Father felt safe. But for someone to come to me, to see me, and what I wanted? It was the first time I'd realized that I hadn't had that in a very long time.

We entered the lab together. Evan was hunched over his table in the corner but he raised his head like a prairie dog and stared at us.

"Sorry to interrupt," I said.

"Oh, don't be sorry, stop being sorry!" said Joey. "I have little interest in apologies, and especially not for Evan. He can be as skittish as he wants, that's his choice."

"Yes, Mister Drew," said Evan in a flat voice.

"I'm going to give young Rose here a proper tour," explained Joey, closing the door behind him.

"You are? Are you sure that's a good idea?" Evan's shocked expression was shocked. Shocked squared, you could say. I pressed my lips together to keep myself from laughing.

"Yes, I am, and if she has any questions going forward, you're to answer them all. Do you understand?"

Evan nodded. He understood. He didn't understand why, that much was clear. He didn't approve, that much was even clearer, but the most clear thing to me was that what Joey said, Evan did. And ultimately that was all that mattered.

"Now, Rose," said Joey. He flipped a switch and a light hanging above the giant square block in the middle of the room turned on and buzzed almost gratefully, like it hadn't been turned on in a very long time. Then he marched over to the bank of televisions and with great theatricality turned them each on. They brightened from small specks to fully lit screens on which played a scene of Bendy whistling while walking along a path in the woods. Each screen showing the same thing. Six Bendys walking. It was mesmerizing. "Come here," said Joey when he noticed I hadn't approached the block yet.

"Yes, sir." I skittered over next to him.

"Are you familiar with Sillyvision?"

I giggled.

"I'm sorry, what's funny?" he asked. He looked confused and a little severe.

"Oh, it's just such a fun name, Sillyvision," I said, trying to explain and feeling painfully awkward. We'd been having such a lovely time, and the temperature of the room had changed suddenly with my small giggle. I needed to remember that. As warm and thoughtful as Joey was, he was changeable like that. Not mean, but he was a genius, and such great minds tended to be constantly on the move in their own brains, and interrupting a train of thought with an irresponsible laugh wasn't fair for him.

"Yes, it is, we do make cartoons after all," said Joey slowly, almost as if he was deciding if he wanted to be annoyed with me or not. He seemed to choose "not" because as he continued his voice got warmer, and he spoke quickly and with great energy. "But despite its name, Sillyvision is actually some rather serious stuff. I was able to invent a new type of ink just before the studio unfortunately had to shut down. It allows you greater flexibility and speed in the creation of new cartoons but, even better, allows you to put yourself into these cartoons as well."

"Like one of those books? Where they replace the main character's name with your own?" I'd never received one, but my friend Dora had got one once for her birthday.

Joey's brow furrowed for a moment, but then he brightened again. "Ha, well, in the most basic, simplest of ways, but surely you can see how changing a word versus adding a whole figure to a moving picture is a vastly different enterprise."

I could see that, yes. I nodded.

"Good! Well, it was all going marvelously, but then, let me tell you—it's just a temporary setback, mind you—but with my studio closing, many things had to be put on pause. Until we can start things up again, which we will! Have no fear, especially once this show is a great success!"

"I have no doubt it will be!" I said. Why wouldn't it? Everyone loved Bendy cartoons.

"This is the next step forward in the Sillyvision goal. Why put an illustration of a person into a cartoon when we can put the actual person into one?" He snapped his fingers then. "Evan, the glasses!" he commanded.

With an obvious reluctance, Evan rose and placed those same glasses I had knocked onto the floor into Joey's outstretched hand. Joey didn't even look at him, just held up the glasses for me to see. "What these glasses do, well, it takes some inspiration from the new 3-D movies, but it's going to be so much more than just an image popping out at you. It'll be like you're in the show with all the characters. As if you are interacting with them. Are you familiar with my memoir?"

"You have a memoir?" I asked. How wonderful to have a life worth telling, worth putting on paper for others to read about.

Joey laughed. "I guess that means you're not. It's called *The Illusion of Living*, and it's not just some fancy title, it's my life's philosophy."

"Oh, wow." Imagine having a life's philosophy.

Joey's smile widened but there was something behind the eyes, a bit of a strain. I worried I was insulting him with my ignorance now. But I didn't know what I could say in this kind of moment. I felt stuck.

"It's a very complicated philosophy. That's why I needed to write a whole book on the subject, but the point is, living is an illusion, and reality is all fantasy. And we need to decide what we do with that information."

That was the sort of twisty mind-bending sentence I had no idea what to do with. "I don't quite understand."

"No, of course you don't," said Joey, his expression softening a little. "You'd have to be a genius to understand without reading the whole book. And even then, you still might not fully appreciate it. But my goal with these glasses is to cross that divide. Imagine a world where you could literally be someone else. What would that do, how would that change everything?"

I didn't have an answer yet, though my mind was spinning with the question. If you could be anyone else, even for just a moment, what would that do for society at large? "That's fascinating!" I said, still thinking hard while staring at the Bendy cartoon loop playing in front of me. Bendy had entered a small house in the forest, with Boris the Wolf inside trying to bake a pie.

Joey smiled at me. "I'm thrilled you think so, kid. Some people find this kind of stuff boring."

"Not me," I said. I was watching the story play out on the televisions. Bendy trying to bake Boris into a pie.

"We are at the testing stage, just in time for the show to premiere. We're going to test it on a beta level first, and then . . . Well, then we're going to ship it all worldwide!"

"It'll change television as we know it!" I said. Bendy was touching the fire on the range, then putting his finger in his mouth, as if he was tasting if it was hot enough. So silly.

"Sure, television, but also Bendy."

I nodded. But I was still thinking about the idea of the technology and it changing everything, like Joey said. What you could do with something like that if you could involve your audience in such an immediate way. Why, it would be terribly fun of course, just like going to a 3-D movie, but if it worked the way he said it worked, it could elevate a person's under-standing and empathy. It could literally allow you to walk in someone else's shoes. Why, you could end conflict as we knew it. If people could see and understand the other side, feel what others felt. We'd never have to go to war again. Suddenly the Bendy cartoon vanished from the screens, replaced with static. A whirling storm of crackling snow. It twisted my train of thought, brought me back to reality.

"And now we come back to you, Rose," said Joey. He moved in front of the televisions and was now silhouetted by the static, a dark figure flickering in front of me.

"Me?" There was something intimidating about him now. It made me feel a little uncomfortable.

"Would you do me the distinct honor of being one of my test families?"

I stared at the figure. I knew my mouth must have been open. I was terribly in shock. Me? My family? Of all the peo-ple in the studio, in the city, in the country, he wanted our thoughts and opinions. "Of course! Yes!" I paused. "What does that entail though?"

Joey clapped his hands together and laughed apprecia-tively. If it hadn't been for the laugh, I might have been a little spooked. The clap was loud and had startled me. I felt a bit like Evan in that moment. Jumping at the smallest noises. I was so very used to things going bump in the night, it was hard to startle me. But it could be done. I thought of Ollie last night in the dark. Yes, it definitely could be done.

"It entails you and your family watching *The Joey Drew Show* with our wonderful new glasses." Joey seemed thrilled, but I had a sudden pang in my stomach. A deep sadness mixed with a little shame.

"Oh, I'm so sorry, but we don't have a television," I said. I wanted to hide my face, but I kept my chin up. Even as the shame burned in my cheeks.

"Oh, dear child," said Joey. He stepped toward me into the light. He was no longer a silhouette but a real person, a man with kindness on his face, and understanding. "I never expected you did. But even if you had one, it wouldn't do you any good. You need our TV to go with the glasses."

"I don't understand." I felt safe and seen, but I still didn't understand.

"I'm giving you a television. And one pair of glasses. That's the funny thing: It's the glasses that are the most expensive. I hope your family doesn't mind sharing."

"We don't mind sharing at all," I said in a daze. Did he really just say he was going to give us a television?

"Then it's settled! I'll have them deliver it to you later this week, before the show goes live Saturday night."

9

There was so much to get done

and so little time to do it. Though I was learning, even in my short tenure in the television biz, that this was pretty normal. Everyone was always running just a little behind, and everyone was always just a little bit panicked. The set builders would get the wrong-sized plank of wood, the painters the wrong shade of green, a lightbulb would burst just as we were starting a dress rehearsal, and so on. When I wasn't in the studio and I wasn't bringing coffee to Evan in the lab, I was sent out on all manner of errands. I would meet other PAs like me in the elevator, all frazzled, always talking about schedules. The more I got to know of the world of television, the more I understood Papa D's gruff bluntness. There was no time for pleasantries here!

"That is the last time I want anyone crossing through my line of vision!" yelled out Joey, stopping rehearsal for the fifth time now. It was Friday night. And by that I meant night. It was already six o'clock and I had just returned with a stack of sandwiches from the diner across the street.

"I'm sorry," stammered the gaffer, holding the roll of duct tape aloft in his hand by way of explanation. "I was told . . ."

"I don't care what you were told. I'm the producer, I'm the star, you only have a job because of me. If I tell you I need silence and stillness to do my darn job, then I better as heck get it!" I'd seen Joey frustrated, I'd seen him be incredibly intense, so intense of course that I had truly thought I was being fired my first day. But I'd never seen him this enraged. I quickly grabbed his sandwich from the top of the pile after placing them on the table and walked into the spotlight.

"I have your food," I said and smiled as warmly as I could. That kind of smile I used when talking to Father in the dark living room. I walked slowly and carefully too, approaching him from the side. I wanted to be all soft edges, not a single threat here. I lowered my voice as I got near; he was still glaring out into the darkness. "He's not the brightest, you know that," I said quietly.

It was true. Dean was sweet but dim. And a terrible klutz. He was the sort of person you knew could somehow manage to knock over the only chair in an empty field. "He meant no harm. Let's take a short break. The sandwiches are really good tonight." I tried to keep the music in my voice, and automatically raised it a few pitches. I always thought a higher voice was a less threatening voice.

Joey didn't turn right away. But he heard me. Then, after a moment, he slowly looked at the sandwich in my hand, then at me. And smiled. "The feminine touch, taming the wild beast, eh?" he said with a laugh. I laughed back in relief. *Whatever it took*, I thought. Whatever got him to smile again.

He took the sandwich from my hand. "Dean, go ahead, tape everything you want. Tape it all down. Tape my mouth

shut, if you need to. Let's take ten and eat. But I *mean* ten."
He laughed and the team around us also laughed. I smiled
brightly, proud of myself to be perfectly honest. As Joey turned
away from the cameras and toward me, he said, "One more
strike and that kid's out on his backside."

I didn't know what to say to that. So instead I asked, "Do
you need anything else?"

Joey looked at me for a long moment, then shook his head.
"I don't suppose you could come in tomorrow afternoon, be here
for the taping." He said it in a way that didn't feel like an order,
but I hated letting him down. I bit my lower lip. "What is it?"
he asked.

"It's just . . . of course if you need me . . . I only thought
that it would be nice to be there when the television arrived.
We're also hosting a viewing party, so Mother will need help
getting the house ready and making food for everyone . . ." I
trailed off. I felt very average indeed saying all this. Not like
someone ready to climb the ladder at work, not like someone
who was interested in new technology and new inventions.

"No, no, you must help out! The greatest help of all will be
your family trying out the glasses." He spoke with excitement
and enthusiasm.

"We are terribly excited, especially my little brother,
Oliver," I said.

"Perfect for a young boy, it's just the thing. He'll love it, I
promise!" He smiled and I smiled back. "Right, I have to collect
my thoughts, so I need some alone time now, Rose."

"Absolutely." I practically clicked my heels together at the
command and quickly slipped back out of the spotlight to join
the others at the snack table.

●●●●●●●●●●●●●●●●●●●●

"It's here, it's here!" Ollie had been perched on the back of the sofa for a solid hour staring out through the front curtains. I think all three of us were rather impressed. He wasn't the sort of kid who stayed still for very long. But he had sat, wide-eyed like an owl, even refusing to come to the table for snack time. And now all his hard work had paid off!

Because, yes, there it was: the television. A large white truck drove up the street, chased by three kids a little younger than Ollie. When it pulled to a stop, Ollie was quick as lightning through the front door to join them, and Mother gave me a meaningful look, so I quickly raced out after him while she and Father observed from the window.

"You're too fast, Ollie!" I said, panting a little when I arrived at his side at the back of the truck. The two large men who had driven it were shooing away the kids, trying to get through to the rolling door.

"Scram, kids!" one of the men said.

The kids scattered a few feet but slowly came closer again, like pigeons trying to snag leftovers from a picnic. I grabbed Ollie from behind, hugging him around his torso, and pulled him back with me to let the men by. But I didn't want to move too far out of the way either. I was as curious as the children, possibly more so since I understood how meaningful this experiment was to Joey.

Together in one swift movement the two men hoisted open the back of the truck. It made a satisfying clang. The inside was relatively empty, I was surprised to see. The moment the larger of the two men hopped into the back of the truck, the kids swarmed, looking over into the truck, their chins perched on top of the serrated metal edge.

"You'll hurt yourselves!" I said. But I knew they wouldn't listen to me. Anyway, growing up in this neighborhood you were expected to come home with a new bruise or cut every day. Adventures in the city were fun, but they were also full of sharp unexpected edges, missed curbs, and roots pushing out through cement sidewalks.

The man pushed forward a giant wrapped package in brown paper. The kids made the requisite awed sounds, but I was more concerned than impressed. I stared as it loomed over us. It was a lot bigger than I'd anticipated. Would it even fit in the living room? Would it fit through the door? I didn't want my parents to feel like their home wasn't up to snuff.

"You gotta get these kids under control." The man was talking to me and I nodded. I didn't want them getting squished by this beast of a package.

"Come on, everyone, back off, back off!" I used my best grown-up voice and pushed Ollie behind me, grabbing the kid right in front of me by the cuff of his coat. "Come on!" He staggered back and shot me an evil glare, shaking himself out of my grip. But he eased off and the other kids did too.

The two men heaved the giant package off the truck and started to carry it toward our steps.

"Golly, Rose, is that really for you?" asked Stevie. I knew Stevie. He could sound as cute as all get-out, but be careful on Halloween or he'd pummel you with eggs.

"For the whole family," I replied. But it *was* sort of for me. It was because of me. I couldn't help but grin.

"That thing's gonna fall right through the floor into the cellar," said some kid I didn't recognize.

"Nuts to you, we don't have a cellar!" called back Ollie.

"Ollie!" I said, shocked by his language. He looked down immediately in shame. I didn't want him to feel bad, but I didn't like seeing him like this. I liked my sweet boy. He wasn't just another child hooligan.

My father opened the door then, just as the men were starting their ascent up the three steps of our stoop. He looked a little pale, but I knew he was doing his best to be sociable and just a regular Joe like every other father on the street. But I knew that all the activity and excitement was hard on him.

"This way, gentlemen," he said with a smile. And the large men heaved the large television through the threshold. There was nothing more for the kids to see, so they turned back to the truck. Stevie even climbed inside to get a good look.

"Come on, Ollie," I said. "Let's go see our new TV!"

Ollie looked at me, lifting his chin way up in order to do so. He smiled now. I smiled back. All was forgiven.

We followed the men inside. I felt a bit like a guest in my own home, seeing it how strangers might. The narrow dark staircase starting almost right when you stepped over the threshold, the arch on the right that led into our small sitting room with the sofa and Father's chair facing the fireplace. As the men heaved the package into the space, I felt at a loss. There wasn't any room for it.

"Where d'you want it, ma'am?" one of the men asked Mother, who was staring around the room just as intently as I was.

"Goodness, I couldn't say," she replied.

I looked for Father but he had disappeared upstairs. So quickly? He'd been doing so much better lately, but he couldn't even manage a few minutes of these men in the house. I felt my insides tighten. Already I felt the heavy weight of this new burden directly on my shoulders.

"If we moved Father's chair next to the sofa, then we could put it there," I suggested. Mother looked at me, worried. I understood. Any change in Father's routine was not generally a good idea. "Or we could move the sofa over to the chair? Put the television in front of the window?"

"Either way works for us," said the other man. His voice sounded strained.

"Would you be able to do that for us? Move the sofa?" I was feeling a little desperate now.

The man looked at me and I must have had some kind of pathetic expression on my face because he sighed hard and nodded. He signaled the other man, and together they placed the package in the archway to the living room and then made their way to the sofa. It was like nothing for them to move, or at least seemed that way. I was incredibly grateful. Then they finally placed the television in its official location.

"Good?" asked one of them, looking at me.

I nodded. "Thank you."

"Good," said the other. They left quickly, probably worried we'd have more chores for them to do, but before they did, one of them passed me a small rectangular package. "Here," he said, not even pausing, just marching out of the room and the house. I watched them from the door as they climbed back into the truck to make their escape, but not before swatting away a few kids from the truck doors first. I looked at the package in my hand and turned to rejoin my mother and brother.

And then we were alone with it, a large looming box wrapped in brown paper blocking half the window, staring at us.

"Should I get Father?" I asked.

"Let him rest."

I nodded. The celebratory mood had turned somber. The puddles had won again.

"Can I open it?" asked Ollie. He was so excited that he was pacing about in place. Leave it to Ollie to raise everyone's spirits.

"Of course you can," I said, glancing at Mother, who smiled at me.

Ollie rushed over to the giant package and tore at it like it was a birthday present. He was such a sweet, soft-spoken kid most of the time, but he was ruthless when it came to wrapping paper. Usually we had to hold him back and remind him that wrapping paper was special and cost a lot, and we needed to save it for the next presents. He forgot often enough that Mother had taken to wrapping his presents in old newspapers. Ollie didn't mind. It wasn't the look he cared about, it was the tearing part.

However, since none of the brown paper had come at our expense, Mother just stood and smiled, shaking her head as her youngest accessed his most basic animal instincts and pulled apart the packaging with glee.

It took a little more effort than I think even Ollie was prepared for, but finally with a big grunt from his gut he ripped the package open.

There it stood, shiny and new. Our very own television. The square screen was contained within a rich, shiny box made of chestnut wood, standing sturdy on four solid legs. It had one large silver knob for changing channels and one slightly rounder and smaller one for turning it on and off and adjusting the volume. The whole thing was about twice the height of the screen itself, as below the screen a mesh made of pale yellow indicated the speaker system. With the added height the legs gave it, it was so tall it hid the bottom half of the front window quite completely, but it made for a rather beautiful view in its own right. It was a perfect-looking TV. Like something out of an ad in the newspaper. If only we looked quite as beautiful as the families usually featured with it. If only we could be that normal. That effortlessly content. No dark secrets, no dark moments.

Even so, Ollie with his mussed-up hair from the violent unwrapping, Mother with her happy but exhausted smile, and me with my general awkwardness, well, there was something nice to that picture, I thought. Something honest and true.

"Can I turn it on?" asked Ollie, breathless.

Mother placed her hand on his shoulder and he turned to look up at her. It was enough of an answer. He nodded and pressed his lips together.

"When we're all together," I said. "It'll be better that way."

"Yes," he said, squaring his shoulders and raising his chin just so. "It will be. What's that?" He noticed the package in my hand, which reminded me I was still holding it.

"I'm not sure. Let's have a look," I replied. I carefully unstuck the tape at both ends and peeled off the paper, revealing a rectangular black box, rounded on the ends, with hinges. Carefully I opened it.

Of course.

"What is it, what is it?" asked Ollie, peering over my hands to have a look.

With one hand still holding the case, I used my other hand to pull out its contents.

"It's the glasses."

10

We still had so much to do, and

Ollie was a wonderful little brother with it all. He even swept up the kitchen (which he had to do three times because he insisted on doing it while we were still getting everything ready). He dusted in the living room and insisted on cleaning the windows. I was pretty sure he only insisted on doing that because it meant he got to clean the glass on the television, even though it already was glistening and pristine.

"He's so cute," I said to Mother, who shook her head. We were pulling out Grandmother's crystal punch bowl and the little crystal cups that went with it from the high shelf in the cabinet above the sink. She was teetering on the stepladder, passing me these perfect little glittering cups while I placed them carefully on the kitchen table. "Are you sure I shouldn't be doing this?" I asked. But Mother shook her head no.

"Rose, you take care of everything. I am capable of some things, you know," she replied. "Besides, I can't trust anyone with my mother's crystal."

Guests started arriving around seven and by then we had set the punch on the dining room table, surrounded by finger foods. Mother had gone all out with pigs in a blanket, deviled eggs, and a variety of savory goodness on crackers. Mother enjoyed putting things on crackers. We had cucumber and cream cheese, we even had some deli meats, and some kind of salmon mousse that had come from a tin. That one I wasn't entirely certain about. But it all looked marvelously delicious. The neighbors didn't come empty-handed either and soon the table was full of sweets as well: brownies, an upside-down pineapple cake, and a giant platter of sugar cookies.

Father joined us around seven thirty, and he looked so dapper in his suit and so calm and cheerful that I wanted to cry. When he saw the television, he was more excited than anyone. "I missed the whole reveal," he explained to Mr. Martin from next door.

"Truck was huge, the exhaust filled up the whole street," Mr. Martin replied, displeased as always. He shoved a deviled egg in his mouth. "Needs more paprika."

The little kids were running wild, playing a game of tag through the house. We had predicted this possibility and hidden most of the breakable items under Mother and Father's bed upstairs. Still, they did a good job at knocking over furniture and almost Diane Smythe herself. "Little terrors!" she called out after them. Of course her son, Timmy, was the ringleader, so if there was anyone to blame . . . I glanced at Father, but he seemed to be doing well even with all the noise and chaos. But I was on high alert. I was always on high alert. Just in case.

I went upstairs briefly to use the bathroom and came back down, pausing on the stairs to look at the scene. My heart felt so full. We were a packed house, everyone standing very closely to one another, eating and drinking, talking and laughing. I loved the liveliness of it all. Our house could be so quiet at times, too quiet. Seeing it like this made me feel like this was what a home was supposed to be like. The kids with their whoops and hollering. The adults were all so colorful, the ladies in their tea-length dresses, the men in their suits. No one was rich around here, and everyone generally wore the same thing to all the parties, but I thought they all looked so grand nonetheless. Everyone in our neighborhood had taken great care before coming to our party, and even if it was humble, there was an honor in knowing they had taken the time. The ladies were gathered by the food, laughing heartily at something Mother had said. There was a circle of men around the television, looking it over carefully, pointing at the knobs, and examining the hookup at the back. Mr. Jackson picked up the glasses case that we had placed on top of the television. He opened it to examine them. I skipped lightly down the stairs to join them.

"This is Joey Drew's latest invention," I said, interjecting.

"Who's Joey Drew?" asked Mr. Jackson, who took the glasses out of their case. He put them on and laughed. "What do we think?"

"You look like your brother," replied Mr. Martin.

"That egghead!" Mr. Jackson laughed hard. "Quick, take 'em back!" He tore them off his face. He was being so careless with them that I quickly reached out and snatched them from his grip. He looked shocked. So did all the men in the little group.

"I'm sorry," I said. "They're just not ours, they're a loan. And they're quite expensive."

"Ridiculous," said Mr. Martin. "I had a pair at the movies just last week. Dime a dozen."

"No, no, these are glass, see," I said holding them up. "And metal. And they don't work anything like the ones at the movies. They are a new kind of technology."

"A new kind of technology, huh?" said Mr. Jackson with a laugh. He reached out for the glasses again, but I pulled them away instinctively. "Now you're playing keep-away."

"Frank, knock it off," said Father. He had his serious voice now, and I knew the men would listen.

"I'm sorry, but we were only given one pair and they are for Ollie to use," I explained.

"Don't worry, Rose," said Father, placing a hand on my shoulder. "He understands."

Mr. Jackson rolled his eyes, and as I walked away over toward the food I heard him mutter, "Should have got enough for all the kids."

He wasn't wrong in a way, but he also just didn't understand. And I didn't think Joey would want me necessarily explaining the ins and outs of his new technology. It might be secret, and quite honestly, Mr. Jackson wouldn't understand it anyway. I glanced at the clock on the mantle. It was almost eight. I made my way over to Mother.

"It's almost time," I said. Mother was always the right person to tell when it came to keeping things on track. She was never scared to raise her voice over the din of a room, and never concerned if she interrupted others, not if there was a schedule to maintain. She clapped her hands together loudly to get everyone's attention. I noticed Father flinch, but he rallied quickly, and soon all the adults were gathering on the furniture that we had put together for our makeshift audience that evening. A few kitchen chairs, the sofa of course, and Father sat in his chair. The grown-ups who didn't get a seat hovered behind, and a couple stayed as close as they could to the punch bowl and food.

The kids gathered on the floor, battling it out for center spot, but I settled that. That place of honor would be for Ollie, especially since he was wearing the glasses. There was some pouting, but generally everyone was accepting of this. Though I think Ollie was a little embarrassed. He had always been taught to share but I'd explained to him before anyone arrived that these were very delicate and special glasses. This would be the one time he couldn't.

Except: "Rose, you should look first. You're the reason we have the TV."

I felt awkward, very much the center of attention now as everyone in the room stared at me standing by the fireplace. "No, Ollie, it's okay."

"Please?" he asked. He held out the glasses for me so I quickly took them and smiled.

"Just for a minute. I really don't need to," I said. Ollie beamed and turned back to face the television. Inwardly I was quite pleased with the offer; after all, I did have a strong desire to try out the technology myself. But it would have felt like taking candy from a baby by depriving Ollie of the opportunity. Besides, didn't Joey want reactions from real people, from his intended audience? That was Ollie in a nutshell.

"Everybody ready?" asked Mother, standing next to the television.

"Let's do it!" announced Father from his chair. I beamed. It was so wonderful to see him in his element like this. In charge and content.

There was a chorus of "Yes!" and some of the kids cheered. Mother laughed and turned on the television. A tiny pinprick of light appeared in the center of the screen. Everyone stared at it as if hypnotized. It grew larger and larger until the entire screen beamed at us. Mother clicked the bulky silver knob to the correct channel. And there was Bendy!

Another cheer from the kids and then laughter from the adults at their enthusiasm for a still image. It was a picture of Bendy, motionless, caught mid-wave with large words "Up Next: *The Joey Drew Show!*" And underneath in a smaller font: "Brought to You by Arch Steel." Seeing Joey's name gave me a small thrill. I knew him! I worked for him! I'd been working on this very show with him!

The screen changed then and there was the man himself, just as we'd rehearsed so many times, standing in his cartoon makeshift artist's studio. On TV it looked so much bigger. You couldn't see where the set suddenly came to a stop and the studio began. You couldn't tell that just over his head was a catwalk where giant lights were hanging. You couldn't see the camera operators, the grips, the sound technicians, all the other people. You could only see Joey, smiling at us.

"Well, hello!" he said, turning around in his chair as if we'd caught him in the middle of drawing. "I didn't see you there! My name is Joey Drew. Welcome to my studio!"

Our little audience applauded and Ollie turned to grin at me. "Rose! Put them on!" he insisted when he noticed the glasses still just hanging from my hand.

"Oh, yes," I said. And I did.

I was instantly transported. It didn't feel like the typical 3-D movie at all. The images weren't popping out at me in my own living room, but rather I was suddenly back in the studio. On the set. With Joey. I gasped lightly and then immediately hoped I hadn't been too audible. Except it didn't feel like I was on a set. It felt like I was in a room with him. It threw me off, and I pulled the glasses up just to look, to remind myself I was still here, in our house in Brooklyn.

Slowly I lowered them again and there was Joey talking right to me. "I thought I'd introduce you to one of my best friends. Would you like that?" I nodded. I turned to look behind me, at what I knew was Lenny behind his giant camera. But he wasn't there. No one was there. The entire studio had vanished. Instead I was staring at another cartoon wall with more bulletin boards and more pictures tacked to it. And next to it, a door. I was inside an alternate sort of reality, this cartoon set that I was so familiar with but now it was complete. Not a set anymore, but a real room. I looked up. There was a ceiling replacing the black void. Everything looked a little yellow, like faded paper. I looked at the door again as Joey continued to talk to my back. I wondered what would happen if I walked toward it, if I reached out to open it. I stretched my arm out and took a step forward.

"This is Bendy!"

I felt a tug on my dress and turned back to Joey. He was still there, as real as day. But black-and-white of course because he was on television, not in color like I was used to seeing him. I glanced down to where I'd felt the tug. Bendy. Bendy himself, with his bow tie and his little grin. He was standing, looking up at me, coming up to about the middle of my thigh. He had pulled on my skirts. How had he done that? He waved. I waved back.

I felt a panic rise within me and quickly pulled the glasses off. I was facing the television, exactly where I had been, my feet firmly planted. Animated Bendy appeared on the television screen much like he had while I was wearing the glasses. This I hadn't seen before. The kids were loving it. But my mind was racing. I turned to Penelope, Diane's sister, who was a year below me in school. "Did I move?" I asked in a whisper.

She looked at me. "What?"

"Did you see me move? Turn around or anything?"

She stared at me. "No . . ."

"Are you sure?"

"Of course I'm sure. Now hush, I'm watching the show." It was a whispered conversation but Mrs. Martin from across the room said, "Shh," and I turned back to look at the television. I took in a few breaths to calm myself. I hadn't been prepared, that was the problem. I had been talking about the glasses for the last week and about the new technology and Sillyvision, and I had understood that this was more than just the average 3-D viewing experience. But I had not fully grasped the magnitude of what Joey and Evan had created. It would change the experience of watching television and films forever.

I felt a little dizzy and then I remembered: Ollie.

"Ollie," I whispered. He turned, his eyes wide and full of excitement. "It's your turn." This was certainly something he needed to experience. As I bent to pass him the glasses over Timmy's and Lollie's heads, I added, "It's a very shocking experience at first. Don't be scared."

Lollie giggled. "Don't be a scaredy-cat, Ollie," she said.

Ollie grabbed the glasses from me and gave me a look. He was such a sweet kid, but he didn't like people thinking bad things about him, just like anybody wouldn't. I felt a little guilty. But not that guilty. I'd rather he be embarrassed by me than unprepared.

He put on the glasses just as the screen shifted to show us a Bendy cartoon. I recognized it immediately. It was "Little Devil Darlin'." I'd seen it before as a little kid in the movie theaters before a feature, and Joey had explained it had been his first-ever cartoon. The kids laughed just like I had when I was their age. Bendy never went out of style. And I felt more calm and at ease now, settling into watching the show just like everyone else. I glanced at Ollie, but he didn't seem to be bothered in the least by the glasses. On the contrary he was smiling almost as big as Bendy.

Which of course made me smile too.

Half an hour later and six more Bendy shorts, it was done. Joey said good night and that he'd see us next week, and then the screen turned back to a card, this one advertising *True or False*. Everyone applauded and Mother turned on the lights.

"That was fun!" said Timmy, bounding to his feet. He looked ready to run around the house for a few more hours, absolutely buzzing.

"It was," said Mrs. Jackson, his mother. "And now it's time for bed!"

That was the cue and the other kids scrambled to their feet as the adults began their farewells. I moved over to Ollie, who was still sitting in front of the television. He was staring at the card for *True or False*. He still had the glasses on.

I touched him gently on the shoulder and he turned abruptly. Then laughed. "Rose! You scared me!"

He took the glasses off and handed them to me. Such a good kid.

"Well, what did you think? Isn't it keen?" I asked.

"Super keen! It was like I was there with them!" He was practically bouncing in place.

"Night, Rose. Night, Ollie!" called out Mr. Jackson. I gave him a perfunctory wave.

"Did you turn around? Did you look up?" I asked.

"I did! I even walked around a little. I drank from the stream even!"

"That's amazing!" I said. It really was. I don't think Ollie fully understood how fantastic it all actually was. Kids take things in stride. Every experience is a new one, something they don't have anything to compare to, so it's all equally thrilling. It was exciting for him, but the magnitude, understanding how new and different this was? The ability for a person to invent such a thing, the science and brains behind it? I don't think that was something Ollie could fully grasp.

Ollie suddenly launched himself at me and hugged me backward onto the floor in a full tackle. "Thank you, Rose! This was the best!"

"Aw, my pleasure, kiddo!" I said, laughing.

I held him tight and smiled so hard. He had no idea how much.

11

I woke with a start. I couldn't
say why. There was no noise from outside; in fact, it was
strangely much quieter than usual. I sifted through my mind,
searching for a dream or a nightmare that might have woken
me up, but I had no memories other than of the evening we'd
all just had.

Still a small, hard, round ball of dread was lodged somewhere in my middle and I sat up, resting on my hands, and
looked around the small dark room.

Father? Maybe that was it. Had he cried out in the night?
All was silent now, but the thought was enough to worry me, so
I carefully pulled my blanket and sheet off and slipped onto the
cold ground. I quickly put on my slippers and pulled my dress-
ing gown from the hook on the back of the door, wrapping myself
up in a manufactured warmth. The house was always frigid on
winter nights. Heat was for waking hours. And even though I
couldn't see my frozen breath like outside, it felt very close.

I slipped out into the hallway. I saw something move out
of the corner of my eye and turned quickly to peer into the
dark. Nothing, of course nothing. Just the darkness playing

tricks with the mind. I took a deep breath to settle my nerves and kept going. I passed Ollie's room and then pressed my ear against the door to my parents'. Nothing. No hushed whispers or quiet sobs. That was good. But the dread still sat firmly entrenched in my insides so I carefully and quietly opened the door, just a crack, just to see.

Mother and Father both slept soundly, I could hear their rhythmic breathing now. I felt calmer. Relieved. I closed the door.

I stood for a moment and then, just to be sure, I went and opened Ollie's door. Sometimes the poor kid would cry out from a nightmare and it was best if I took care of him in those moments. It was too much of a burden on Mother to have to soothe another member of her family back to sleep in the dark of nighttime.

I opened the door to an empty bed. My breath caught in my throat and my head felt light. I stared at the sheets tossed to one side, the covers fallen onto the floor, and it took me all the strength I had not to cry out. I was simply surprised, I told myself. That was it. I had expected to see his little face and then hadn't. That was all.

That was all.

I closed the door. I now had to find him even though I knew it didn't really matter that I did. It was a small house. He was safe. Unless he had fallen down the stairs maybe, bumped his head. What a series of nonsense; I put those thoughts aside. I walked quietly but quickly along the hall, glancing into the bathroom to see. Ollie?

I stopped and stared. No, the room was empty. I took a step toward it and looked around the door at the bathtub. But we weren't playing hide-and-seek. And Ollie wasn't hiding in the shadows. He wasn't there.

I backed out of the room and then I turned the corner to make my way down the stairs.

I stopped.

There was light. A cold glow flickered into the staircase and the downstairs hallway. It lit the space in a ghostly blue, casting long drawn-out shadows of the banister on the wall. Tall and thin bars. Like a prison cell.

I felt a chill, separate from the cold in the house. A chill that came from deep within.

I walked slowly down the stairs, craning my neck to see around the wall. Halfway down I uncovered the source of the light. The television. Of course. The television was on. But nothing would be on at this time of night, surely.

I stepped off the last step and walked slowly over to the arch that led into the living room. I stared. I stayed quiet as I stared, not fully able to understand what I was looking at.

I had, at least, found Ollie.

He sat there, on the left, cross-legged and in the middle of the rug very much how he had sat during the screening last night. He was staring at the television, perfectly still, utterly engrossed. His expression was blank, not the giddy joy he'd had when we'd watched the show, but neither was it bored or impatient. It was all consumed.

I couldn't see his eyes.

He was wearing the glasses.

He glowed bright and monochromatic in the television light.

And he just stared at the screen.

It took me a moment to even think to look at the television itself. There was something in Ollie's trancelike state that froze me to the bone. Together we were a pair of statues. I could barely move to breathe. But again I saw a movement in the shadows and I was shaken back to the present moment. Once again I looked but all I could see was the bright screen and the darkness of the drawn curtains behind it. There were no shows at this time of night. Everything was done, the world was asleep. All that Ollie was watching was flickering static. Just there. Just glowing.

I turned back to look at Ollie. It was unnerving. His still-ness, his focus. The dark that crept in around the pool of light, the blackness of the sofa behind him, of Father's chair.

"Ollie?" I said softly. I don't know why, but I was nervous to make any sudden noises or sounds.

He didn't move.

I took a small step closer, still standing in the hall, strangely wary of crossing the threshold into the living room.

"Ollie?" I asked a little louder. I heard a creak from above and I quickly turned my head to look up the stairs. I didn't want to have woken Mother or Father.

No one. Just a black emptiness at the top.

I didn't feel alone though. I very much felt like something was on the fringes of my senses. Something that I couldn't quite catch. I couldn't quite see.

I turned back.

Ollie was staring right at me.

I didn't cry out, but I covered my mouth with my hands. I had learned my lesson from the other night. But my heart was pumping fast from the shock.

I still couldn't see his eyes, and lit as he was from the side by the TV, the glasses almost made it look like he was staring out of large round hollows. As if he didn't have eyes at all.

I tried not to look at them and instead focused intensely on Ollie instead. I crouched, trying to see my sweet little brother in all the strange, eerie ghastliness.

"Ollie, are you okay?" I asked softly, gently, like I was speaking to a frightened stray dog.

He stared. He just stared.

I bit the inside of my cheek, just to feel the sting of pain to stay calm.

"Ollie, can you hear me?"

Nothing.

I reached out carefully, slowly. He didn't move, didn't even seem to notice my actions at all. I didn't like this. I didn't like it at all. My fingers made contact with the arm of the glasses and in one swift motion I pulled them off his face. I almost feared what I'd see underneath, but as I pulled back, I could see Ollie's eyes, wide and confused, and then he closed them, bending his head down and rubbing his hands against them.

"Are you okay?" I asked again. I moved a little closer. His natural response to the glasses coming off comforted me greatly and gave me confidence.

"Yes?" he said quietly, more to himself as he continued to rub his eyes. He stopped and opened them again, looking first at me and then at the television. "Is it over?" he asked.

"Yes, it was over hours ago, remember?" I said. I had moved in right next to him and sat cross-legged beside him. "I think you might have been sleepwalking, kiddo," I said.

He stared at the television in confusion and shook his head a little. Then he looked back at me. "I sleepwalk?"

It was my turn to shake my head. "There's a first time for everything."

"What time is it?"

I glanced at the clock on the mantel above the fireplace. It flickered in the glowing artificial light of the snow. "Three thirty, kiddo."

A little gasp. "I've never been up this late, Rose." I looked back at him; his face was aghast. I couldn't help but smile. I felt such a relief seeing any kind of expression on it in the first place.

I reached out and pulled him into a tight hug. He melted into my arms and I finally felt fully at ease. "Well, what do you think about being up so late?"

Ollie wrapped his arms around me, hugging me back. "I don't think I like it. It's spooky."

"Well," I said, looking up at the dark room, which still had that ominous glow to it. "Spooky" was definitely an appropriate word, but I didn't want to worry the kid. "I think it's probably just the television. How about we turn it off and get you back into bed."

Ollie nodded into my arm and together we helped each other to stand. I looked at him just for a moment. His kind eyes had a warm but still-confused expression. I couldn't help but give his hair a tussle.

"No!" he whined, but he smiled also.

"Shh," I said. "Why don't you get into bed? I'll take care of things down here. Be up in a minute."

Ollie nodded and turned toward the stairs. He was so quiet you couldn't even hear him climb them, and he was so light that they didn't make a single squeak.

Good kid.

I turned back to the television and made to cross the room. My foot grazed on something cold and I pulled it away quickly.

Thank goodness too, because I realized only then that I had almost crushed the extremely expensive 3-D glasses. I picked them up carefully and folded the arms back against the lenses. I held them for a moment. There was nothing truly sinister about them. They were just glasses. Maybe it was just the lateness of the hour, the staring, the wide black circles, empty, emotionless.

A shiver went down my spine and I turned now to the television. Enough of this. I walked over and placed the glasses on top of it. Then in one quick motion I turned off the knob with a satisfying click.

The room went dark.

I felt a wave of relief. It was strange to find the dark comforting after all these years of dreading it. But I did in that moment. And then I felt tired. So very tired.

I went upstairs and found Ollie tucked under the covers all the way up to his chin. I let out a little laugh. "Comfy?"

He looked at me and nodded.

I sat beside him and ran my fingers through his hair.

"Stay with me until I fall asleep, Rose," he said. He didn't ask it. He didn't demand it either. But there was a sort of need in how he said it.

"Of course I will."

And so I did. Until I could hear his breathing become regular and see his head fall slightly to the side. I kissed him on the forehead and quietly made my way back to my room.

Only then did I lower my face into my hands.

And cried.

12

The rest of the day was for recovery. It was cold and gray outside, and I felt very much the same on the inside, even as I tried to buck up an exhausted Ollie. We didn't mention our nighttime adventure to Mother or Father. We both knew how to keep certain secrets. Besides, we didn't get much of an opportunity to anyway. Father for his part stayed in his room all day, and Mother, Ollie, and I had spent the day cleaning up after all the excitement. Then it was early to bed for everyone, which no one, not even Ollie, complained about. But I couldn't fall asleep. I just lay there, waiting for Ollie to sneak out to the television. I was on high alert, just in case. But he hadn't left the room. Not once. No one had left their room except me. I couldn't help it. I had to make sure. I stood at the top of the stairs but I didn't see a glow. And I was too scared to actually climb down them to confirm the TV was indeed off. The darkness would do. The unsettling darkness could be a small comfort.

I went to the bathroom and drank some water. I stared at my face. Worn and tired. Bags under the eyes. This weekend had taken it out of me. I felt as exhausted as I looked. This would not do for tomorrow. I needed to look professional, peppy, like good ol' Rose. I saw something on my face then, just beside my nose, and leaned closer. A small speck of black. Like ink from a pen. I touched my face to rub it off. Somehow the speck grew larger, into a dark smudge, like I was spreading dirt. What was going on? I needed to get rid of it. I needed it gone. I was feeling a slight panic as I rubbed it again. And I saw to my horror the skin beneath my fingers pull apart, just a small gash on my cheek, but enough to see a dripping black ooze from the wound. I gasped and stepped back.

I heard a noise to my right.

"Ollie?" I turned to look into the dark hallway. I listened. But nothing. There was nothing. Just my own heart pounding.

I turned back to my reflection and it was gone. The wound was gone. The black was gone. I leaned in close, not even a speck. I closed my eyes. I tried to calm my breathing. Too little sleep, too much darkness. The puddles were winning tonight. I needed to go to bed. I looked at myself again. Still nothing. Just me and Bendy.

Me and Bendy.

I whipped my head around to look behind me at the shelf above the toilet, but of course there was no Bendy sitting there waving at me as he had been in the reflection. Because of course he hadn't been in the reflection. Because cartoon characters aren't real. Because it had all been in my mind. Because I needed rest. I needed rest before tomorrow, before going back to the studio.

I was so tired I wanted to cry. But I was all cried out.

I turned off the light and went to my room. To my bed. And somehow I managed a few hours' rest. Somehow.

And then it was Monday.

And it was time to go to work.

When I couldn't find Joey the next morning in the film

studio, I knew exactly where to look. I was exhausted, but the need to tell Joey all about how incredible the glasses were had given me a jolt of much-needed energy. Even as the image of them on Ollie's glowing face still haunted my memory. No, I had to remember the good in them, the magic, the science. The reason I had been given them in the first place: I was a test subject and my job was to report back, and report back I would! I walked determinedly down the dark hallway, refusing to acknowledge the slightest movement from the corner of my eye or flicker from an ambitious lightbulb. I didn't need any reminders of the strange waking dream that was Ollie and the television. Or of my exhausted visions last night in our bathroom.

Because I was so intent on my goal, I almost flew right into the lab before I stopped myself. No. In spite of not getting fired, I had learned my lesson to ask permission, and what was a knock on the door if not an ask for permission to be allowed inside? I raised my hand but, as I did, I heard a voice, and pulled it back. It sounded frustrated, almost angry. "Leave me alone!" it commanded so strongly I couldn't help but wonder if it was me being ordered even though I hadn't made my presence known yet.

I stepped back. I was pretty certain it was Joey himself. Had he and Evan got into some kind of argument? I definitely had no desire to interrupt that.

I felt a sudden hand on my shoulder and whipped around with a gasp.

"What are you doing?" It was Evan, full of his usual intensity and obvious distrust of me.

"I was going to knock on the door," I replied. "I thought you were inside."

"Obviously I'm not." He scowled at me, then said, "Come with me."

"But . . ." And I pointed toward the door. I needed to tell Joey all about the delivery, about how thrilled and grateful we all were. How amazing the technology was and how much both Ollie and I had enjoyed it.

Ollie and the television. And the static. And big round hollow eyes.

Evan grabbed me by the elbow. I tried to pull back but he held fast, and I worried if I pulled too hard, I might wrench my shoulder out of its socket. "Stop it."

"Come with me now."

I had been ordered around plenty of times on the job, but the physical part was brand-new. I was a little stunned but did as I was told. I had to admit I didn't entirely hate it when Evan paid attention to me, as odd and gruff as he was. I allowed him to guide me as he pulled me back down the corridor toward the elevator bank. Upon our arrival I finally pulled my arm out of his hand and stepped away from him.

"What are you doing?" I asked.

"Why can't you just follow directions like you're told?" he hissed back.

"What directions, what's going on?"

Evan slapped the elevator button, just launched his arm out to the side and smacked it hard. It made me jump. "Go back into the studio, but stay away from the office."

"Why?"

Evan shook his head, turning his back to the elevator, and stared at me. I didn't think I was being obtuse. I just didn't understand his frustration. Unless it was as simple as he didn't want me to ask any questions. I remembered back to Papa D's instructions. I had wanted to be so good at the time, follow them to a T. I had forgot. And it truly seemed that people in this building really never wanted a person to ask why. Which of course made me wonder . . . well . . . why.

"Weren't you just listening at the door? Don't you understand why?" he finally said.

"I wasn't listening . . ." I said. Not purposefully at any rate.

"He's in a mood; he doesn't want to see anyone."

And again. "Why?"

The elevator made a ding and the doors opened. I stared into the black behind Evan as he turned to step inside. Then something within me, something made of pure instinct, took over and I grabbed the back of his shirt and pulled at him.

My heart was racing and my face was hot and flushed.

"What the heck?" said Evan, stumbling backward. He turned to me, pulling himself free, and stared daggers.

"Look!" I said. I said it at the same time my mind informed me what my instincts already knew. I pointed at the void.

Evan rolled his eyes at me and turned once again, completing his full circle, and then I heard him gasp. Though my body was still coursing with adrenaline, there was a part of me that couldn't help but smile just a little. There was something in that gasp that felt human and vulnerable for the first time. Like Evan wasn't just this mopey presence, but a real-life person.

"Are you kidding me?" he asked, staring down.

I joined him at his shoulder. I didn't feel safe standing beside him. Before us was an empty elevator shaft. Two pairs of thick, taut wires strung up before us plunged into the darkness below. Evan took a step forward and placed his hand on the edge of the elevator doorframe. He leaned over just an inch to look down at the drop below.

I didn't dare. I wasn't scared of heights, but I was definitely concerned about falling. I didn't consider myself a steady enough person to not accidentally tumble to certain doom. But I could visualize it, in my mind's eye. Seven stories down. That was some drop.

"What happened, do you think?" I asked.

Evan shook his head. He was quiet for a moment. Then, "You saved me."

"Oh," I said, feeling a little embarrassed, "I suppose I did."

He stepped back from the open doors to look at me. "No, you saved my life. I'd be dead." He spoke so seriously and so bluntly, as he always did. Even though I was fully aware that his statement was an accurate description of the situation, something about the directness of it made me suddenly afraid. Afraid of what might have been. I suddenly saw his body, twisted at the bottom of the elevator shaft, his head facing the wrong direction, his bones broken and bent. It was as real as if I was staring at it in front of me.

"What's wrong with you?" Once more the blunt-edged voice. Cutting through my vision this time, bringing me back to reality. I stared at Evan staring back and I was overcome, seeing the living, breathing man in front of me. I reached out and grabbed him into a tight hug, fighting back tears. "Geez louise. You're a weird one, aren't you?" said Evan, not hugging me back, but I didn't need him to.

I pulled away. "I'm sorry, I'm just glad you aren't dead."

"Yeah, well, me too." He said, smoothing out his shirt and shaking his head. "I need to get out of this building." He marched to the staircase exit and pushed open the metal door. I nodded. I didn't blame him. I was feeling pretty overwhelmed myself. He looked back at me. "Are you coming or not?"

13

We sat in the small diner across the street from the building, a real dive of a place, with grimy walls, coffee-stained tabletops, the smell of cigarette smoke always in the air. The food was too greasy, the drinks watered down, the coffee burnt. It was only really good for quick service. Definitely not polite service, that was for certain.

"Here," said the waitress Delores as she dropped two cups of coffee in front of us, the liquid sloshing around dangerously and spilling over onto the tiny saucers below. She stormed off as if being required to do her job was the very last thing she needed right now.

I picked up my coffee and blew on it. Evan chugged his down in one large gulp. I wondered how that made his insides feel. The coffee might not have been any good, but it was blisteringly hot.

We had arrived just after the breakfast rush so there were only a few stragglers sitting about. I didn't really pay close attention to them. They were a motley bunch: the old man sitting by himself staring out the window and wiping his mouth at random intervals, the fellow at the counter with his overcoat on and his fedora low on his eyes. He had glared at us through a pair of sunglasses he was wearing inside as we'd entered as if we were invading his personal home. But otherwise, we were alone. It was a weirdly private and intimate setting, and despite the fact that Evan and I had been alone together before, I felt a little unsure about how to act, how to talk now, in our current situation. It almost had the feeling of a date, but that was of course a very silly thought and most untrue. Well, not that silly. I didn't exactly dislike him; I just thought he was odd. Yes, he was a few years older, but it wasn't that large of an age gap. He was even cute in his own unique way. I shook my head to stop that train of thought. What was wrong with me today?

Evan leaned back and sank into the red plastic banquette. It was torn just above his shoulder and some foam poked through, almost touching his ear.

"How are you feeling?" I asked, finally taking a sip of my coffee. I winced. Still too hot.

"Can I be honest with you?" he asked.

I nodded. Absolutely, he could. "Of course! Honesty is one of my favorite things."

Evan shook his head a little. He leaned forward onto his elbows, lacing his fingers together, resting his chin on top. "Okay . . . you're weird as heck. You know that, right?"

That surprised me. It was such a strange and impolite thing to say, but that was quite normal for Evan. I was more flummoxed, however, that I came across as anything other than a mild presence. I certainly didn't think I registered to anyone generally in any meaningful way where they'd have an actual opinion about me aside from my immediate family.

I placed the coffee in its saucer. "Really? What do you mean?"

Evan sat up again. He was antsy, moving from pose to pose. He now gestured with a hand toward the window beside us and out to the gray, cold world beyond it. Or at the least the street. "This whole positive, sunny, happy-go-lucky Pollyanna thing you do?"

"Pollyanna? Really?" That was a first.

Evan continued, "It's weird. It feels fake. How can you trust someone like that?"

This was just getting all the more confusing. And, not the least, insulting. I tried to maintain my composure. "But it's not fake, and I'm very trustworthy." Why on earth would anyone think otherwise? Had I not proven myself reliable in the past week? Was I not a good worker? And who was he to tell me that who I was and how I behaved was anything other than authentic? I started to feel a little angry—just a little, not enough to truly consider myself mad, but it did all seem rather unfair of him.

"It just seems like you've lived this sheltered life and you don't understand that things can be hard sometimes," he said, "or that things aren't always positive or have a happy ending."

I shook my head. That was simply untrue. "Oh, no, but I do understand that."

"How old are you?"

"Almost eighteen." I hated that my age mattered so much to people in the city. In Brooklyn people assumed I was a mature and responsible person no matter what my age. No one had asked me my age in forever. Maybe when it was my birthday.

"So you're a kid. That's my point: You haven't seen things." He talked quickly, not with a nervous energy but with such a confidence in his own rightness. I didn't have time to put two thoughts together, couldn't defend my honor, before he moved on to his next question: "Tell me, are your folks still alive, still together?"

I knew he was leading the conversation somewhere, but all I could do was play along at this point. "Yes," I answered kind of dumbly.

"So there you go, that's the first thing." He pointed at me and didn't quite smile but looked rather validated. "My dad never came home from the war. My uncle lost his leg. You ever seen a severed limb before?"

What did that have to do with anything? "No," I said, but then my brain finally caught up to the conversation and I realized that wasn't entirely true. "I mean, well, I've seen men with missing body parts as much as anyone. Just because I don't have your experience doesn't mean I haven't seen things."

Evan waved that off. "You have a home? A house, apartment?"

"A house." Somehow I knew that answer was only going to fuel him further, but I still said it. After all, I did like honesty.

"See, that's swell too."

Now that didn't feel particularly honest. "Did you grow up without a home?" At this point I already knew the answer.

Evan sighed. He leaned back again. I stared at the tear again—it was now so close it might tickle his ear. Did he see it? The rip in the seam? "We moved a lot," he said, a little more thoughtful. "I sometimes had to stay with friends when things weren't so hot for Mom. Look, the facts are the facts. You had a home, a family, you were raised right. You had it good. There's no shame in that. But you need to understand that most of us raised in the real world, well, we don't trust people like you." He turned and flagged down Delores. The casual way he said something that felt like a punch to the gut and then moved on to something unrelated like coffee was so very purposeful, I noted. And unkind.

"That's not fair," I said. I was tired of feeling attacked like this and I was done trying to be a polite conversationalist. I felt embarrassed I'd ever thought he was a little dreamy. "First of all, my world is the real world. It might not be your real world, and I'm sorry for it because it sounds like you went through a lot, but it doesn't mean I don't exist here. And you don't know anything about my family, about what we've been through. About my father and puddles."

He turned back as Delores made her way over. "Puddles?"

Oh dear, had I said "puddles"? That had certainly not been my intention. My insides tightened. What a slipup, a silly childish reference to something far too complicated for someone like Evan to understand. I felt very visible all of a sudden, like everyone in the diner was looking at me. I glanced at the man in the trench coat. Was he staring at me from behind those sunglasses? No, he was probably just looking outside. "No, not puddles. No, what I meant was you don't know. You just don't know me. I'm not a Pollyanna because I don't know that there is sad stuff in the world. I am who I am because of it. Because I choose to see the good around me and in other people. Even you."

Delores arrived with a pot of coffee and refilled Evan's cup. For my part I still hadn't taken another sip. "Oh, even me?" He smiled at that. The first time I'd ever seen him smile. I hated that I liked it. Especially since I wasn't liking him very much at the moment.

"I'm sorry. That sounded mean."

Evan shook his head and downed his second cup of coffee in one gulp. "Hey, it's maybe the first time I've kind of liked you."

I shook my head and felt my cheeks burn. "Well, that's awful. You should like me for me. Or because I saved your life."

"Any other options?"

I shrugged. "I'm a person, that's all, and I think before you judge my life, you should know a little about it."

He clanged the coffee cup back onto its saucer. "Okay, so tell me."

"Oh." Then suddenly I realized I had absolutely no interest in doing so. If I wanted to impress him, I'd have to tell him sob stories, and my sob stories were not ones I was keen on sharing. Besides, I didn't think he'd understand. No one understood. Not really. Maybe at first they had cared, but now nearly eight years later, it was abundantly clear that everyone in our community thought my father should be well past whatever issues he had come home with. "I don't really want to."

"That's okay, kid. I don't really want to know."

There was that "kid" again. Clearly Evan had spent a little too much time with Joey. And I didn't much like Evan thinking of me as a kid. Especially not as a kid. "I'm sorry, but could you stop saying that, please? That's what Joey calls me because he's old enough to be my dad, maybe even my grandfather. You can't be much older than me, so it's weird. Or at the least condescending."

"I'm twenty."

"There you go."

"But I've lived."

"I've lived too. I'm here, aren't I?" I knew he didn't mean it literally, but I also knew it was a silly game of one-upmanship that was getting tedious. Yet, I couldn't stop playing.

Another lean back. I noticed he did it almost predictably when his energy changed. "It's just different. I dunno. I've seen things. Life-changing things. Where I used to work, the stuff we did there, it was terrifying and exciting. It was going to change the world. I thought Mister Drew had a grand vision, that's why I came with him here. Now I'm stuck in some closet." It was a surprising shift in the conversation. From cutting me down, now he wanted to share all this with me? Maybe, I wondered, that was the point of all this? Of his invitation out for coffee in the middle of the workday. Of his small insults about my character. Maybe all he wanted was to share something on his mind and he had to work his way to it through a maze of pointless interrogation. Some people needed to communicate as if by accident, I marveled. It couldn't seem purposeful or too eager. Maybe that was why I liked Joey so much—he was so ready and excited to share. He had no secrets.

If this had been the point, I certainly was curious to follow through. "Did you work at the studio?"

Evan shook his head. "Nah, that was before my time." He turned his gaze out at the street. "I worked at Gent."

"What's Gent?"

Immediate eye contact. "You don't know what Gent is?"

I was startled by the sudden intensity. I felt bad in my ignorance. "No," I confessed.

Energy was pumping through his veins again; he was like a cart on a roller coaster, only I couldn't see the track. I had no idea when we'd be going up or down. I just had to hang on for the ride, I supposed. He leaned toward me, eyes bright and shining. It was intense and I pressed my lips together hard to keep myself from looking away. "It was this amazing factory where we did real science, worked on true technological advancements. It was nothing like these stupid gimmicks with these 3-D glasses. It was real-world stuff."

That didn't seem fair. "I like the 3-D glasses. They're wonderful!"

He furrowed his brow. "You tried them?"

I nodded. "I did. I mean, only for a moment. My little brother wanted them of course."

His stare only intensified. "You did, and how do you feel?"

It was a strange question. "I mean, fantastic! In awe! Mind boggled, I suppose. It was so exciting to watch TV that way. I think Joey is really onto something."

Evan shook his head. "No, not about the glasses. How do *you* feel?"

Well, that was an even stranger question. "I don't know. What do you mean?"

He looked at me closely for a moment longer, and I had absolutely nothing to say but stared back anyway. Then he shook his head and, once again, predictably leaned back. "Never mind. Look, I'm just telling you, Mister Drew used to have these big plans, these grand ideas. Ever read his book, *The Illusion of Living*?"

"I haven't! But Joey told me about it. I really should." I liked talking about Joey.

"You probably won't be able to get your hands on a copy. It went out of print ages ago."

"Oh."

"Anyway, point is, he had these amazing ideas and that's what inspired Gent to go in the direction they did and set everything into motion. But he didn't have guts. I dunno. He didn't follow through. He was so darn focused on those stupid cartoons. As if that was the point somehow, but that was never the point."

"I don't understand." I was feeling a little tired now. It was all so much, and I felt woefully ignorant about all of it. Maybe I wasn't tired actually; maybe I was just a little disappointed in myself.

"I know. I'm just venting. I'd never expect a girl like you to understand."

And then Evan again managed to find a way to spark that little bit of fire inside me. "It's hard to understand when you don't actually say anything. When you skirt around the subject. It's easy to feel superior when you don't share."

He raised both his hands in mock defense. "Okay, okay, cool your jets. All I'm saying is Gent really took things to the next level. When the studio went under, they kept going, you know? They understood the mission statement. And then, well, then the factory had to shut down, and I guess I thought when Mister Drew invited me to work with him that we'd be starting again, looking toward a bright and exciting future. But it's all been, well, it's all just TV. Show business. Numbers and audience viewership and sponsorships. Commercials. It's not what I want. It was never what I wanted."

"But you're still here."

He paused and thought for a moment. Then sighed. "True. Well, what can I do? No one's doing what Gent did. No one. It's like an alcoholic. You might give up the hooch but a taste is better than going cold turkey."

"I don't think it works like that."

"You get my point though."

I nodded. It wasn't the best analogy, but I definitely understood the meaning behind it. "I do. I actually do. I think in a way maybe it's the same for me."

"You?"

I laughed. "You think I like fetching coffee when you get to invent brand-new things that the world has never seen before?"

"I dunno. I thought so, yeah."

It made sense he'd assume that. "No, I like having a job. I love working in TV. But I'll admit it, I do get a little envious of the work you and Joey do. Even the work Papa D does."

"Who the heck is Papa D?"

"He works upstairs, it doesn't matter. I just think having a goal and working toward it is marvelous. Having a real purpose, a real drive. I've always wanted to find that purpose, and so, even while I figure it out, getting to see you all, well, it's like that little sip of alcohol you mentioned." I paused for a moment. "I think . . . I think I like technology. I think I wish I could know more. Learn more." It was the first time I'd truly formulated this thought. It came together as I said it, like the words were putting all these mixed-up thoughts and feelings I'd been having into one solid idea. I felt butterflies in my stomach.

"Yeah?"

"Yes," I said. I felt excited now. But also at a total loss. Now what? Now with this new realization, what on earth what? "I guess maybe I could go to school for it, but I wouldn't know where to start."

He waved off this idea. He liked to do that. "Oh, forget school. They teach you what they already know, and what they know is never that much to begin with. Nah, you want to learn? Well, stick with me, kid.

"Rose," I reminded him.

"What?"

"Call me Rose. Please. It's Joey's thing; it doesn't suit you."

He shook his head at me again. But I felt now like we had some kind of an understanding. That we had come out of the other side of this strange diner experience with something new, something positive.

"You do like your honesty."

"I do." I smiled.

"That's okay, I guess." And he smiled too.

"You'll really teach me?"

"Sure, why not? I have nothing better to do."

Joey greeted us in the lobby

of the building. It reminded me a great deal of the first day we'd met. And he was just as enthusiastic about this meeting as he was at our initial one. I couldn't help but smile widely when he came up to us, waving and excited, no hint of an angry or frustrated person. Of the man who'd been yelling behind the closed door, or who Evan had wanted to escape from this morning.

"I couldn't wait! I need to hear everything! How was it?" he asked as he held open the door to the stairs. There was now a proper "Out of Order" sign on the elevator doors. Still, it seemed to me he was so excited and full of energy, even if we could have ridden up, he would have insisted on walking. I was okay with that. I had pretty strong legs. Evan seemed less than thrilled.

Then again, he was always "less than" generally with all his emotions, I was learning.

"It was amazing! I've never experienced anything like that in my life. You've created a whole other world! I have no idea how you did that. One second I was in my living room, the next I was in your studio. It was like magic."

Joey was beaming so brightly I thought I might want to borrow that man from the diner's sunglasses. It made me smile all the brighter.

"Tell me more, don't spare any details!" he said.

"Oh gosh, but the details are so tedious," I said as we made our way upward.

"Oh no, the devil is in the details!" he replied.

I was overwhelmed by his joy and not sure exactly where to start. "Well, we had some neighbors over to watch . . ."

"Neighbors! I love neighbors!" He was walking up ahead backward so he could look at me.

"You do?" asked Evan dryly, not turning around.

"Tell me more!"

"And we sat to watch it. And my little brother, Ollie, got to wear the glasses of course."

"Of course!"

"And he just loved it!" I said. I paused then, thinking about him staring at the static, the cold house, the cold glow from the TV, the cold in my very bones. No, that certainly wasn't the kind of detail Joey was looking for.

Joey arrived at the second-floor landing and held his hand out for me as if that extra step would be just too much for me to handle. It was a grand gesture, something old-fashioned and smart, so I took it. When I arrived on the landing, he took my other hand in his. Then staring me down, he said, "And?"

"And, well, he loved it as much as I did!" Possibly too much. My enthusiasm had turned artificial now.

"Tell me more."

Evan continued the journey upward and I glanced at him briefly as he trudged along. Joey really cared about my experience. Really, really cared. I wanted to find it charming and flattering, but it did feel a bit strange too, I had to admit.

"There's not much more to tell. It was exactly as you described it would be. He told me it was like he was with Bendy and everyone, like he was surrounded by the cartoon world. He drank from a stream, he said." I thought for a moment. What else could I share? What would interest him in a scientific kind of way. "Oh, here's a neat thing," I thought of at last. "When I was wearing the glasses, it wasn't black-and-white."

"What do you mean?" asked Joey.

"Well, on the TV without the glasses it was black-and-white obviously. But when I put on the glasses it was yellow-and-black."

Joey nodded; he seemed to already understand this. Shoot, so it wasn't any particularly new information for him. "Yes, that's the tint on the glasses."

"Oh, of course, the tint."

He was still looking at me closely, still holding my hands. I could hear Evan above us, traipsing up the stairs, one heavy footfall at a time. Resentment in every step.

"I really don't know what I'm supposed to say," I finally said.

At that Joey released my hands and smiled. "No! There is nothing you need to say, you've said it all perfectly. Come, let's climb." He turned and extended an arm for me to join him. We started walking again, side by side, each holding on to our respective railing. I felt a little relieved but still like I had let him down.

Joey had started to huff and puff. I could see sweat forming at his brow. "You young people, it must be nice to be so effortlessly strong."

I nodded. "It's not an easy climb for me either," I said, wanting to make him feel better.

"In my youth, my goodness I was spry. I was in the army, you know, in the Great War."

I immediately thought of Father. "I'm so sorry."

Joey gave me a funny look then. I couldn't fully read it. "Sorry? No, my dear. It was wonderful. Every young man should have the opportunity to fight for his country."

I wasn't entirely sure he was right, but I nodded again nonetheless. "Were you in the trenches?" I asked.

"Metaphorically, yes," he replied.

We had arrived at the fourth-floor landing and he stopped for a moment to catch his breath, bending over at the waist, his hands on his thighs. Evan's purposeful footsteps had faded from hearing.

"Oh," I said. What else could I say?

"No, no, not now," he said, turning to look at something to his side with a wave of his hand.

"I'm sorry?" I said. What had I said wrong?

He looked back up at me in confusion, then stood straight and smiled. "Never be sorry! Remember that! Always move forward, never look back. Any mistakes we make are merely lessons we take on to the next chapter." Suddenly he looked sharply to his right again. "I said not now."

I nodded and pressed my lips together, utterly confused. And, if I was being entirely honest with myself, a little scared.

He glared into the distance for a moment and then turned back to me. Immediately his expression brightened. "Say! Say, how would you like to go to a party?"

"Right now?"

Joey threw his head back and laughed. It didn't feel like I'd said anything funny, or if I had, it didn't seem like it would be quite that funny, and it made me feel strange. Uncomfortable. Like I was being laughed at, not with.

"Wouldn't it just be swell if we could just go to a party right now, eh?" he said, grinning at me. "No, no, I meant this Saturday. The night of the show."

"The night of the show?"

"We were in such a rush to get the thing on air and get the technology in place, well, we plum forgot to have an opening-night party! But there's no rule that says you can't have one at a later date! After all, it's all about celebrating our accomplishments, and that never goes out of style."

I nodded. I was nodding a lot. What else could I do? Something dark moved in the corner of my vision and it was my turn to look. My turn to stare at nothing.

"So, what do you say?"

I turned back. "A party."

"Yes. My old pal Nathan Arch is hosting it at his home on the Upper East Side. Swell fellow, a major sponsor of the show. Arch Steel."

"Oh, that's him," I said, remembering the name on the place card before the show came on.

"That is him. It'll be grand: music, all the movers and shakers in New York, good food, good drink, good times! What do you say?"

It sounded lovely. It sounded a bit overwhelming as well. I'd never been to a party like that in my life.

"Is everyone going?" I asked. Maybe if some of the staff were there, then I wouldn't feel too out of place.

"Nah, it's exclusive, very exclusive. Evan, though. Hey, that's true, Evan will be there."

That didn't sound too bad. It actually almost sounded nice. I hated that a single butterfly flitted across my middle at the thought. *Stop it*, I told myself. I focused on the party idea instead. I reminded myself of what Mother had always told me, that I had to take every opportunity that came my way and grab it hard. Without risk there was no reward, after all. Even if it might seem scary. And of all the scary things in the world, a fancy party with fancy people had to be one of the least.

Though. Still. A little scary.

"Okay," I said quietly.

"Okay?"

"Yes, of course yes. That's wonderful really. I'm honored you'd invite me," I said. I smiled then, because really I was. Now that I was thinking about it more, it was quite special, wasn't it?

"Please, it's nothing. You have shown gumption and smarts, and you're fun to have around the studio. I respect people with innate talent, you know," he said.

"You think I have innate talent?" I wasn't so sure about that. Well, maybe talent for doing grunt work, I supposed.

"You ask good questions, and you're interested in the right things." The right things. "Never had any kids, but I could see the appeal, if they were as bright as you, say," he added.

That made me beyond flattered. It was hard to accept these accolades when I hadn't really done anything, I didn't think, but it was a kindness and I wasn't going to reject it and make him feel bad.

"I think we'd better continue our arduous journey," he said, looking up through the tower of stairs winding around itself. "But it's not so bad when you have company."

I smiled. "No, it's not so bad at all."

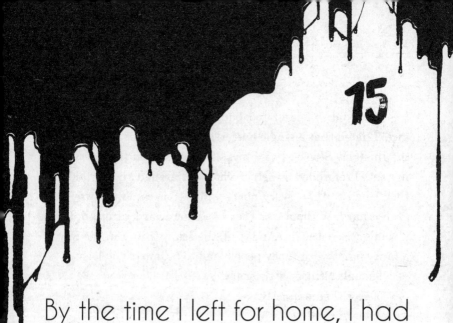

15

By the time I left for home, I had

that wonderful feeling you get from being completely exhausted but exhilarated after a good day of work. That feeling where you are ready to turn in, but not so eager that all you do is look at the clock. It had been a truly full day. Evan was now a friend, even if he probably wouldn't define me as one, not yet, and Joey had invited me to a fancy party. And beyond all that, I was working in television, and though maybe in the future I might get bored with that fact, today was simply not that day.

I stepped out into the cold air. It was pitch-black outside, and my breath froze when I exhaled a happy sigh. The lights beamed out of the windows in the tall towers above me, and the diner, as cheap and run-down as it was, positively glowed across the street. I smiled. I loved the look of the city at night, of the cozy interiors and the signs of life going on all around me. It made me feel warm even on the coldest nights.

I drew my coat closer to me in a hug and sighed. I watched as a pair of men trudged past me deep in conversation, heading no doubt to a bar to complain about their bosses. I couldn't relate; I liked my boss just fine. In fact, you could argue that he was just dandy.

Then I noticed a flash of movement out of the corner of my eye.

Again. There it was again. That something just in my periphery. But this time I'd caught it. This time I'd seen a glimpse. My subconscious had been ready for it.

But for the life of me I couldn't believe what I just saw.

No. No, it couldn't be.

I turned and looked to the left of the diner where I had seen it. Nothing, of course, nothing. Always nothing. But I still stared and squinted through the dark. Because I knew what I'd seen. This time, I knew where to look.

There it was again. It ran right across my line of sight.

I took in a deep breath, my skin was buzzing; I felt light-headed. And that familiar dread was sitting low within me. And again. There it was again. It darted out from behind a trash can and down into the alley. How was I seeing what I was seeing? This wasn't possible. This couldn't be real. I was completely petrified and yet somehow at the same time my body was drawn to it. I had to know, I had to see. I wanted to call out. I almost stepped right out into the street after it, but I stopped short as a cab whizzed by. When the coast was clear, I ran across the street and over to the alley. It loomed narrow and dark. High brick walls, a fire escape on one side, a creak-ing of metal on metal. Trash mixing with slush. I took a step toward it and looked but saw no one, nothing.

"Bendy?" I called out. My voice echoed in the emptiness, high and strained. The moment I said it I felt instantly foolish. I shut my lips together hard and shook my head. No, this was all very stupid. I couldn't have actually seen Bendy . . . I was exhausted. A long day, a weekend before it with little sleep. I remembered the Bendy in the bathroom and could feel the flush of embarrassment rush through me. I spun on my heel to run away from the scene as quickly as possible.

And right into someone.

I bumped into him hard. Hard enough that he grunted and I staggered back a few steps and held my head with my hand.

"I'm so sorry," I said as I looked up.

The figure silhouetted in front of me didn't say anything back, just a man standing there, staring at me, in a trench coat and a fedora. He was blocking the exit to the alley, and I felt frightened in a new way. He wasn't doing anything, but I didn't like being cornered like this. I didn't think anyone enjoyed the feeling of being cornered.

I raised my chin to show I wasn't scared, though I could feel my hands trembling, and walked toward him. "Excuse me, please," I said with all the confidence I could muster and aimed myself for the gap between him and the wall. But he sidestepped into it.

Now a deeper fear set in. This wasn't an irrational emotion inspired by some animal instinct, this man was actually a threat and trying to prevent me from leaving. I quickly darted to the other side but he blocked it as well.

"You work for Joey Drew," he said. He had a working class English accent. It was irrelevant to anything, but it stuck out in my mind as unexpected. If he thought I was going to engage him in polite conversation . . . I made to dart right again, but as he moved, I changed direction and went left, slipping in the tight space between him and the wall. I ran as fast as I could out of the alley and down the street toward the subway, my heart racing as quickly as my feet. I couldn't help but look back over my shoulder. I saw the man in the light of a streetlamp, watching me. I couldn't see much of his face but I did see now that he was wearing sunglasses. At night. I remembered him then, from the diner that morning. What on earth?

He wasn't following me, but I wasn't about to take the risk. I turned back to face the direction I was heading and ran the entire way, even down the stairs. I flew by the other commuters and only when I was on the platform did I feel safer, surrounded by people. I made a point of standing next to a very large man reading the newspaper. He glanced at me but then returned to reading.

My heart was going a mile a minute, and I looked around, staying vigilant even as I boarded the train. As I stood holding tight to the pole, my knuckles white from the strength of my grip, I was grateful for the crowds, those crowds that so many people in the rest of the country couldn't understand. I found them so comforting right now. To be surrounded by people. They might not all be good, they might not all be polite, but they were all witnesses.

Suddenly the image of Evan broken at the bottom of the elevator shaft burst into my vision and I gasped.

"Hey, watch it!"

"I'm sorry, I'm sorry," I said to the man whose foot I had inadvertently crushed with my step back.

This was the problem with the puddles: They could find you at any time, but most especially when you were already vulnerable.

He didn't fall, he isn't dead, you saved him, I told myself. I tried to remember that elated feeling of being a hero, of saving the day. But it was buried deep inside now.

I just wanted to get home.

When I finally made it inside our small house, I was completely drained. Staying vigilant was hard work, and my body felt achy and sore as I pulled off my coat and hung it in the front closet. I had been holding my body so tight, I hadn't even noticed. Every one of my muscles was clenched. I took in a deep breath and let it out slowly and focused on letting go.

Letting go of the tension in my body, of the images in my mind, of the fear in my gut.

Whoever that man had been, he hadn't chased me. Maybe he had just wanted to talk and I'd overreacted. But who follows a young woman down an alley? Who wears sunglasses inside and at nighttime? No one decent, certainly.

I made my way back to the kitchen where happy sounds of dinner preparations were floating toward me down the hall. Somehow they had an ominous twinge, almost as if they were an echo of a memory and not a present and real thing. I entered and there was Ollie at the table doing homework, and Mother at the stove stirring some sauce. Very real indeed. I smiled softly.

"Oh, you're home. I didn't hear you come in," she said as I approached her. She leaned her cheek toward me as I kissed it.

"I can be so sneaky," I replied.

"That's what I tell everyone. 'Have you met my sneaky daughter, Rose?'" She raised the ladle and gave the sauce a taste. "It needs something more," she said.

"Rose!" Ollie bounded toward me and I gave him a big hug.

"What a greeting, that's real brotherly affection," I said, holding him against me. "Or maybe someone doesn't want to do his homework."

"It's so boring," he said, pulling back with a grin.

"It's not," I replied. I didn't have the usual pep talk within me to say much more. I sat down at the table as Mother made her way to the fridge, opening it and thinking as she stared into it. "Garlic?" I asked.

Ollie, meanwhile, had moved over to the stove, I could see out of the corner of my eye. Sometimes he helped Mother cook; he wasn't bad at it even. He gave the pot a smell. "Smells good to me!"

Mother turned and waved him back with her spoon. "You keep your nose out of that!" We all laughed and Ollie moved back along the oven to the other side. "I have no idea. I'm going to chop some green beans." She closed the door and sat opposite me, bringing the cutting board and green beans over. "Will you be the executioner?"

I smiled and grabbed a small pile, carefully going through and breaking off the tops and bottoms.

"How was your day?"

What a complicated question that was all of a sudden. How *had* my day been? I didn't want Mother ever to worry about me, but I also didn't like hiding things from her. "It was good. Evan was nice to me, and Joey invited me to a party."

"Oh, he did, did he?" replied Mother, grabbing my green beans and chopping them into small pieces with her knife.

"Mother!" I said, reaching for more. "He's older than Father!"

"I'm teasing," she replied. "What kind of party?"

"A party for the Bendy show."

"Bendy!" said Ollie. I smiled and glanced at him. He was pointing at the stove. I looked to see if the pot was boiling over. It was fine. I turned back to Mother.

"Yes, I guess they've been so rushed they didn't have time for a big premiere party last week, so it's this week," I explained.

"Oh, so it's going to be a big television party. Very done up, I imagine," said Mother.

I nodded and reached for more green beans. "Yes. I imagine." I was thinking now about the man in the trench coat again for some reason. He wouldn't leave my mind.

"I can see you're worried," she said.

I saw her looking at me, and I quickly shook my head. "No, I'm not worried about anything."

"Of course you are. I would have been at your age. A big fancy party, nothing to wear. But you can wear my black tea dress."

Oh, well, I hadn't actually thought of being concerned about clothes yet, but she was right. Now that I thought about it, with all those rich TV types, fashion would be an important consideration. And of course with Evan there too. No, not of course. He probably wouldn't care a fig what I wore. Silly. I smiled. "Thank you." It was a very pretty dress. Mother had never offered it to me before, not even for prom. She must truly have understood the importance of the event. She seemed to understand its importance even more than I did.

"Bendy!" said Ollie again. It was a little strange, and a little infantile of him, and I turned in my seat. I wasn't planning on scolding him, just to remind him that he was seven now and interrupting conversations with nonsensical outbursts was a little childish.

But instead I found myself mute, rooted to the spot. I was watching something as if in slow motion. I couldn't fully process what I was looking at. Ollie was standing by the boiling pot, his fingers sticking underneath it, into the fire from the burner. Just holding his fingers there, not making a sound. I stared. I just stared. It oddly reminded me of the cartoon that had been playing that day in the lab, the day Joey had asked me to test the glasses. Bendy in the forest. Boris making a pie. Bendy touching the burner and tasting his finger. Suddenly I snapped out of it. I jumped to my feet in an instant and grabbed him by the shoulders, pulling him back away from the fire.

"Ollie!" I cried as I did, and we fell back into a heap onto the tiled floor.

"Oh my goodness," said Mother, breathless, rushing over.

Only then did Ollie cry out. He screamed in agony and held his hand with the other. He stared at it. And I stared too. Red and white blisters were already bubbling up. His skin was peeling on all four of his fingers. It was horrific.

"Why on earth would you do that?" It came out louder than I had meant it and made Ollie cry even harder. "No, no, it's okay. I'm sorry, Ollie. It's okay, everything will be okay!"

Mother bent down immediately and looked closely even as my stomach turned. I wanted to cry too, but I held on to Ollie from behind, hugging him as he wept.

"I need to take him to the hospital," she said. She had turned into pragmatic problem-solving Mother. The one who had to always be ready for anything in case Father slipped into the puddles again. "Rose, you finish up dinner and make sure your father eats something."

"I can take him," I said. I couldn't think to let go of him. I didn't want to.

"No, please, just do as I say."

She pulled Ollie out from my arms and up into hers. He was too big to really carry, but she was able to hold him close and lift him up. He wouldn't stop screaming. Why wouldn't he stop screaming?

Tears burned in my eyes as I helped them to the door and out into the night. When I closed it behind them, I slid down to the ground and cried into my arms. I saw his little fingers, I smelled that smell, that awful smell of burning flesh. It made me nauseous and so scared. He had to be okay, he would be okay.

I took in a deep breath and looked up. The kitchen was waiting for me at the far end of the house and I knew I had a duty now. Duty was the one saving grace, the thing that would get me through this. Father would be home soon, and we both needed something to eat. Even if the thought of eating anything made my stomach turn. It wasn't about me right now. It was about my family.

I entered the kitchen with purpose and made my way to the pot. The sauce was sticking to the sides, turning a little brown, likely burning at the bottom. I picked up the large ladle and stirred.

I glanced to my left. To where Ollie had been standing, just watching. Where I had just ignored him in favor of talking about a party dress. In my mind's eye he morphed into Bendy. The cartoon demon stood on our tile floor looking up at me with that stupid grin on his face.

"This is your fault," I said, though I had no idea why. But it felt right and so I said it.

Bendy nodded back.

16

It was close to midnight when my mother and Ollie came home. Both Father and I had stayed up to wait for them; neither of us would have been able to sleep anyway. We'd spent a quiet evening in the living room together, not really talking. We tried to turn on the television, but there was something about the artificial happiness of everyone on-screen, from the presenter on the quiz show to the actors in the advertisements, everyone's bright, too-wide smiles, that just made me feel worse. It was all my fault. I should have been keeping a closer eye on my brother, and now he was hurting.

He fell asleep in Mother's arms as she cuddled him close in bed that night. Father slept fitfully; I could hear him from my room. And I, well, I knew I wouldn't be sleeping at all tonight and didn't. The next morning at work I walked through the day as if in a dream, but no one seemed to notice. For the first time since I'd started, I felt indifferent to the goings-on, and when I was sent to fetch Joey from the lab, I didn't even knock, just opened the door.

"Leave me alone!"

That shook me out of my daze and I backed away, closing the door as I did. "Oh, sorry."

Joey turned just as I was about to shut it. "Oh, not you, Rose. Come in, come in."

"Okay," I said. I didn't have the brainpower to question the interaction.

"I was talking to Henry." He casually waved toward an empty stool and I nodded. It didn't strike me as particularly delusional. I just assumed some genius make-believe was at work. Or something. I honestly didn't care.

"Who's Henry?" I asked, propping myself up on the large center table, sitting so my feet were dangling beneath me. Why was I here again?

"A traitor," he replied.

"Oh, I hate traitors." Not that I had any in my life, but the concept of them was lousy, so I figured I did. Besides, again, I didn't really care.

Joey turned fully around in his seat. "Exactly. Nothing worse than someone you thought you trusted just abandoning you."

I nodded and felt my stomach clench. Just as I had abandoned Ollie, just ignored him in favor of talking about fancy parties and stupid useless things.

"And now he has the gall to just sit there and judge *me*. Me! I stuck around, you know, I actually did it."

I nodded again. "You did." Maybe I was dreaming actually, maybe I had fallen asleep after all. None of what Joey was saying made any particular sense.

Joey turned fiercely to the stool and pointed at it. "You see! Even she sees, and she's a nobody." He paused, finger still aloft. His brow furrowed. Then he leaned back in his seat, his legs slipping out so that he was almost lying backward, hand to his forehead. "Forgive me, Rose. I haven't had much sleep. My old nightmares haunt me in my waking hours now."

"I know the feeling." Had he just insulted me?

"Henry was . . . well, that's no matter. It's no matter." He brought up his other hand so they both covered his face, then drawing them down to his chin, pulling the skin with them, he let them drop to his side. "I did another pass with the ink last night. I think this Saturday is going to really bring in the crowds. I can't wait for the feedback from our test group." He looked over at me and smiled. "Do you know what I mean when I say that?"

"Test group?"

"No, about the pass with the ink?"

I shook my head. I felt like I had a spring for a neck again and it was just bobbing all about. But this time not from elation but rather a detached indifference.

"The ink for the film for our show. I put it through another Sillyvision treatment. I was working on it all night, tweaking things, perfecting things. And I think it's going to be something even more impressive."

"It was already very impressive. And immersive," I added.

He snapped his fingers and pointed at me, much in the same way he had been pointing at the stool. "Yes! Immersive! Excellent word. Rose, you are good with words. You should be a writer. I could hire you as a writer. When we start making original cartoons again. When I open up my studio again."

"Thank you." I felt rather stupid at the moment so I wasn't sure exactly what he was talking about. Suddenly I remembered. "They want you on set!"

"Ha! *That's* why you're here. Okay, then, let's go to set." He hopped out of the chair, suddenly full of energy again. I was envious. I was still sitting there on the table like a sack of pota-toes. I heard the sound of the door open and then slam shut behind me. I turned. He had left. Just like that. Not waiting for me or anything? I was alone in the lab. I slipped off the table and looked around, approaching Joey's desk. I saw drawings, sketches of some kind of cartoon hallway.

"Of course you're here." I spun on my heel. Evan stood, like he tended to, framed in the open doorway.

"How do you open doors so quietly?"

"How are you always in my space?"

I had no answer. But I also hadn't done anything wrong. "Well, you said you were going to teach me, remember?"

"It was yesterday, so yes." He sauntered into the room and rolled his eyes at me, dropping a heavy stack of round metal containers, the kind we kept the film reels in, on the large table.

"Tell me about Sillyvision," I said, walking up to him. His presence invigorated me somewhat, and I felt slightly more energized.

"I thought you already knew all about that." He pulled open a drawer within the table and produced a roll of masking tape and a marker.

"Well, how does it work with the glasses?"

Finally he glanced up at me. He didn't seem particularly enthusiastic to share, but he had made a promise to me. And I could see that mattered to him. "It's a symbiotic relationship."

"I don't know what that means."

Evan wrote something on the tape, ripped it off, and placed it on the first metal container, then shoved the container aside.

"It's a natural phenomenon where two things coexist in order to support each other. They need each other to function."

"So the glasses and the Sillyvision."

"It's not Sillyvision. Please stop calling it that. I despise that name." Rip. Tape.

"Joey said . . ."

"Joey doesn't understand his own technology. He came up with an idea, but I made it real. And now he calls it by the same name he used to call something else. Just because we use the same ink doesn't mean it's the same thing."

"But . . ."

Evan slammed the tape onto the table and glared at me. "Look, Rose, I'm dealing with a lot. Do you know what he did overnight?"

"Something with the Silly—with the film processing?"

Evan stared. He seemed surprised I had an answer to his obviously rhetorical question. "Yes. He insisted that we reprocess the cartoons for this week's show. He completely redid them. We haven't tested them at all with the glasses. We have no idea if it will work the way we want it to. The way he wants it to. It's expensive, it's risky, he could have destroyed all the originals. The cartoons are old, Rose, some over two decades old . . . Ugh, I don't have time to educate you and get everything ready by Saturday." He threw up his hands.

"Can I help?"

"Help?

"I can help. I can do the tape, maybe?" I pointed at the tape clutched in his hand that looked like he was trying to press through the table itself.

He looked at me, then shook his head like he always did whenever he looked at me. "Sure. Okay. You can do the tape."

He slid it over to me quite violently, but maybe because I was too tired to think, I managed to catch it by reflex alone.

"Just do what I ask, and otherwise leave me alone!"

"Okey dokey!" I said with a small laugh.

He marched past me while still looking at me over his shoulder. "Are you drunk?"

"Oh no, never touch the stuff." I pulled out the tape and ripped it. I held it up, stuck to my index finger, letting it dangle like a worm on a hook. "What should I put on this?"

"'Bendy and the Pie Contest V 2.'" He sat at his desk hard with a sigh.

"As in the letter V and the number 2?"

"Yes. Version two."

"Oh! Yeah, that makes sense."

Even looking at the back of his head, I could tell he had absolutely rolled his eyes at me again.

Joey didn't seem to mind that I wasn't properly PA-ing in the studio that week. I barely saw him at all, to be honest, but the times he came into the lab he seemed happy I was helping Evan. He seemed quite happy in general. Despite his starting the week in a foul mood when he'd been yelling at his imaginary friend Henry, clearly this new plan of his, this new version of the film reel, was thrilling him.

"Why aren't you more excited, Evan? This is going to be spectacular!" He laughed, slapping Evan on the back heartily.

"I can't believe we're testing this on Friday night. We need more time," replied Evan.

"Work fills the time allotted," replied Joey.

And then he'd practically skipped out the door, leaving me alone with an ever-grumpier Evan. Not that I particularly minded.

"At Gent we had time; at Gent we were doing something real," muttered Evan to himself.

"And what exactly was that?" I asked, hoping this time he'd say.

And as usual, he offered no answer.

My spirits had risen by midweek. Mostly it was down to Ollie, who was getting better and stronger every day. He still felt the worst in the evenings and he hadn't gone back to school yet, but he was able to come downstairs to join us for breakfast now, even as he avoided the stove, walking as far away from it as he could to do so.

But there was also another reason for my happier state, though I wished it was just Ollie and Ollie alone: I hadn't seen Bendy again and, most importantly, the man in the trench coat hadn't returned. The lack of both these individuals in my life made me feel a bit silly by the end of the week that I had been so upset by them in the first place. As the latter had clearly been someone needing Joey and, who knows, maybe he'd even managed to find him and speak with him. And the former, well, the former was a figment of my imagination. Something that happened when you were tired at the end of a long day, and you were in the dark, and very, very likely was a giant rat.

Of course it didn't prevent me from yelping when I opened the door on Friday to Bendy sitting on the giant table in the middle of the room.

"What's wrong with you?" asked Evan.

I didn't want to say anything as I approached it, but as I came into the light, I felt so stupid and ridiculous. It was a large Bendy stuffed toy. Not the real thing. Because of course there was no such thing as the real thing. Bendy wasn't real; he was a drawing.

"Nothing. Where did this come from?" I asked.

"Your best pal," he replied.

"Joey?" I asked.

"Of course." Not once in this entire conversation did he turn around to acknowledge me. But I was used to it. I knew the back of his head better than the front at this point.

I leaned over and picked up the toy. It was very soft. "But why?"

"It's for your brother," he said.

I had mentioned something offhandedly to Joey the other day about him not being well, not the specifics of course, but just some general small talk I'd felt instantly guilty about. But he'd remembered. He'd remembered.

I hugged the Bendy. "That's so nice of him."

"Sure, it is. Rose, come on, you know tonight's the big test night for me. I have a lot of work to get done."

"I'm sorry. Yes, of course. Do you want me to grab you any dinner before I leave?"

There was a pause. And then: "Yes, that would be nice, thanks."

"Always happy to help."

I squeezed the Bendy tightly again.

I got home after eight that night and quietly removed my boots and coat, moving Bendy from one hand to the other to slip off the sleeves. As I was hanging it in the closet, Mother approached me, wiping her hands on her apron. "And who's this?"

"It's for Ollie. From Joey."

"That's just lovely of him, isn't it?" Mother beamed and gave Bendy a little pat on the head.

"Is he still up?" I asked.

"Should be," she replied. She leaned forward and kissed me on the forehead. "There's leftovers in the fridge."

"Thanks," I said. And I immediately made my way up the stairs to his room. I knocked gently on the door. "I have someone out here who wants to meet you," I said. I didn't hear anything so I opened the door slowly and held the plush Bendy doll through the crack. "Hello, Ollie! Your big sister tells me you're very brave!" I said in a high squeaky voice.

"Bendy doesn't talk," said a quiet voice from inside the room.

I pushed open the door farther and looked inside. Ollie was lying on his bed in the dark room, his arms over the covers, and I could see his bandaged hand. It all reminded me too much of Father. I wanted to flip the switch for the light and let the room flood with brightness. But I had to be gentle with him, poor thing.

"I guess you're right, but you don't think it's a little funny hearing your sister sound so silly?" I asked.

Ollie didn't look at me. He just kept staring at the ceiling.

I came over to the bed and sat down as gently as I could beside him. I reached over and pushed his hair on his forehead back up. "How are you feeling, kiddo?" I asked.

"I'm okay," he said. I watched as his eyes flitted back and forth almost as if he was watching something. I glanced up, but in the dark I couldn't tell if maybe there was a spider or silverfish crossing the ceiling.

I looked at him again. "Does the hand still hurt?"

He nodded. "A little."

I still had the Bendy in my other hand, hanging down over the side of the bed. I put it up next to him on his pillow. "Isn't he cute?" I asked.

Finally Ollie turned to look at the toy. A faint smile. "He's pretty cute, yeah," he said.

"Why don't you give him a hug."

Ollie thought about it for a moment and nodded. He reached out with his good hand and I passed Bendy to him. He squeezed him tight between his arms and turned onto his side to face me, holding him close.

"Rose?" he asked.

"Yes?"

"Do you ever see things in your imagination?"

The question sent a chill over me, and I had to remind myself that Ollie was a sweet little boy who didn't know anything about the puddles. He was just asking a typical little kid question. One of those big questions that always felt really tough to answer but you tried anyway. "Do you mean like when I close my eyes and I imagine things? Like what it would be like to visit Hawaii or own a pony?" I asked.

"I don't know," he replied. He looked so sad, but he still held fast to the Bendy and that made me feel better.

"I see things in my mind a lot, like pictures. Things I wish I could see, things I've seen in the past and want to see again." And then there were things that had never happened and I wished to never see. Like Evan's broken body. Or things that could not possibly exist, like Bendy himself walking down a dark alleyway.

But I didn't say that.

"I see things in my imagination a lot," said Ollie. "Ever since I was little."

"I think it's a family trait," I replied with a smile, even as my gut dropped. "It's fun to play pretend."

Ollie nodded again. "How do you know what's real and what's pretend?"

Wow, he really had tough questions today. Answering them felt impossible. "Well, real things are real. You can see them, but you can also touch them, and smell them, and hear them. I guess if your other senses can participate, that makes things real?" I was asking myself more than him. I'd never thought about it in such specific terms before.

"Can you imagine smells?" he asked.

"I don't think you can," I replied, but I didn't feel certain about that.

"What about sounds?"

I didn't know. I thought about dreams and how real they could be in the moment. How you could have conversations with people and it really seemed like you could hear them speak. I thought about if I had dreamed about eating cake, say, wouldn't I dream I could taste it? Smell it? I think I would. I didn't know what to say, and I was worried I was getting it all wrong.

"Are you real, Rose?" he asked.

That just about broke my heart.

"Ollie, of course I'm real."

"And Mother and Father?"

"Yes, yes, of course."

"And Bendy."

I paused then. The question was confusing. Ollie had long ago learned the difference between the made-up characters on the big screen and radio plays and real-life people. He was a little too old to be asking this. At the same time, I didn't want to discourage him or make him feel bad. "Well, Bendy is a character in a cartoon and that's all made up, but the toy you're holding, that is very real."

Ollie looked at the toy Bendy and gave him a little pet. "He's soft."

"And squishy," I added with a smile.

"But not real."

I shook my head. "No. No, the character of Bendy isn't real."

"Not real."

I felt strangely uncomfortable, a little like when your skin is too dry, or the air is too warm. "Hey, kiddo, can sisters get hugs too, or is that reserved only for Bendy?"

Ollie gave me a little smile and carefully placed the Bendy to one side. He reached out his arms. "Sisters always get hugs!"

I pulled him in close, careful not to irritate his hand. "This is real," I said. "This is the best kind of real."

17

I stood in the dark and cold. I had pulled my scarf down to my chin so I could watch as my breath puffed in the air. To my back was Central Park, a looming black void with the lights of the West Side peeking out through the trees. And in front of me was the Arch residence. Home of Nathan Arch, steel magnate, investor and backer, and party host. I was freezing in my stockings and kitten heels. Mother's dress was a pretty and simple, sleeveless, black silk tea dress that poofed out nicely to just below my knees thanks to an old, yellowing crinoline. Covered by my wool coat, I still felt like I was wearing practically nothing in the winter weather. But for some reason I wasn't ready to go inside yet.

I had never been to a house in Manhattan. The city was made of towers, like the toy blocks I played with as a child. To be honest, I really hadn't visited anyone's home on the island, just in my little borough. But of course it was quite obvious that everyone on the island lived in the sky. Especially in the evenings when you could see the lights glowing from all the windows and silhouettes of the people living there passing by. All kinds of people in the same building, all with different hopes and dreams and day-to-day business. I thought it was marvelous.

But a proper house?

Not until that moment. And in that moment, staring up at the six-story structure before me, I could hardly imagine all this space could be for one family alone. It seemed grand but also a little sad. A little too empty, I imagined. I wondered if it was possible to go a full day in there and not see another person.

I took in a deep breath and climbed the steps to the large oak door, ornately decorated with a cornucopia of harvest-time foods carved around its border. I saw a large door knocker in the center, but to the right there was a bell. I chose the bell. Almost exactly as I withdrew my finger, the door was opened by a tall man with white hair wearing a tuxedo.

"Oh, are you the butler?" I said, not really thinking. How thrilling; I'd never met a butler before.

He looked at me, and had it not been beneath him, he very much would have rolled his eyes at me. That would have been fine; it had been a silly kind of outburst to say. Music and laughter floated over the threshold to greet me, and I tried to look beyond his shoulder into the home. Finally he moved to the side to let me pass, and I stepped into an ornate glittering entrance.

"Thank you," I said, but it barely managed to escape my lips before a stunned silence overtook me. I didn't want to disgrace the space with the descriptor of "foyer," for it was far grander than that. I had entered a massive room with a marble-tiled floor in which danced thousands of sparkles reflecting off the enormous chandelier hanging from the ceiling above. It rose above my head at least two stories, if not more, just as the wide marble staircase before me did, taking you in two directions at the top landing. At its peak hung the largest painting I had ever seen, the size possibly of someone's living room, or at the least mine. It was of some king or noble warrior, wearing swaths of fabric blowing in the wind as he held a sword aloft, his foe prostrate at his feet. It was a lively picture, full of movement and emotion, and I found it fascinating that a two-dimensional image could evoke such easy feeling when Joey was working so hard to create in all three dimensions. Perhaps, I wondered, it wasn't altogether necessary. But of course, no, no, it was. It was necessary if only for the need to experiment and see. To discover.

Still. I marveled.

And that wasn't all! Because before me, right there, right where I was standing, just before the stairs, there was a fountain. An actual working fountain, inside, like something you'd see in a park, with three-tiered large bowls on top of one another, carved stone cherubs and angels looking up where the water exploded out of the top.

Two very finely dressed people rushed by then, a man and a woman, he in a tux and she in a long blue gown. I felt the cold on my ankles and realized only now that what I had assumed was a cocktail party indeed was not. My cheeks burned but I couldn't let embarrassment ruin this moment. Even if I had known it was black tie, I certainly would not have been able to dress for it. I would have come as I had or not at all. And despite my nerves, oh dear was I glad I had come.

"Beautiful room," I said.

"Immaculately restored. One of the few remaining jewels of the Gilded Age so thoughtfully taken care of," replied the butler. He seemed pleased with my reaction and indeed looked at the grand entranceway with a personal pride. As if it was he who had done the restoration himself.

"How wonderful," I said. And he nodded.

"It is. Come, miss, the party is in the drawing room."

A drawing room. How marvelous!

I followed him across the entranceway and along the same path as the pretty couple, down a short hallway on which hung another huge painting, this time a portrait of a man with kind eyes, and a boy, perhaps his son? The boy looked right at me as if he could read my innermost thoughts. How unnerving, but how impressive, again, at what a good artist could do with a little bit of paint.

We arrived then at the party, another giant space. It was decorated in soft greens and blues, the walls sparkled in the light of another magnificent chandelier, and I noticed the pale paisley wallpaper must have had some sort of iridescent threads within it. A carved white marble fireplace the size of a car stood on the opposite wall and burned brightly so that the room was very hot. But of course the many people added to that. Such beautiful people, all beautifully dressed and laughing and eating finger food being passed around on silver trays by beautifully dressed staff. I looked to see if I could spot Evan. I wondered if he too was wearing a tux.

"May I take your coat?" asked the butler.

I nodded, still staring, gaping if I was honest. I quickly unbuttoned my winter coat and he very elegantly helped me step out of it. I felt a little childish in my mother's tea dress, but I kept a smile on my face and thanked the butler as he left.

"Champagne?" asked a waiter materializing beside me.

"Oh no, thank you," I said, though the glittering glasses filled to the brim with golden bubbles did look very tempting.

"There she is!" said a booming, jovial voice. Joey. I felt suddenly so much more at ease. He emerged from the crowd dressed in a perfectly tailored tux, beaming as he made a bee-line right for me.

"Hi, Joey," I said as he arrived.

"You look stunning, just stunning," he said, and it really did seem he meant it.

"Oh no, nothing like your other guests. I'm so sorry, I didn't realize it was black tie." I nervously smoothed my skirt.

"Let me tell you a little secret," he said, linking his arm through mine in such a familiar fashion I almost felt a little shy, and turning to face the room in the same direction as I was. "The more effort you can see in an ensemble, the cheaper it is."

I didn't really understand.

He gave a nod at a woman in a purple dress covered in what looked like diamonds. "What do you say? I say that dress is worth half the value of what she's wearing." He indicated the woman beside her in a simple dark green velvet gown.

"Oh," I said. I still didn't understand his point.

"Those who show up to parties overdressed, in my opinion, have made far worse social blunders than an elegant young woman in a classic little black dress. You outshine everyone. Because you don't care." He grinned at me. It was comforting and kind of him to say. But . . .

"But I do care."

Joey laughed. "Well, everyone does. It's all about the appearance of not caring. The illusion, my dear, the illusion."

I smiled, but again all I felt was a little confused. I supposed he was just trying to make me feel better, and he had in a way. And yet, that purple dress still looked pretty spectacular to me.

"Come, I want to introduce you to someone very special, and who you already know in a way," he said. He gave my arm a small tug and I followed the pull toward a white baby grand piano nestled perfectly in a large bay window alcove where a professional pianist was playing "The Way You Look Tonight." Leaning up against it, perfectly within the dip, was one of the most beautiful women I'd ever seen, wearing a sleeveless full-length white gown made entirely of sparkles. Sequins of course, but it looked like stardust or that it had been hewn out of diamonds themselves. She wore white elbow-length gloves and held daintily onto a glass of champagne as she sang softly along with the song, loud enough that I could hear her perfect voice, but not so loudly that she was commandeering the attention in the room. A small crowd had gathered nonetheless, and when she finished just as we arrived, they appreciatively applauded while she beamed her gratitude in return.

"Allison, my angel, please meet my newest employee, Rose," said Joey. He unlatched his arm from mine and gave me the tiniest of pushes in her direction. Not that I needed it. I was drawn to her like a magnet.

"Rose, what a pretty name," she said, switching her glass to her left hand and extending her right. I took it and we held hands for a moment.

"It's a pleasure to meet you."

"And of course you know who Allison is," said Joey.

I smiled and nodded but I had to admit I had absolutely no idea. But I didn't want to let him down, nor insult the stunning woman in front of me. Allison smiled brightly.

"Now I need to find Nathan. You two get to know each other!" he ordered and then he spun on his heel and marched off.

"He has this way of making you feel like the center of the world one minute and the next like you've disappeared in a puff of smoke," said Allison as we watched him go.

I turned to her. "I'm fine," I said.

"Of course you are," she said. "I'm Allison Pendle by the way. I'm the voice of Alice Angel."

Of course! That was it! I knew I recognized her from something. But how embarrassing. Incredibly so since she knew I hadn't remembered her.

"I'm so sorry," I said. A waiter passed then with some crackers with a pile of tiny black balls on them and I grabbed one hastily. "I do recognize you now, of course. You're wonderful."

"I find that context changes everything. Besides, it doesn't help to be all done up like this. I don't really feel entirely like myself in any way tonight, but Joey insisted I go all out. I feel like I might have overdone the white."

"Oh no, it's perfect. Very glamorous," I said, surprised she'd feel at all uneasy.

She smiled almost a little sadly. "Well, that's the job, I guess. Being glamorous and performing for the guests. Even when you're supposed to be one. You're always expected to be on, as an actor."

That didn't sound like that much fun. "Do you never get to enjoy parties?"

"Depends on the party. I do wish he'd allowed Tom to come, but . . . well, obviously not. Still. It helps when you have a friend with you."

"Oh yes, I understand that." *Where* was Evan? I wondered.

"Well, we shall be each other's friends tonight, then." She smiled so warmly at me that any of the lingering cold from outside I was feeling disappeared in an instant. "Are you going to eat that?" She nodded at the cracker that I still held awkwardly in my hand.

"Yes. Yes, I am." I took a bite. It was deliciously salty. "What is this?" I asked.

"Caviar. You either love it or you hate it. I take it you are the former."

"Definitely the former." So this was caviar. This was the quintessential rich person's food. Everyone had heard of caviar, but here I was actually tasting it. "This is Nathan's house, right?" I asked after brushing the crumbs off on the tiny napkin that had come with it. I balled it up in my hand and then looked for a place to put it. There was no place to put it.

I just held on to it.

"Yes, a very successful businessman, old friend of Joey's. He's probably the biggest sponsor of the new show," she replied, taking a sip of champagne.

"That's nice of him," I said.

"Yes, to have such friends," she said with a smile. A waiter passed by just then and she placed the empty glass on his tray and he vanished before I could think of disposing of my napkin likewise. I squished it harder in my hand. I was feeling very awkward.

"What's it like to be famous?" I asked. Well, that was a silly thing to say.

But Allison gave the question due consideration, which hadn't been necessary but made me feel a little less stupid. "I don't think that I am. I suppose it is lovely when people recognize me, for any of my work, not just Bendy. It's wonderful to know you've done something that lasts in the world. That has a real impact."

I nodded enthusiastically. Yes, that must be the best part. Knowing you made some kind of a difference. Like how I was helping change the face of television. I didn't need to be famous for it, but knowing something I had been a part of had changed the lives of others was a thrilling idea. "What do you think of the new technology?" I asked.

"Which new technology?" she asked with a smile.

"The television and the 3-D glasses." There was a great deal of technology out there in the world, I supposed. Specificity was a good idea.

"I do enjoy a good 3-D movie. It's so real," she replied. She started swaying a little to the new song the pianist was playing, a lilting melody I didn't recognize.

"Me too. But I meant Joey's 3-D glasses."

"I'm not sure what you mean?"

I wasn't certain how exactly to explain it any better. I was confused by her confusion.

"Allison, darling, you said you'd tell me where you got your clutch." The infamous woman in purple suddenly appeared between us. Up close I had a better sense of what Joey meant; there was something a little unrefined about her outfit that translated generally to her entire appearance. Her rouge was a little too red, her hair a little too stiff. But I didn't find anything particularly bad about it. Her wanting to put in an effort for Joey surely was more of a compliment than anything.

Allison gave me an apologetic look and I nodded back. It was time for her to be "on" again. I didn't mind the interruption in fact, as I was still feeling perplexed.

"It's a custom piece, a present from Joey, but I'm sure he could introduce you to the designer," she said, and they slowly melted away into the crowd together.

I squeezed my napkin again. I could feel it falling apart from the sweat in my palm that had by now permeated my thin gloves. I now had no choice but to keep my hand tightly closed or, I feared, shower everyone with confetti.

I stood there, on my own, and watched the room. Joey had vanished and I didn't see anyone I recognized from the office. Evan had not made an appearance yet and I was starting to feel stupid that I'd cared at all if he would. I felt very alone and awkward. Should I go up to someone and just start speaking. It didn't feel like my presence would be welcome. Not here. Not at a party like this. It was amazing how you could feel so lonely in a room full of people.

Suddenly I heard a sublimely familiar voice. "Don't walk away, man. Do you think I can survive on half a cracker! *You're* crackers."

Turning, I saw Papa D, wonderfully grumpy Papa D, over by a large vase. He had cornered one of the waitstaff and was eating directly off the tray. I quickly skipped over to him. He was too distracted by the food to notice my appearance so I said, "Hi there, Papa D!"

The man started and then began coughing, spitting a few flakes of pastry toward the poor cowering waiter. Papa D turned to look at me. "Just like you to appear out of thin air. Are you trying to kill me?"

"No, of course not." I was grinning though. How could I miss this gruff man, but evidently I did. "I didn't know you'd be at this party."

"Well, I didn't know I'd be here either. Stupid internal politics."

I noticed then that he wasn't even wearing an evening suit, but one of his regular work suits. I liked that; it made me feel more at ease.

"Internal politics?" I asked.

"When the top brass isn't impressed by the numbers, gotta keep an eye on their investment. It's ridiculous." The waiter slowly started to ease himself away as Papa D was distracted by me. But his movement caught Papa D's attention. "Don't you dare," said Papa D, grabbing another salmon puff violently off the tray. He shook his head as he swallowed. "Disgusting."

"What numbers?" I asked. I smiled at the waiter apologetically, trying to emulate Allison in the gesture, though I think it came across far more pained than hers. I took a puff off the tray, half expecting Papa D to block me, but he allowed me the privilege.

"Viewership. I told them. I told them no one wants cartoons in the evening, who are they even trying to appeal to? But they liked Arch's money, and Joey Drew is a salesman, that's for sure. Look, what does it matter to you anyway?" He was glaring at me now, and I found it delightful. Though the content of what he was saying alarmed me a little.

"Well, it's only been one week. We shall see what happens tonight," I said.

"They do like to jump the gun, you're not wrong. What time is it?" I shook my head and looked around the room for a clock. I couldn't find anything. "I gotta stay till seven thirty. Then I'm gone."

"But the show isn't on until eight."

Papa D shook his head. "Sweetheart, if you think anyone here is actually gonna watch the darn thing, well, you're more naïve than I took you for. And I took you for pretty gosh darn naïve."

"Isn't this a viewing party?" I asked. It didn't make sense.

"It's a party. That's all anyone here wants. To mingle, to talk to the right people, to suck up to Arch."

"Nathan Arch," I said, clarifying it for myself.

"That's the man. You think any of these stiffs are gonna wanna sit and wrinkle their pretty outfits to watch some kids' cartoons?"

No, I didn't think they would. Maybe Allison. Definitely Allison would. But the rest of the company here? That was feeling unlikely.

"Well, Joey certainly can convince them," I said.

"Sir," said the waiter quietly.

"He knows which side his bread is buttered on." Papa D grabbed another puff and then just stared at the waiter, who was staring back. "What?" he barked.

"It's, it's seven thirty, sir," replied the waiter, his voice cracking.

"Good." Papa D grabbed the remaining puffs and, stuffing them into his jacket pocket, stormed off without so much as a farewell.

We had passed a few minutes quite nicely, I had thought, but now that they were over I was back to square one. "Miss," said the waiter. I looked at him.

"Yes?"

"There is a television set up upstairs in the library for those interested." He sounded a bit more confident now and I felt sorry for him. Not everyone was prepared for a Papa D encounter.

"Oh, wonderful, thank you!" I said. "Where do I find it?"

"Up the stairs and to the left. The door will be open." He smiled, then looked down at his empty tray. "I'd better get a refill."

I nodded and then, realizing, said, "Wait! Can I leave this with you?" I opened my hand to reveal the destroyed napkin. He nodded and I put its remains on the silver tray before the waiter walked with a rather quick step out of the room. Probably wanting to avoid any other strange individuals. Like Papa D. Or me.

18

I retraced my steps through the giant room. No one seemed the least bit interested in chatting with me and Joey was nowhere to be found. Once more I glanced around for Evan, but of course nothing. I felt a combination of anxiety and boredom. So I wandered back into the extravagant entranceway and climbed the massive stairs. I gazed at the huge painting once I reached the top. It was extravagant in a way that made me wonder how much money it had cost and wonder if potentially it could have been put to some good use elsewhere. But the painting did look old, and maybe the purchase of it was a preservation in its own right. Not every museum could afford great works of art. As I stepped closer, I could see the energy behind the artist's brush, the wild strokes and a thick application of paint. There was a passion there, and even if the painting didn't entirely please me to look at, I appreciated that.

There was a peel of laughter from downstairs in the drawing room and I remembered why I was here in the first place. I turned left and walked down the wide hall with vaulted wooden ceilings. There were many doors but I was supposed to look for the open one, which I did and which I found. I peered around the doorway and indeed was met with the sight of a library. A beautifully vast room with floor-to-ceiling shelves all packed full with books. I enjoyed books, though no one would ever call me a great reader, but seeing so many in one place was quite intimidating. How could anyone possibly read this much in one lifetime? What a grand goal.

And how odd, too, to enter a room full of books in search of a television.

It was like walking through a maze as some shelves came right out into the center of the room, creating walls and nooks and crannies. There were a pair of leather chairs when I turned one corner, with a large globe on huge brass casters standing between them. And around another I found a chess board on a table with two wooden chairs on either side, paused mid-game. One of the chairs was pushed back away from the table as if someone had left in a rush. Or perhaps a huff. Like Ollie would when he was losing at Chutes and Ladders.

I saw a flickering blue light on the wall around the next corner and felt satisfied I'd finally found the television. I quickly made my way around the next bend and, sure enough, there it was. Quite small, smaller than the one Joey had given my family, sitting on an elegant table. On the screen was that quiz show, the one that aired just before *The Joey Drew Show*, but the volume was turned all the way down. There were about six chairs around the table, and I drew back the one nearest me and sat so that I was at the head and the TV was the foot. Or perhaps the other way around. It did feel a bit as if the television had called this meeting and not me. It was a silly thought.

That's when I noticed the 3-D glasses sitting in the middle. One pair. Just one. Sitting as if an invitation or possibly, strangely, a dare.

"So I'm not alone after all," said a voice. I turned abruptly in my seat to see a man leaning against the bookshelf on the far wall. He was holding a book open as if he'd been reading while also watching the screen. He was tall and thin, maybe in his late twenties or early thirties, possibly older, possibly younger. It was hard to tell with his thinning hair and the flickering light. His voice had a rasp to it, as if he had smoked one too many cigarettes.

"No," I replied, "unless you wish to be." I stood quickly, not wanting to intrude.

The man shook his head. "Of course not. Why does everyone always want to leave me alone?"

I had no idea what to say to that. "Do they?"

The man coughed, unfolded his arms, and took a step toward the table. I could see him a bit better now, and I still couldn't entirely make out his age. "Sit down, please," he said with an elegant gesture of the hand.

I did, but I felt reticent now. "Will you join me?" I asked.

The man shrugged. "I prefer to stand."

There was an awkward silence and I folded my hands together in my lap. I had attempted to escape the uncomfortable downstairs by seeking out the television but now I felt all the more out of place. I looked back at the television. There was something almost spooky about the screen flashing images with no sound. A bright light, a dim light, a bright light again. I thought back to the night with Ollie and that same ghostly glow. My stomach turned. I glanced up at my companion. His face seemed to change shape in each new light as the shadows grew and diminished, highlighting his sunken cheeks, his focused gaze.

"I'm Rose," I said. I hadn't planned on making an introduction, but the silence had overwhelmed me.

The man turned to look at me. "Wilson," he said with a small nod. "Wilson Arch."

"Oh, are you related to Nathan Arch, then?" I asked. I still felt ill at ease but at least here was something we could talk about.

"I am," he replied, closing the book. "He's my father."

"Well, that's lovely," I said.

"Is it?"

"I think so, yes." I felt on the spot and stammered out my answer. "He's a very generous man, your father." Wilson stared at me now. I couldn't stare back. Though I was able to maintain eye contact with so many strange and new people—Papa D was an excellent example—for some reason I couldn't with him. For some reason, I felt a little cold. I averted my gaze back to the television.

"He's generous, I suppose. Foolhardy, maybe? Too trusting, too invested."

"Oh." The man on the television grinned and pointed at a cue card that had the number fifteen written on it for some reason.

"Most businessmen are ruthless, but not my father. He's obsessive, but far too lenient, far too hopeful. I admire him in a way."

"That's nice," I said. It felt like I had to say something, but I didn't really mean it. I didn't want to participate in this conversation anymore at all. I really wanted to just get up and leave, but something held me rooted to the spot.

Now fourteen and now thirteen. *Lucky number thirteen*, I thought.

An arm appeared between me and the television. I glanced up at Wilson. He had picked up the 3-D glasses and was looking at them intently. As he stood upright, the television suddenly changed. Bendy, on the screen, waving at me. It was the "Next Up" card, the same as last week. In exchange for the glasses, Wilson had left the book in its place. My eyes were drawn to it. *The Illusion of Living*, it said on its cover. Joey's book. The one Evan had been talking about. It was right there, in front of me, so close I could reach out and touch it.

"Show's on soon," said Wilson.

"Yes," I said. I kept him in my peripheral vision, still studying the book cover, and noted as he stepped out of view to the side. It was so quiet I could hear him breathing, wet and raspy. It was far more unpleasant than the awkward silence. "Do you like Bendy?" I asked.

"You know, I don't think I do," he replied. His voice was now behind me. I made to turn but he stopped me with "Don't. Keep facing forward."

I did as I was told. I felt in my gut I should probably be doing the opposite but I was frozen in place. I just stared at Bendy, also frozen, in his wave, with that smile.

"Keep watching the screen." I started at that. It was a whisper, right in my ear. He was directly behind me now and I felt myself hold my breath. I didn't like this. I didn't like this at all. I could feel my pulse quicken; I wanted to bolt from my seat, run down the hall and out the front door. But I couldn't. I was stuck. Glued. Immobile.

Then the glasses materialized in my view. I could see them being lowered over my head in my periphery, and carefully, almost delicately, he placed them over my eyes, hooking the arms over my ears. Bendy drew himself toward me. He was standing on the table in front of me. His wave wasn't frozen anymore, he beckoned me with a finger as in "Come here, Rose, come here." For some reason I closed my eyes.

"Watch, you'll see. Just watch." In my ear again, that rasp, that almost cough.

"I've seen it," I said, also in a whisper.

Suddenly I felt the glasses torn away from my face. I opened my eyes to see the regular Bendy on the screen and then the image cut to Joey standing at his artist's desk. The show had started.

"What on earth are you doing?" asked Wilson. He was farther away from me now and I felt the ability to move again. I stood and turned all in one motion, knocking over the chair.

"Could ask you the same thing, bub," said Evan. He was there, standing across the table, holding the glasses and staring absolute daggers at Wilson.

"Evan!"

"Rose, come on, let's get out of here," he said, pointing toward the exit.

"But the show just started." I didn't mean to argue. I wanted to leave more than anything, but I felt numb and kind of stupid all at once.

"She wants to stay," said Wilson, reaching out for the glasses, and Evan pushed him back. Shoved him more like—a hard shove, a violent shove.

I didn't mind that. In fact, it shook something inside me, and without any more instruction I immediately turned and made my way hastily toward the exit. I looked back and saw Evan marching not too far behind me. I felt good about that and stopped to wait for him in the hall. The brightness was welcoming, and I could feel cool air flowing now that we were out of the confined space. It made me realize all the more how strange and unpleasant that entire interaction with Wilson had been. It sent a shiver up my spine.

Evan emerged and walked past me, and somehow I knew I was to fall in step with him. So I did. He still carried the 3-D glasses with him.

"Are you okay?" I asked.

He laughed one of his wry knowing laughs. "I'm not the one who . . ." He stopped then, so I did too. He seemed to think something and then turned to me. "Are *you* okay?"

He genuinely looked concerned, which was quite nice of him. Indeed, very nice of him.

"Yes," I said.

He nodded. Then he looked at the glasses in his hand for a long moment, so still, thinking something. And then threw them onto the floor. There was the sound of glass cracking but that wasn't good enough. He stomped hard on them.

"Evan!" I cried out. "Your invention."

"Exactly. I made them, I can destroy them."

"Is that what you want?" I stared at the poor things, all shattered glass and twisted metal.

"It is." He looked back at me. "So, now we're even."

"Even?"

"You saved me, I saved you."

I couldn't help but laugh a little, though he looked deadly serious. "I saved you from certain death, Evan. I don't think this was quite the same thing."

"No, I agree," he said, turning and starting to walk again. "This would have been far worse."

I caught up to him at the top of the stairs under that massive painting. I had to grab his arm to stop him, and he turned and shook me off with a scowl.

"You can't just walk off like that," I said, "not after what you said."

"I don't have time to explain everything," he replied.

"The time you've already spent on this conversation is time you could have spent explaining 'everything,'" I replied.

He shook his head and leaned in. "How about I don't want to do it now, to do it here? Does that maybe work as an excuse for you?"

I felt another shiver up my spine—they were following each other in quick succession, like a waterfall flowing backward. "Yes," I said.

"Good."

"So let's leave, and then you can," I added.

Evan looked at me with that indignant look of his. I couldn't tell if he absolutely couldn't stand me but I was just going to assume with the week we had that he liked me. Or at the least tolerated me.

"Rose, not tonight, not . . . I don't even quite know what I'm doing, okay?" he said. He looked worn out suddenly, and I saw him differently then, not this young man made of sharp edges and an even sharper tongue, but someone exhausted and drawn out. Worked to the literal bone.

"There are my two favorite employees!" called out an all-too-familiar voice.

As one, we both turned to look down the grand staircase to Joey standing at the bottom like the lead in a musical, arms outstretched up to us while striking a fine pose. Neither Evan nor I said anything. We just stared. When we didn't move, Joey sprinted up to join us, taking the steps two at a time. He was sprightly for a man in his fifties. It was quite admirable.

"Did you watch the show? Is it over yet?" He beamed at us and it was hard to not smile back, so of course I did.

"We started to," I stammered. Joey nodded and glanced down the hall toward the library. Then his brow furrowed. He stepped between us, pushing us apart without having to actually touch either of us. We moved the moment he did, an innate act of respect for him. He walked down the hall and stared. At the broken 3-D glasses. I heard Evan take in a sharp breath beside me. Joey looked back up at us.

"How did this happen?" he asked. His voice was stern, like a parent asking his two naughty children who broke an expensive vase.

I was struck silent. I had no interest to get in the middle of these two men, and furthermore, well, I felt a strange kind of loyalty to Evan. He and I were more like a team now, in a way. Surely.

Evan for his part spoke up immediately. "They broke."

Joey stared at Evan for a moment and then turned back to the glasses. Carefully he bent over and gingerly picked them up, including the small pieces scattered around them on the floor. He placed the pieces of glass in his jacket pocket and held the frame in his hand. Then he looked at us again.

At Evan.

"They did, didn't they," he said.

He made his way slowly back toward us, and Evan, still in his superhero mode, I suppose, subtly placed his hand on my arm, indicating I should move behind him. Which I did because honestly Joey's intensity was starting to truly scare me.

"Of course," said Joey, arriving at Evan as they met each other, eye to eye, "the question remains: how."

Evan stared right back. They were evenly matched in height, but Evan still looked so much more like a child in relation to the well turned-out Joey Drew. I noticed he, like me, was wearing something borrowed, a suit that clearly belonged to a friend or family member. It was a little too big, the sleeves a little too wide.

"They fell," replied Evan.

"And someone accidentally stepped on them?" asked Joey.

"Precisely."

Joey took yet another step closer and I held my breath. I flashed in my mind to Wilson, right behind me, intimidating me yet doing absolutely nothing wrong, nothing that you could put your finger on. I didn't like seeing Joey behave in a similar manner. It was out of character for him.

"I stepped on them. I'm so sorry, Joey," I said, the words tumbling out of my mouth. He turned his glare on me. It felt as if someone had actually knocked the wind out of me, a real punch to the gut, and yet, again, nothing tangible had happened. "I dropped them and then as I tried to pick them up I got all turned about and accidentally stepped on them. And I'm so sorry."

Joey just kept staring. Then with an uncomfortable calmness he said, "You are too good, Rose. I wouldn't be that good. It's dangerous." He turned back to Evan. "You're fired." Then he swept past us both and I followed him with my gaze as he marched down the stairs and back under the archway toward the drawing room. He didn't run, he showed no large emotion, but he did it with a speed and focus that made my insides drop.

He was angry. He was very angry indeed.

I turned back to Evan. "I'm so sorry," I said. Evan kept staring in front of him, where Joey had been. Had chastised him. Had fired him. "Evan, please, I'm so sorry. This is all my fault."

He still didn't look at me. But he spoke. "I broke them, Rose. It's entirely my fault." Then finally he turned to look at me. "Let's see him do his grand plan without me." He laughed a little then, to himself, not to me.

"Evan, what's wrong with the glasses?" I asked.

"Nothing," he replied. He was still amused by something I knew he'd never share with me.

"Evan. What happened last night, at the test run?"

He looked at me again. "I don't know, Rose. I can't decide if it was something very wrong or something very right. I just don't think someone like you should wear them."

"Like me?"

He shook his head. "Like Pollyanna." I didn't say anything. I didn't know what to say. And I didn't feel like this was an appropriate moment to argue with him. Not after he'd just lost his job. "Well, I better go," he said. "See you in the funny pages." Then he laughed to himself again. "Maybe literally."

He winked at me, and I had no idea what it meant, and then it was his turn to take the journey down the stairs, only this time he made his way past the fountain to the front doors. The butler materialized and opened them for him. He had no coat, no hat, no gloves.

And then he was gone.

I stood there. By myself. I could hear the sounds of a happy party off in the distance, but even thinking of all those glittering people, I felt desperately alone. It wasn't a literal aloneness. It was an aloneness inside me, in my heart and soul. Evan had become a kind of ally and now he was gone. But even then it wasn't the greatest cause for concern. It was Joey. I had to confess to myself that it was all Joey. I had never heard him speak like that, I had never seen him act like that, and while I completely understood him wanting to fire an employee who ruined company property, it was the attitude behind it. The coldness. And the stare. But it hadn't been a stare, not really. It had been something more disturbing, at least the way it seemed to me. It had been a man reading my innermost thoughts. And I have no idea what he'd seen in there. In my mind. *Could he dive as deep as the puddles?* I wondered. Could he get that far?

Had he?

Another shiver and then another reminder. I turned and stared at the hallway leading to the library. In my mind I saw the book *The Illusion of Living* sitting on the table, with the frozen Bendy waving at me from the screen just beyond it. I needed that book. It would explain, if not everything, then at least something. Something important. I felt it in my very bones. But I was absolutely not going back into that room, not with Wilson still in there. That would be like walking into a snake pit.

Instead I left.

I just left.

I walked down the stairs and

even before I arrived at the door the butler appeared with my
things. "Thank you," I said as he helped me put my coat on.

"Of course, miss."

And then I was out on the cold street staring down Fifth
Avenue as far as I could see. I crossed the street to the park
side and stopped then. To stare up at the house. The light from
the windows no longer called to me. It felt instead like I was
being stared down, challenged.

"Joey Drew girl," said a familiar English accent.

"No, absolutely not," I said. I didn't even have to turn to
make sure, but as I started walking away quickly, I could see the
shadow of the man following me from behind. The wide fedora
gave him away just fine. I simply did not have the time to deal
with my terrifying stalker, not after someone had breathed on
me and my boss had just read my deepest secrets and fired my
one friend in the office. I was fueled by adrenaline and fury as
I picked up my speed. Even as the man in the fedora kept pace.

"I need to talk with you!" he called out from behind. He
had fallen farther back but he was still there.

"I don't care! Stop following me!" I picked up my pace even more and began jogging, running away from him again.

I heard his footsteps get faster. He was jogging now too. Finally the fear returned, and as tired as I was of feeling afraid, I let it push me faster. I just had to get to the subway where there would be people. That was the trouble with Fifth Avenue at night: No one casually spent their time outside, sitting on stoops, playing on the street, in this neighborhood even on a summer's evening.

Finally the glowing lamps of the subway entrance materialized and I turned my run into an all-out sprint. I made it to the stairs and held the railing tight as I flew down them. They were covered in wet slush and my feet slipped as I went. But I refused to fall over. I couldn't hear the Englishman anymore, but I didn't want to risk the time it would take to turn around. So I barreled through the gates and onto the platform.

Where I found myself completely alone.

As I stood there, panting hard, feeling the sweat on my brow and collecting under my scarf, I remembered that the other thing about the Upper East Side was how underused the subway was at certain times of day. I felt myself start to shake, and though the Englishman was nowhere to be seen, I nonetheless walked myself backward up the platform to keep an eye on the entrance. I glanced at the exit I was approaching, the small one on the far end up the platform, but as I got closer I saw that it was chained up, a sign indicating that the exit was closed on the weekend. I had nowhere to go. Nowhere to run to. But darn it all, I wouldn't be caught off guard.

I heard then the distant sound of a train approaching. I felt my heart race as I sensed an actual race beginning between its arrival and the arrival of the Englishman. Who would make it first? I turned my back on the entrance to lean over the edge of the platform and glance down the tunnel. I saw a pinprick of light. It was coming.

I turned quickly and horror quite overwhelmed me. The Englishman had arrived on the platform. There he was, far down the other side, standing there staring at me. I still had no idea what he actually looked like, but that fedora and that trench coat, they had become so familiar to me.

The sound of the train was getting louder and I moved as far up the platform as I could go, as if the few extra feet would make any kind of a difference.

I refused to look away as the figure started walking toward me. He was in no rush; clearly he didn't feel a need to race the train, even as I expected he ought to. The train got louder and louder and light started to fill the platform. The Englishman kept walking, but I was ready. The moment those doors opened I was diving onto that train. I didn't care how foolish I might look to my fellow passengers.

I took a step closer to the edge to prepare myself. The man kept walking.

The train burst into the station all light and noise and a rush of wind. As it slowed to a stop, I turned to face it, watching as the doors flew past and gauging where mine might land so that I might immediately board.

I glanced back at the Englishman.

He was running. He was running right for me.

I took in a deep breath and faced the train. It stopped, the doors opened right in front of me as if the train knew I needed the help. I made to step aboard. And was grabbed firmly from behind around my middle and pulled back onto the platform. I flew away from the train. I kicked out and screamed, hoping some passenger might see. I flailed with my arms, hitting out, and managed to twist myself free, pushing myself off the man behind me and staggering backward. He was wearing those sunglasses, those horrible sunglasses.

"Stop!" said the Englishman.

But I still had time, the train hadn't left. I turned to leap on board, my full body weight behind me, and found myself facing an empty platform. I skidded to a stop, throwing my arms out in front of me and falling, my head over the edge of the platform where a train had once been. I held on to the edge with my fingers even as my body continued to slide forward. Then there was a hand on my ankle and a pull as my upper torso fell over the side. My view was nothing but the train tracks.

I had stopped.

There was another pull on my legs and I realized that the Englishman was trying to bring me back onto the platform. As much as he terrified me, in this moment I allowed him to hoist me up. I let go of the edge that I was barely managing to hold on to, and once my chest was back on the cold tile floor of the platform, I pushed the rest of myself back and up, turning around so that I could sit upright.

The Englishman sat opposite, his hat on the ground, his coat a tussled mess. His sunglasses had skidded across the floor. I stared at him, aghast. Without his sunglasses I could see what he'd been hiding. His eyes were black. Not that he had very dark brown eyes, but that the entire eye, the whites and everything, was completely black. They looked almost hollow except for the glint from the artificial light in the station.

I shivered, reminded of Ollie wearing the glasses. His hair was deep black also. It lay against his face almost as if it was dripping down the sides of his head. It lacked any kind of texture or structure, it just was a black form. But it moved like hair—hair in slow motion, that is—when he shook his head and leaned back, breathing hard. His skin was a jaundiced yellow. I wondered if he was sick. I wondered if he was catching.

I wondered what the heck had just happened, and most of all, what had happened to the train.

"Are you alright, miss?" he finally asked after we had both calmed down.

"What just happened?" I asked. I had no idea if I could trust him, but he was the only witness I had.

He shook his head again and again, his strange black hair moving slowly in response, almost as if he was underwater. There was something about it that reminded me of something. But I couldn't think of what. "I'm sorry, miss, I didn't mean to manhandle you. I just couldn't let you jump like that."

"Jump?" I asked.

"Onto the track, like. I know I scared you. I'm sorry about that. I am not entirely good at being a person anymore. But running away up into the tunnel would have been so dangerous for you." He spoke softly, almost warmly, but I didn't dare let my defenses down. Besides, what he was saying were the ramblings of a madman.

"I wasn't trying to jump into the tunnel. I was trying to rush on board the train." How could he not have understood that?

"What train?" he asked.

More madness. I pointed at the track without looking at it. "That train. The one that was there."

He opened those black hollow eyes wider, confusion perhaps or shock? It was hard to read on a face like his. I noticed black wetness now at the corner of his mouth, like he'd eaten something and forgotten to wipe. The gash on my face. The black ooze. I suddenly understood my memory. His hair, his eyes, the wet on his lip—it was the same kind of blackness as that vision I'd had of myself in the mirror. My breathing got shallow, my head all fuzzy. "I promise you, miss, there was no train. I saw you move to the edge as I came close and then you was going to jump onto the track and I pulled you back."

A tear had formed in the corner of his left eye. A black teardrop, perfect, almost as if it was drawn by hand. I was mesmerized by it even as it horrified me.

"Please don't run," he added. But I couldn't run. I couldn't move. I felt dizzy and also heavy. I realized aside from the one cracker with the caviar on it I hadn't eaten anything all evening.

"There was a train," I said quietly. I needed to convince myself more than anyone, more than this strange Englishman on the ground with me. I noticed movement out of the corner of my eye. Not now, Bendy, please not now. But when I turned I saw instead two men walking onto the platform in the distance. I was suddenly aware of how public this whole scene was. I needed to stand. This wasn't right.

"Let me help you," said the Englishman. He leapt up onto his feet and was quickly at my side, offering me his hand. The nail on his thumb was black, as if he had polish on it. I looked up at him. His face was so close now, I could see each individual strand of wet black hair on his forehead. His eyes . . . his eyes.

I took his hand.

I stood.

"There was a train," I said again. But now I wasn't so sure. If there had been a train, how had it just vanished into nothing like that? And now that I thought harder, there had been something off about it. I closed my eyes, searching for answers in my memory. I saw the words "Silverlane Express" now on the front as it rushed to the platform. I opened my eyes. That was odd. Trains for the subway didn't have names like that. They had numbers and letters. Not names.

Not names.

The man had gone to retrieve his hat and I saw him pick up his pair of sunglasses too. I thought of the 3-D glasses then, smashed on the floor. I saw Joey slip the sharp shards into his pocket. The man put on the glasses and hat, hiding his eyes. And hair.

"Who are you?" I asked.

"My name is Archie Carter," he said. "But who I am? Well, I'm a nobody. Someone you wouldn't even notice on the street."

"No, I think I'd notice you," I replied.

"Come, let's sit on this bench." He could see I was shaking. He could tell my knees were weak. I felt vulnerable and alone. But also very tired. I was tired of being scared and tired of being told what to do and only given half the story. So I didn't move. "I need to talk with Joey Drew," he said, seeming to understand I needed more.

"Well, why didn't you?" I asked.

"What?"

"You were outside the studio that night, you were outside

the house tonight, you were waiting. Why didn't you wait a little longer? For Joey himself. Why chase me?"

Archie Carter stopped to ponder the question. "I suppose . . . well, I suppose I didn't think he'd want to have anything to do with me. And you, well, you seem like good people."

What had Joey said? That my goodness was dangerous?

"I'm a nobody too, you know," I said. "If Joey won't give you the time of day, well, there's nothing much I can do about that." Suddenly he had both my hands in his. I couldn't pull free, I didn't have the energy. I heard the sound of another train approaching. Or did I? "Do you hear that?" I asked.

"You have to try. I have to tell him about Gent," he said.

"Gent?" There it was, that name again.

"Yes, I have to tell him." I could see my own reflection in his sunglasses. I looked small and pathetic, and not like a girl who'd just come from a fancy party.

"Do you hear the train?" I asked back.

"Please."

"Do you hear the train?" I shouted it now because the sound was so loud, but I worried there was no sound at all. That I was just screaming on an empty subway platform at a man who wouldn't let go of my hands.

He nodded. "Yes. Yes, it's coming. It's behind you."

I turned even as he held on to me tight. A train blasted into the station. I turned back. "I have to go," I said.

"Tell him I need to speak with him. I'll be at the diner all day every day until he comes. Please, Joey Drew's girl, please." Even though I couldn't see those black eyes, I could still see the pain in his face. I nodded. He let my hands go free.

"I have to go," I said, turning. The doors opened as I walked carefully up to them. I paused, staring at the open space and the subway car beyond.

"It's real," said Archie.

I didn't turn around but I nodded that I had heard him, then I took a step and it was. My foot landed on solid ground. It was real. I turned, and as the doors closed, I called out, "My name is Rose!"

Archie nodded as they clanged shut. Then we stared at each other as the train started up, and I watched as he slowly slipped away as the train disappeared into the dark tunnel.

20

I lay in bed wide-awake, star-ing at the ceiling as the light crossed in a wave as a car drove down our street, rumbling over the pothole that the city had no intention of ever filling. I had never felt quite so overwhelmed. Nor quite so scared. To sift through everything that had hap-pened in one short evening felt like digging a hole in dry sand: The more I dug the more it was filled in by everything sur-rounding it. My body wouldn't stop buzzing, my mind wouldn't stop racing. I needed to relax. Breathe, I told myself. I took in a long cool drag of air and held it within me. I exhaled.

But it felt impossible to calm down. So much had happened tonight, but of all the things—the party, Papa D, the creepy Wilson, Evan and Joey, and Archie—the thing that wouldn't release its grip, the thing that held on most tight, was the train. I was utterly petrified by the thought. I could feel the cold grip of terror tighten around me every time I tried to focus on something else, anything else.

It wouldn't let go.

Was it something passed down from parent to child? I had always thought that combat fatigue was specific to people who had been through traumatizing experiences. That is, at least, what the doctor had explained. The kind one, the one who had taken time with us all, who had listened to Father. Not the first one. Or the second one, the second one who was so ancient I assumed leeches were probably his medicine of choice for all ailments. Of course Father wasn't the only person out there who had to contend with it, so it wasn't unique to our family tree or anything. It was, unfortunately for all involved, quite common.

But what if . . . I clenched my fists under the covers, felt my stomach turn over, and curled over onto my side in a tight ball. Maybe I could try to squeeze the horrible feelings out of me. It wasn't doing any good though.

What if there was something special . . . or maybe not special . . . different, different about us? What if there was something in our biology that made us more susceptible to visions? To mind games. To delusion. I had spent so much time over the years taking care of Father that the notion I might be next in line, well, it hadn't ever occurred to me. Why should it? I'd never been to war. I lived my whole life in this small little neighborhood, with my small circle of people. Did leaving it for the first time this month spark something inside my soul? Inside my brain. Did something snap? Did something come to life that had been lying within me, waiting for the right moment?

Was I going mad?

I squeezed my eyes shut hard, trying not to cry, but I had already cried so much recently. I didn't have time to lose my mind. I had people depending on me. I had an injured little brother, an unpredictable Father, and a mother who had far too much on her shoulders to take care of it all herself. I had to stop seeing things. I didn't want to see Bendy anymore, or hear bumps in the night, or see my face peel away, or encounter ghost trains. I didn't want anything else.

I certainly didn't want to die.

Archie had saved me. That strange man—something was very wrong with him and yet he seemed to have more sense than I did. He knew something about Joey. Just like Evan. They all knew something. Even that terrible Wilson Arch, why he had Joey's book. *The Illusion of Living.*

The Illusion of Living. The illusions. In my mind. In my very being. What is true and isn't true?

Ollie asking me if I'm real. I am real. I know this. I know I'm real.

I sat up, the covers slipping off my shoulders and pooling around my waist. I could feel the cold on my arms, seeping through the sleeves of my nightgown. The book. I had to find the book. I certainly couldn't go back to the Arch house. I would never go back there again. But books are in libraries, and books can be found on forgotten shelves in attics and schoolrooms. Books don't disappear into the ether, they last. Even ones you've never heard of before, they are out there, somewhere, existing.

If I found *The Illusion of Living,* that would be something. Maybe there was an answer in there for me. Joey was so smart, even as he was unpredictable and strange at times. Maybe he understood something that would help me. Would help all of us.

I lay back down. I wasn't satisfied or content, but the buzzing had lessened. I felt more calm, which was a small something. Something that would help me finally rest. Even a fitful sleep was better than nothing, and I needed a well-rested mind. Or at least the approximation of one.

I did somehow manage to fall asleep because when I opened my eyes again daylight was filtering through the curtains. A dreamless sleep. Like a snap, I had gone from night to day and it must have been quite late for the brightness outside. I looked at my little alarm clock: 9:00 a.m. Mother had let me sleep in.

I joined the family in the kitchen. There was a lovely happy feeling in the air. Mother was sipping some coffee and Father was reading the Sunday paper. They greeted me and looked so very much like a normal couple with no problems beyond paying the bills and raising a family. My heart ached.

Ollie bounded up to me, dragging the Bendy stuffed toy with him. He'd had him less than a week but the wear and tear was already visible. A sign of love. "Did you watch it last night?"

No. But that was no answer for him. "Of course! Did you!"

"Of course!" He laughed. "I love the glasses."

The glasses. A sudden vision. Broken glasses, smashed underfoot. Something dangerous, something bad. I felt like a cold bucket of water had been dumped over me.

"I think, maybe next week you should try it without the glasses," I said carefully.

"No! They're the best part." Ollie looked indignant.

"I think the best part is the cartoons," I replied.

Ollie shrugged. "Yeah, I guess they're fun too. But when I'm wearing the glasses sometimes, I don't even watch the cartoon. I walk somewhere else."

I glanced up at Mother and Father, who shook their heads with a smile. It wasn't some fanciful imagination though. I understood what he meant. The ability to walk around within the world was very real. And very odd.

I was still tired, and I was still feeling sorry for myself, so I let it go, for now. "We'll see," I said. I thought to myself, worst comes to worst, I can always hide them.

"Have some breakfast, sweetheart," said Father. "I'm making pancakes." He made to stand up but I quickly arrived at the stove before he was able to put the paper down.

"It's okay, Father. I can do it, thank you." There was mix in the bowl ready for me and I wondered what had happened last night to put everyone in such a good mood. Father didn't make his famous pancakes just any Sunday morning. "Everyone is so happy," I said.

"Are we?" asked Mother. "I suppose so. How was the party?"

What a question to ask. What a question to answer.

"It was fun, very fancy, everyone was so beautiful," I replied, pouring some batter into the hot pan. It sizzled in a very pleasant way that I couldn't fully enjoy.

"I'm sure you were the most beautiful of them all," said Father.

"Well, you have to say that," I replied with a laugh, still watching the pancakes fry, the little bubbles materializing around the edges.

I heard the fridge open and saw Ollie carrying the carton of milk over to his spot at the table. "Still hungry, son?" asked Father.

He was quite occupied by the task of opening it, and even as my pancakes bubbled in the middle, now indicating they were ready to be flipped, I watched him, exhausted, in a haze, and strangely wary. I didn't say anything though. Just stared as he stood up and then upturned the carton over Father's head, spilling milk all over him.

"Oliver!" said Father, jumping to his feet and grabbing the container from his bandaged hand.

"What do you think you're doing?" asked Mother as she took the milk from Father quickly. "You can't do things like that. You especially can't do them to your father."

Especially not to him. No surprises. None. Never. Not even a "boo!"

Ollie looked a little stunned and sputtered, "He said it would be funny."

"I certainly did not. What a thing to say!" said Father. I could see he was shaking a little, but he maintained composure, he didn't disappear into the puddles. I was proud even as I felt like I was in a dream watching it all.

I just continued to stare. I felt a little dizzy in fact. And I could smell the burning pancakes beside me. Still I didn't touch them.

"He told me to do it!" Ollie was getting teary-eyed. His bottom lip quivered as he looked at Father standing over him while Mother grabbed a towel and tried to clean everything.

"We do not lie in this household," said Father.

"Who did?" I asked.

He turned to me, eyes red, tears on his face. "Bendy."

"Go to your room, Ollie," said Mother. She was on the ground, soaking up the spilled milk.

I stared at Ollie, he stared back.

"He said it would be funny. That we'd all laugh."

"Bendy doesn't talk," I said. Of all the things to focus on, *that* was the thing I chose?

"I know. But he still says stuff. Like I can't hear it, but I know it."

And I just kept staring at him.

"Ollie! Now!" Mother ordered, her voice fierce and her face as stern as I'd ever seen it. It shook Ollie out of his trance staring at me, and he looked at her, then at Father.

"I'm sorry," he whispered.

"Ollie, just go to your room, okay?" I said.

He nodded, still watching Mother clean up his mess. Then he turned and quickly dashed out of the room, dragging the Bendy doll along the floor behind him, its head bouncing all over the place like its neck was broken. I could hear him run up the stairs and slam his door shut. Only then did Father collapse into his seat. Only then did he put his head in his hands. Only then did he start shaking properly.

"Rose, the pancakes!" Mother pointed as she stood up, the sopping-wet towel bundled in her hand.

I turned and saw smoke rising. I quickly turned off the burner and moved the pan over to the other one. Mother went to the window above the sink and opened it, then she immediately returned to Father's side. "Do you want to lie down?"

"I'm fine," he said, sitting upright and taking in a deep breath. Mother looked at him carefully, placing a hand on his shoulder. He placed his hand over hers. "I am, I promise. Just a little sticky." He gave me a smile. But I didn't think any of it was particularly smile worthy. "I think I'll take a shower." And he slowly rose, giving my mom a peck on the cheek, then left the room.

Mother wiped her brow with the back of her arm and then placed her hands on her hips, looking at the chaos in the kitchen. "What on earth happened?" she asked, looking at me.

I didn't have an answer. But I felt a deep dread in my gut. Something I couldn't share with anyone. I could see Bendy and, evidently, it seemed Ollie could too.

"I don't know," I said, turning to the stove again and picking up the pan to scrape its contents into the garbage.

I had to find that book.

I started by putting together a list of the bookstores and libraries I could find in the phone book. I collected almost ten, and I felt quite confident that one would provide the book for me. After all, on my list was the New York Public Library itself. An institution in the world of libraries, it had been around forever, and beyond that it was massive. The building took up an entire city block in Manhattan and had huge columns at the entrance. It was a gorgeous place that I enjoyed visiting a lot as a kid. The giant stone lions standing sentinel, the wide steps that people would use to just sit on and picnic. Inside you had vaulted rooms with painted ceilings and shelf after shelf of books on multiple floors. It made the Arch library look like a small, dusty corner bookstore.

And yet, "I'm sorry, love. I can't seem to find this book. Are you certain that's the name and the author?" The woman on the other end of the line was warm and friendly, certainly nothing like the stereotype of the harsh, brusque, matronly librarian.

"Yes. *The Illusion of Living.* By Joey Drew."

"Well, I've been through the card catalogue, but I'll ask some of my colleagues as well. Stay confident, my dear. If there's a book out there that was published in this country, chances are we have it."

I thanked her and hung up. I was more disappointed than I'd expected to be. I supposed it shouldn't be that easy, but as the woman on the phone had said, oughtn't the book just be there? The fact that it wasn't felt more pointed than perhaps it ought to be, and I was still on edge from everything the night before.

Come on, Rose, not everything has some profound meaning. Some things just are. And in this case, well, the reality is that this book clearly was not very popular. That was all.

That was all.

I readied myself for future disappointment. Good thing too, because sure enough every store I contacted, every smaller library, all of them came up empty-handed and promised to call me back if they found anything.

I feared now there might only be one solution and it involved returning to the Arch residence. This was not something my stomach was too thrilled about and I was barely able to eat a bite of my sandwich for lunch. The idea of returning to that house made me so uncomfortable that I stood in a rush and said, "I'm getting some air."

My parents stared at me, and I could feel them watching as I ran down the hall to the front closet. "I'll be back soon," I announced.

"Okay, dear," said Mother. I could tell from her voice she was confused. I was confused too, for that matter.

I stepped into the bitter cold and felt some relief. Only then did I realize I didn't have a destination. I thought, well, there was the used bookstore on Waverly Ave. That might be an excellent place to start. I could use the walk and maybe I'd be lucky. Maybe the bookstore just around the corner might turn out to have a copy of *The Illusion of Living*. Maybe it would be standing up in a display even, with a little light, glowing and ready for me. Or maybe I would be digging through a pile somewhere hidden in the back, and then just as I was about to give up, I would unearth it, like a jewel or a dinosaur bone or . . .

"Rose! Oh good, you're still here. There's a call for you," said Mother. I turned to see her standing on the stoop in the open door, wrapping her sweater tight around her small frame.

"A call?"

"Yes, do you want to take it?"

I nodded and turned around, making my way back into the house as Mother closed the door behind me. I picked up the receiver and stood with my legs pressed against the radiator that held the shelf in the hallway that the phone sat on, along with the monthly calendar and other little odds and ends, warming myself as I said, "Hello, this is Rose."

"Hi, Rose," said the voice on the other end. "I saw a note from my boss that you were looking for *The Illusion of Living*."

Such elation, my whole body warmed in an instant, forget about radiators and such. "Yes, yes, I am."

"That's very interesting. May I ask why?" said the voice. The woman on the other end had a very straightforward way about her, the tone direct. Not mean, but not warm either.

I felt a little put on the spot. I couldn't very well tell her actually why, now, could I?

"No . . ." I said. I held on to the word for a moment and felt absurd the second I said it. But somehow I couldn't remedy the situation, I couldn't come up with an excuse for such rudeness. I just stood there awkwardly cradling the receiver in the crook of my neck. Waiting.

There was a significant silence but then the pragmatic voice spoke again. "That's fair, I suppose. I think you should come to the store. Sooner rather than later."

I was relieved and also thrilled. I quickly reached for a pencil and notepaper. "Absolutely, what's the address?"

"126 Mulberry Street."

"I've got it, thank you."

There was another silence. Then, "You're welcome. I'll be here when you arrive. Please ask for Dot."

"Is that you?" I asked, adding the name to the address. I smiled. Just looking at it all written down had given me so much hope.

"Yes," she replied. "That's me."

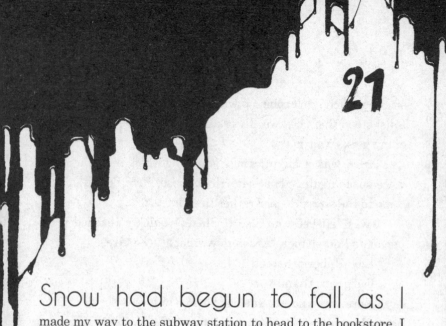

21

Snow had begun to fall as I made my way to the subway station to head to the bookstore. I was feeling great trepidation, not about meeting Dot, but going back down underground to take the train. I was grateful that my journey was one I was enthusiastic to take, because otherwise I wasn't sure if I would have been able to do it. I almost asked for Mother or Father to join me, but I couldn't do that. Not in small part because Father was uncomfortable taking the subway and preferred always to travel aboveground, but because what on earth could I tell them? *"I tried to take a train last night that didn't exist and now I need you to make sure that all future trains I try to board are real."*

No. That didn't sound like a sentence I would be saying anytime in the near future. What I had planned on doing, and indeed what I did end up doing, was following the lead of everyone else on the platform. If others stepped toward the slowing train, if others got on board, well then, so would I.

Unless, of course, the people were also figments of my imagination.

BENDY: FADE TO BLACK

I was indeed fortunate that I was desperate to get a copy of this infamous book, otherwise I might have never left the house again.

In the end, I did survive the trip, I did ride an actual subway train, and the people around me did seem to be real enough. The man muttering to himself, the pair of little old ladies in their Sunday best. The kids running up and down the center of the car and their parents utterly ignoring them. They were all there. They were. I knew it to be true.

It had to be true.

When I arrived in the city the snow was flying about. Not the soft pretty white flakes floating down from above, but a whirlwind of white obscuring the city streets and the tall towers. My breath caught in my chest, but there was something about the feeling of being truly in the present, in the reality of the moment, that I appreciated. And currently the reality of the moment was cold, and wet, and unforgiving.

I arrived at 126 Mulberry Street. It was a small narrow shop and in the whirl of white could have easily been missed. I actually walked by it at first. I opened the door, and the little bell rang. A small bent old man sat behind the counter at the front. He glanced up from his book to appraise me and peered at me from behind the thickest pair of glasses I had ever seen. They made his eyes appear twice the size.

"Hi," I said, approaching him. "I'm looking for Dot?"

He nodded. "In the back." And he returned to his book.

The store was small in width but seemed to carry on indefinitely toward the back. There were no customers, and I did wonder where you would put them anyway, as the place was overflowing with used books on shelves, piled on the floor, sitting on the steps that led up to the second story. This was not any kind of organized chaos. It was an explosion that hadn't been cleaned up, that would probably never be cleaned up.

I made my way to the back and finally saw a pair of shoes at eye level through a shelf that jutted out at an awkward angle. I sidestepped it and turned a corner that revealed a young woman who appeared to be in her mid-twenties standing on a stepladder, carefully shelving a large stack of books. An activity that seemed entirely pointless to me but she took it with a great deal of seriousness. She was wearing a plaid skirt and a white button-up shirt, the sleeves rolled up. And a pair of cat eye glasses off which dangled a gold chain. Her hair was blonde, and though she looked to have taken the time to curl it, it was quite disheveled now.

"Dot?" I asked.

The woman looked down at me immediately, still holding aloft the book she was in the middle of shelving. "Rose?"

"Yes," I said. "Yes, I'm Rose." It felt almost reassuring to say so. I was Rose.

"Good," she said. She turned and efficiently shelved the book and then hopped off the ladder in one jump. It was a small surprise to see, but it definitely made me like her almost instantly. "Follow me."

I did and we walked quickly through the shop toward the front, where she grabbed her jacket off a coatrack behind the counter.

"I'm taking my fifteen, Arnold," she announced. Arnold made a slight grunt in response and turned the page. "Come," she said to me. And once again I was following her. She was very good at giving commands.

Back out into the whirling snow we went and we hiked our way up the street to a small café on the corner. Inside it was painted a sickly green and seemed no warmer than outside; in fact, it almost felt more damp. I glanced at the brown water mark on the ceiling as we walked under it and past the empty display case by the counter. Fortunately, for our purposes, its bleak interior meant that the café was virtually empty, and Dot led us to a small table in the corner, away from the window and door.

"So," she said as we sat. "You must be very confused by all this. I'm sorry. A coffee, please."

The waiter had arrived so suddenly I jumped. "And for you?" he asked in a morose, almost resentful tone. How dare we actually want a coffee at a café.

"A tea maybe?"

"Up to you."

"Right. Yes, please. Tea, sugar, no milk, please." He wrote it down on a little pad and then sighed, leaving us with his shoulders hunched.

"You have to understand that anything to do with Joey Drew sets me a bit on edge. To say the least," continued Dot as if we hadn't been interrupted. I quickly nodded, though I didn't understand any of it. "Why are you looking for the book? How did you hear about it in the first place?"

"Well," I said, and for a second I wondered how honest I should be. Considering this woman clearly had some sort of issue with Joey, could I trust her? Then again, I wasn't sure there was any reason to concern myself with questions of "trust." I had no secrets, or at least none about Joey, that needed to be kept. And as for my personal needs about the book, well, I could just not share those. So I answered her questions: "I'm looking for the book because a colleague of mine recommended it to me. And I first heard about it from Joey himself."

"Joey?" Dot cocked her head to the side. "First-name basis, I see."

Why did I feel like I'd stepped in it somehow? "Oh, I guess, yes?"

"So how do you know . . . Joey?" she asked. Her gaze was firm and difficult to read.

All this for a book? "I just want to read the book, is that okay? Do you have it?"

"I have it," replied Dot just as the waiter returned with our drinks.

I looked at my tea. I felt this great exhaustion come over me. Why did people have to be like this? Why couldn't conversations be straightforward? "May I buy it, please?"

Dot sighed and then took a sip of coffee. "How old are you?" she asked me.

Again being asked about my age. I felt like saying "I don't know" because what did it matter? "Seventeen."

Dot nodded. "That sounds about right."

I sighed. "I can't do this. I just can't. I know there are games that must be played and ways of talking, but I'm so very tired. Can you just tell me if I can buy the book or not? I don't think I can handle any more of this."

"Any more of what?" Dot looked concerned.

"You seem so straightforward and to the point. But even you can't answer a direct question. It seems like no one in his orbit can answer a direct question." I looked up at her. I felt the tears form but I was quite frankly too tired to care.

"You speak very well," she said.

"Thank you."

Dot took another sip. "I'm sorry. I don't want to be like those people. I never want to be like those people. I think the only way to explain my hesitation is to simply tell you a little about me. And about Mister Drew. Would that be okay? I don't think I can tell you if I am willing to sell you the book until you understand me better. And until I understand you."

It wasn't ideal, but at least it was to the point and an actual answer to a question. "I'll tell you whatever you'd like."

"Tell me about your relationship with Mister Drew," she said.

I plopped a sugar cube into my tea and stared at it as it slowly started to dissolve. "I work for him. I started work at the Kismet Production Television studio two weeks ago, and then I was assigned to work specifically on *The Joey Drew Show* with him. He liked me for some reason. I'm just a production assistant, I'm a nobody. But he likes me. And, well, I guess also you should know my family is one of his test families." That felt like an honest kind of answer.

"Test families?" Dot furrowed her brow.

"For his new technology. The glasses. Well, that's where the whole *Illusion of Living* thing comes in, you see. He keeps referring to it in relation to the glasses. And I think I ought to read it, to understand better." Another reasonable answer. And the truth. Not all of it, but all of it was true.

"I'm sorry, I'm very confused about all of this. *The Joey Drew Show*. Test families. Glasses. I feel like you're speaking another language."

"I don't know how to be more plain."

Dot nodded and sighed. "No, it's me. I just need to sift through all this. Joey Drew has a show? A television show?"

I nodded. "Yes, part of the trouble is it seems no one actually knows the television show exists. The numbers are low," I said, remembering what Papa D had told me last night. "I'm not surprised you don't know about it. It airs Saturday nights. It's only been two weeks."

"Joey Drew has a television show. But they shut down his studio, I know that for a fact."

"The animation studio. Yes, that shut down a few years ago."

"Yes, 1948 to be precise."

"Oh well, sure," I said. "But he is now with my television studio. It's a different studio. It isn't his. We produce his show. If that makes sense."

"That snake," said Dot.

I was floored when she said that. "That's not very nice."

"Maybe not, but it's accurate. He's back again, just trying to slither his way back . . . and what is this new technology? Does it involve the Ink Machine?"

I shook my head. "I don't know what that is, but I don't think so. Unless Sillyvision has something to do with the Ink Machine."

"It does and it doesn't." Dot looked downright angry now. Though not at me, no. It didn't seem like she was upset with me. So I continued.

"It involves a new kind of 3-D glasses. A new visual experience. It's quite something."

"You've tried it."

"I'm a test family."

"Which is?" Dot leaned in now, her gaze still firm. I couldn't help but lean back a little.

"Joey gave us a TV and the glasses and we watch the show, and I tried the glasses but mostly my kid brother uses them."

"And what do the glasses do?" Another lean-in.

Somehow I was feeling cornered, and even though the glasses weren't secret, there was something about sharing exactly what they did with a complete stranger who really seemed to dislike Joey that made me uncomfortable. She was pushing too hard. It was starting to bother me. "First tell me about you. You said you would, and then you didn't."

Dot leaned back then and turned her cup of coffee so the handle was facing me. She bit her lower lip. Why was she so unsure all of a sudden? She'd seemed so confident. Joey. That was it. The answer came as quickly to me as the question. She didn't trust me, because she clearly didn't like Joey.

"Joey fired someone yesterday," I said. It was inelegant, and I felt awkward in how I said it.

"He does do that," she replied, still staring at the cup.

"It was very strange. I'd never seen him like that before. Normally he's happy and excited, but he was so cold. He fired someone just like that. Without even thinking about it." Dot nodded. She seemed to respond well to this subject. "And he gets so angry with the crew on set. If things aren't perfect." And this is where I lied. I was desperate to get this book, and after the night I had, I was willing to do just about anything.

Even if it meant going against everything I believed about honesty. "I think I might quit soon. I just don't think it's worth it. He's so unpredictable."

Finally Dot looked up at me again. "You should. You should leave while you still have the chance." She spoke passionately and intensely. It was almost frightening.

It also made very little sense to me. Why wouldn't I be allowed to leave a job? "Please tell me about yourself. You're scaring me." That, at least, wasn't a lie.

Dot made a furtive look around the empty café and then leaned in. "I'll tell you, but it might sound unbelievable. I promise you, however, it's the truth."

I leaned in as well since we were sharing secrets. "I understand."

Dot took in a deep breath and then, finally, made the decision to share. "I worked for Mister Drew. I worked at his animation studio. I was a writer and very young. Around your age. But from the moment I arrived it all felt off to me."

"How so?"

"It's hard to explain. It was mostly to do with Mister Drew himself. His changeable nature, as you just described, but also his need for perfection. His need for attention. He wanted more and more. I think most businessmen do. He claimed to be an artist, but it was always about expanding things, bringing Bendy to the world. He was obsessed with Bendy. I met a boy there." She stopped talking. A shadow seemed to pass over her face. "The same age as me, young, much more naïve in some ways. In many ways." Her voice caught in her throat. She stopped again. "Forgive me, I haven't ever said any of this out loud before. It's harder than I thought it would be."

I felt a natural impulse and reached across the table for her hand, the one still nervously playing with the handle of the coffee cup. I took it in mine and she let me hold it for a moment, but she quickly withdrew it into her lap. "Thank you," she said in her perfunctory way. "I'm fine."

She wasn't fine. My stomach was in knots. I felt for her, but selfishly I felt for me most of all. It was the first time I had even considered the possibility that I might be in any kind of danger. Though I had no idea how I could be or what her story was yet.

"His name was Buddy, and we became friends. He was an artist. It's my fault really. I brought him into everything. It actually really is all my fault. He was the kind of person who just wanted to keep his nose to the grindstone, who wanted to make money, go home at the end of the day. He wanted to survive. I wanted more." Her voice was shaking.

"What did you want?"

"I wanted to know everything. I wanted to see inside every locked room. I wanted to know why the strange things that were happening at the studio were happening. Why that woman died."

"Woman?"

"A musician. She was found dead. Covered in ink."

"Ink?" Like Archie. Like my face. I was starting to feel light-headed. I shouldn't have absolutely believed her—I didn't know her at all—but I did. Even if what she said was so strange and unbelievable.

"I'm talking in circles, this is ridiculous. It's so hard. You don't understand the years I tried to find him. The toll it took on me. How hard it is to try to forget, to just let go. These things stay with you, pull you under when you least expect it."

Oh but I did understand. I understood too well.

Dot took in a deep shivering breath. She calmed herself. "I'll be plain with you: There was a monster. A real monster. Not a metaphorical one, or a man who behaved monstrously. But somehow an actual beast of a monster."

"Impossible," I said, because it was.

"Yes. It ought to be. It really ought to be." She lowered her voice to almost a whisper. "I just know that somehow Bendy is real, and he's not cute."

"Bendy?" The idea of Bendy being real hit far too close to home for me.

Dot nodded. She kept talking in that low voice, drawing me in. "The monster . . . is this large, twisted version of Bendy. He's huge, with his grin, and he has claws and sharp teeth. A long, lean, inky body. And a wail . . . I'm sorry. I need to stop." I could see she was shaking, physically shaking. Again, instinct took over. I stood and went over to her. I bent over to hug her. I held her as she shook in my grasp. I felt like I was holding Ollie after one of his nightmares. "It killed Buddy," Dot said into my arms. She was crying now. "It tried to kill me, but he saved me, and it killed him. And I don't know what happened to it. I don't know what happened to him." She pulled away and looked up at me, her eyes red, her face wet. "I ran away. I was so scared."

"I would be too." I felt like crying myself after seeing her like this.

"No, not from the creature, from Mister Drew. I couldn't stay there. I knew he knew. He knew I knew."

"Did he know about the Bendy monster?"

Dot pushed me away, not violently but forcefully enough that I could see I had upset her. "You don't understand, do you?"

"I'm really trying to."

"Joey Drew made the monster!" She was staring at me with fire in her eyes, pure white-hot hatred.

"No, that's not possible," I said.

"You just think a Bendy monster appears out of thin air?"

"Of course not." Though now I did wonder, did Dot have puddles of her own? Was there maybe a kind of madness that happened to you when you worked for Joey?

"There's a machine, it's called the Ink Machine. Mister Drew had it made and brought to the studio. That's where the monster was born."

"A machine."

"Yes." She watched as I returned to my seat. She was keeping such a close eye on me I felt almost naked. "You don't believe me."

"I believe you believe it," I said slowly. I didn't look at her; my mind was going a mile a minute. I could barely trust my own perception of things these days. How on earth could I trust Dot's?

"So it's all just a fantasy I'm making up for fun. Would you like to visit Buddy's mother? I still see her from time to time. We tried so hard to find out if there was any trace of Buddy left. We spoke to men at City Hall, we spoke with scientists, we spoke with mediums, we spoke with newspaper reporters. In the end we had to come to terms with the fact that we were it, that we were the last trace of him."

"Dot . . ."

Her eyes were all fire. "Or his grandfather's grave, maybe? The man survived untold horrors during the war but died from heartbreak losing his grandson. He was very real, his tombstone, very real. Or shall we break into the old studio? I know it's been boarded up. No one else has moved into it. Why wouldn't they, do you think? It's prime real estate after all."

I shook my head. "No, that's not necessary."

But she continued in her rant. "I have no idea where he's put the machine, but we could make a visit to the Gent factory. I bet they might have blueprints. Proof that it exists."

"Wait, what?" I looked hard at her now.

"Blueprints. For the machine. It was a stunning invention. I'm sure they didn't throw those away."

"No, you said Gent. You know what Gent is?"

"Gent built the machine, Rose."

I tried to steady myself by taking a sip of tea, but I couldn't swallow. I had to spit it back out into my cup. There was a long silence after that. I could hear Dot panting faintly, catching her breath while I sat there, light-headed. Overwhelmed.

Finally: "Are you okay?" asked Dot.

"Evan worked for Gent," I said, more to myself than her.

"Who's Evan?"

"Evan followed Joey to the TV studio. He invented the glasses. At least, I'd always assumed so. I believe Joey out-sources his ideas to others and they do the work." As I said it, I knew it to be true.

"That is how he does business, yes."

"Evan destroyed the glasses. He was fired over it. Evan worked for Gent." My head was spinning. All I could think over and over was that Gent made a monster, and if they made monsters, what else could they do? "We need to talk to him."

"He left Gent to follow Mister Drew. I wouldn't trust him."

"No, he left because they shut down. He was quite miserable about working for Joey."

"They shut down? When?"

I thought back to wearing the glasses, looking around the fake art studio. It had been an uneasy feeling. Unnatural. "Last fall, October, I believe."

"It's been so long since I've looked into any of it. I'm utterly out of the loop. Gent is gone?" Like me, Dot was putting things together by speaking out loud to herself. I didn't fault her for that; I was deep in thought as well. Dot noticed. "Rose, what are you thinking?" I looked up at her. Her face was still a blotchy red but she was no longer in tears. She was investigating me now. She saw something inside me, she saw I was holding back.

"I'm thinking . . ." But I had no answer for her. I wasn't even sure what the answer was. I was a tornado of thoughts, but not one in particular.

"Why do you want *The Illusion of Living*? And don't tell me it's to get to know Joey Drew better, because it isn't that at all, is it?"

It wasn't. She knew it wasn't, I knew it wasn't. I had to trust someone eventually, didn't I? Maybe not my parents—they couldn't handle it—but this stranger, this person who seemed to understand that unbelievable things can and do happen? More than anything I wanted to trust her. I needed to trust her. "I want the book because I think it might explain why I am experiencing all these strange things. I want the book to prove I'm not crazy."

There. There it was. Laid out on the table like my cup of cold regurgitated tea.

"What kind of strange things?" asked Dot.

To the point, and utterly terrifying to answer. "I don't think I can talk about it yet," I said. Talking about it meant revealing my family's secret, and that was a bit more than I was fully willing to share with my new trustworthy stranger friend.

She seemed to understand and accept that. "Well, I don't think the book will help with that. But it might be worth a read, just to get to know your employer a bit better. I wish I'd had it when I got the job."

"But what about the illusion part?" That had to be at least a clue for something, anything. I needed it to be.

Dot sighed. "The Illusion of Living is a pseudo-philosophical belief entirely invented by Joey Drew, and the motivation behind everything that he does. The idea that life and fantasy are not far apart from each other, and that you can make anything real because nothing is. It's all nonsense. It has inspired him to push the boundaries between fact and fiction. But it isn't a real philosophy, Rose. It's an excuse for him to play God."

She was biased of course. I had to keep that in mind. "But pushing the boundaries is my question. How does he do it? Can he do it?" *Did he do it to me?*

"I think he has in his own way. I think that's where the monster comes from, yes. But I don't think it's anything more than complicated science. I don't think even he understands how it works. He just gets other people to do it for him. The idea that life isn't life is wrong though. He wants it to be whatever he wants, and he can live in that fantasy. The rest of us end up stuck in the reality of his decisions. We don't get the luxury of just thinking about ourselves and assuming the world revolves around us."

"No," I said. The weight of that sat heavy with me. "We don't."

"Rose, I can give you the book if you'd like. I'll give it to you for free. But I think more than anything in that book that you need to get away from Joey Drew."

She was convincing, but I didn't think that would solve my problem. He might be responsible for terrible things, but that also meant he maybe could undo them. Or at the least, help me understand what was happening to me.

"Here," she said when I didn't say anything in response. She pulled a paper bag from inside her purse and handed it to me. "Take it. Just remember everything I've told you. And if you ever need me, for anything, please call me."

I took the bag and looked inside. The book. *The Illusion of Living*. Black cover with a title on it, and a pair of drawn horns. Like Bendy, I supposed.

"Thank you," I said, feeling far less satisfied than I thought I would when I finally got my hands on it. "I will."

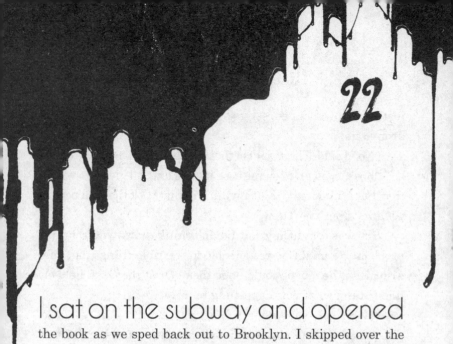

22

I sat on the subway and opened the book as we sped back out to Brooklyn. I skipped over the introduction to chapter one. "The What," it was called. I read:

"What is the 'Illusion of Living'? That's the big question, and that's what this book of mine will answer for you."

Well, that was good, as that was what I was curious about. And yet as I continued the chapter, I didn't feel any closer to understanding. Not even when he wrote: "So, in the briefest of explanations: The Illusion of Living is the art of mimicking real life on the big screen. An understandable concept, I would think, and yet it is not! The more you dig down into reality, the more complicated it all gets." None of that actually said anything. I flipped through the pages. The first part was labeled "A Question of Reality." Ah! Surely that, that would have some kind of key.

But I already felt unconvinced. More and more I believed that Dot was being wholly honest with her interpretation of the text.

I noticed then the doors were closing at my stop, and I quickly stood and dashed out between them just in time. I watched the train vanish down the tunnel and held the book tight to my chest. Then I followed the crowd up the stairs and back out onto the street. The snow had stopped and the world was blanketed in a cozy white. It was so fresh that there were even parts of the sidewalk with not a single footprint at all. I had to step out into the street to walk in the path made by tire tracks.

As I turned the corner, I could see the neighborhood kids up ahead in the middle of a snowball fight. My heart instantly sank knowing that Ollie had to stay upstairs and couldn't join in the fun. There was nothing quite like fresh snow to play in, especially when it was packing snow like this and you could make snowmen and snowballs.

Though that did also make them more painful weapons.

"Ow!" A cold, hard projectile got me smack in the face.

I looked to my right and there was Timmy, grinning like a fool, his cheeks and nose as red as his hat and mittens. He waved, not at all pretending he hadn't just thrown a snowball right at my head. He thought he could get away with it, did he?

I shoved the book into my purse, and hooking it over my arm bent down to collect some snow. I still remembered how to make a quality snowball. Timmy didn't run—he didn't think he had to—but when I got him back smack-dab in the kisser? Boy, was he surprised.

The other kids laughed and pointed as he scowled at me. "Where does a girl learn to throw like that?" he pouted, trying to make a snowball quick, but I was quicker. Another one, exploding on his shoulder. He fell back. No mercy, I didn't care that he was a kid. There were some games you played to win.

Snowball fights were one of them.

"Same place you did! You think only boys can play baseball?"

Suddenly I had the sense that I was surrounded. Oh dear. I had forgotten the most important rule. Even when there are opposing teams, you gotta all join up against the grown-up. It's the law.

I raced down the street along my tire track path, dodging successfully and not-so-successfully a barrage of snow. By the time I reached our house I was sweating and soaking, but also laughing for the first time in what felt like forever. A real, easy, straightforward kind of fun. The kids had followed me, laughing too, and I held up my hands. "I surrender!"

"Ollie, no!"

Lottie called out then. I looked to her. She was staring up beyond my shoulder, so I turned and there was Ollie. Standing outside his window on the ledge in his pajamas and bare feet, he was taking a giant step off it with a big grin on his face. He wasn't looking down; he didn't even seem to notice us.

"Ollie!" I screamed. I dove forward as he fell from the sky, reaching for his falling body. He landed with a thump into the snow, and I rushed over to his side. I looked down at him, my head swimming. All I could see was Evan's broken body at the bottom of the elevator shaft. I felt faint and saw stars. I stumbled forward and fell to my knees. The cold was like a slap to my face and I was suddenly very aware again.

Ollie groaned and looked up at me. The other kids had gathered around too.

"Is he okay?" asked Lottie.

I saw him now, not Evan, but him. He wasn't bent or broken, he was lying there on his back. The snow had helped cushion his fall. He looked at me and then at the other faces looking down at him.

"Where am I?"

"You fell," I said, reaching over.

"You jumped!" exclaimed Lottie. She was crouched down by his side too.

"Yeah, right out the window. What was it like?" Timmy of course, speaking in awe.

"Give him some room, please," I said. And they were good kids, and they knew it was all a little scary, so they backed off quickly. I moved closer to him. "Can you wiggle your toes?"

"I'm cold," he said.

"Well, you're in your pajamas, kiddo. Wiggle your toes for me." I didn't know a lot about the human body, but I knew if you could wiggle your toes, it was a good sign that you hadn't done anything to your spine.

"Okay." He bit his lip. "I wiggled them."

I felt a wave of relief. "And what's your name? And when's your birthday?" A test I'd been given many times as a kid after having hit my head on something.

"Ollie. January 24th."

"Good. Okay, let's sit up." I reached out as he pushed himself up, his hands sliding on the snow. I held him with shaking arms. I felt like I was in a dream; maybe I was. Maybe I would be lucky and this was another one of my hallucinations. I helped him to sitting, and then up to standing. I turned to the other kids. They had formed a wide semicircle and were staring at us, all with grave concern.

When we came inside, Mother was vacuuming the foyer. She looked up as we came through the door and then dropped the handle of the vacuum, a beast roaring at us as she ran over.

She crouched down and examined Ollie closely, pushing

the hair up off his forehead. "What happened?" she said, speaking over the motor of the vacuum. "Why were you outside in your pajamas? Why are you soaking wet?" When he just stared back at her, because of course he didn't have any kind of real answer, she looked at me. Not that I had one either.

"I don't know," I said quietly. "I'm going to take him upstairs."

She looked so confused, so scared. What a day she had had with him. She stood up and backed away, not saying anything, and picked up the vacuum. I gave Ollie a little shove and he obediently made his way to the stairs.

His room was freezing, his window still wide open. As he sat on the bed, I went over to close it but not before looking out. From this height it was even more terrifying. The ground looked so very far down. The kids had stopped playing. Everything was still and silent.

"We should run you a bath," I said, turning back to him. Ollie nodded. But I didn't move, just stayed there leaning against the windowsill. "Why did you do it, Ollie? What possessed you?"

Ollie sat there, staring at the empty space in front of him. "I wanted to play. But I was grounded."

"But jumping out a window . . ."

"I wasn't planning on jumping."

"Ollie."

"I was supposed to walk. In the air."

I shook my head. "No, that's nonsense and you know it." I knew I was sounding harsh but I was so frustrated and so scared now.

"I did it before."

"No, Ollie. No, you didn't."

"Yes, I did!" he turned and shouted it at me. His face was flushed and angry. He'd never yelled at me like this in his life.

"Ollie!"

"The clouds turn into stairs and you can walk on them."

Suddenly I had a thought. "Ollie, did this happen the other night? When you were watching the cartoons?"

Ollie squeezed his eyes shut tight and balled up his fists. He opened them again. "They aren't cartoons, Rose. I was there. I was in Bendy's world, it's a real place. And he comes and visits ours. And he can show me things. He can do it. So can I."

I went over to him and sat beside him. "Ollie. Bendy doesn't come into our world." Except for when he did.

"Yes, he does." He was so upset with me. I just wanted him to trust me.

"Okay, well, let's think about this logically. This morning, when you poured milk onto Father . . ."

"I said I was sorry."

"When you poured the milk onto Father, you said 'he' told you to do it. Was that Bendy?"

Ollie nodded but didn't look at me, just stared at his feet.

"And was he in the kitchen with us?"

"Of course he was," he said with a huff.

"Okay, so you saw him in the room. But Ollie, I didn't. And I know Mother and Father didn't either. If we couldn't see him, that means he wasn't really there."

"Yes, he was," said Ollie. I saw a tear roll down his cheek.

I grabbed him gently by the shoulders. I understood his frustration. I wasn't sure I was entirely convinced my Bendy encounters had been completely fictional either and I was almost a full grown-up. For a kid to get it? "Ollie, look at me." He did. His eyes were glistening. "You remember when you asked me what was real? Well, I think this is a good test. If you're the only one who can see something, then it's probably not real. Especially when it's a cartoon character and we know cartoons don't exist in the real world."

"But he was there." More tears now. And he was shaking. He was still in his wet clothes, but I somehow knew it wasn't from the cold.

"I know that it feels like he was, I know it really well. You know, I've seen things sometimes that aren't there either. It feels real. And it's scary to learn that it isn't."

I couldn't finish my thought as Ollie grabbed me tight around my middle, holding me close. Shaking so hard. "Am I crazy?"

"No, no, you're not crazy. You just have to be careful. And remember that if a cartoon character tells you that you can walk in the sky, it's not true, okay? You have to do the opposite, okay?"

I could feel him nod against me. "Okay."

It was what I needed. It was a small comfort, very small, but it was something. If I couldn't be there to protect him all the time, then I could give him some tools to protect himself. If only my situation was so easy.

But even though I had seen Bendy too, I hadn't seen him at the same time as Ollie, so that meant he was also just in my mind too, right? I asked myself.

Right?

23

I stayed up late into the night reading the book. It was, as Dot had told me, quite useless for my present situation, aside from an explanation at the end about Sillyvision offering a little more information than I already had. Though there was a section under "Joey Drew's Seven Rules to Animate By," the very last and seventh rule that instructed artists that "Your Animations Should Haunt People," that felt strangely literal. It was just an explanation of how to make cartoons compelling for an audience, but still.

One thing I did learn, however, was that Joey had never actually been overseas to war. He had worked on base in a lab as some kind of scientist. But a real battle, no, he'd never seen that. He'd lied to me about that. Or, well, not entirely. He had insinuated otherwise, but he hadn't actually said it. Still. It had upset me more than I'd thought it might.

Monday morning arrived with a thud. The enormous weight of all that had happened over the weekend sat on my chest, heavily pushing me down into my bed, making it almost impossible to get up and get going.

I had no idea how I managed to get to the studio, but I did. I made my way directly to the lab, a deep-seated dread sitting somewhere in the middle of my torso. I didn't want to see Joey. I didn't want to see anyone for that matter. But I had a job to do and, more than that, I couldn't risk Joey being upset with me. Not more than I thought he already was.

But he wasn't there. I was surprised. He was always in the lab these days. It couldn't be possible that he'd gone right to the studio. I didn't think it would be likely, but I had nowhere else to look. So I closed the door to the lab and turned around.

I pushed the heavy door open to an empty studio. I was surprised by this. Normally the place was buzzing with activity at this hour. The work lights were on so everything was very visible and kind of drab looking. It wasn't the first time I'd seen it like this, but somehow today the boring reality of how a show is manufactured hit me hard in all its garish reality: tape on the floor everywhere, a stray coffee cup upturned in a corner, the faded black of the floor from so many people traipsing across it. I glanced around; no one was there. No one, that is, except for Joey himself, pacing back and forth on the set, his back to me.

I held the door open behind me. I didn't feel comfortable yet walking into the room. Instead, I watched as Joey huffed and puffed, all anger and bluster, like a tiger pacing about in a cage. He stopped suddenly and then pointed at the table. "No! Not like that, how many times do we have to go over this!"

He reached down and swept his hand over the table, almost as if he was clearing it of dust or debris. Of course there was nothing actually on it. He crouched down and stared at the empty space in the chair. "Do it again. Do it right this time.

Look at me, see my face, this is what I look like. This is what I want put in there."

Then he stood and resumed his pacing.

Distracted by the strangeness, I let the door close. It made a small clang. Joey whipped around and looked right at me. He was all fury in his gaze, but it was different than the night of the party. It didn't feel personal or like he was reading my thoughts. It was wild and almost confused. Dangerous in its own way, but nothing to do with me.

So I said, "Good morning, Joey." I said it with my high voice, with the lilt. The voice for Father. The voice for people trapped in puddles.

Joey furrowed his eyebrows. Then something shifted, he was coming back to now. Whatever puddle had taken hold of him was letting him go slowly, almost like he was climbing out of a grate from the sewer.

"Rose?"

I smiled, not too toothy, not too broad, but warm, kind, soft. "Yes, it's me. Goodness, I seem to be early."

Joey turned to look back at the desk, then back at me again. "I gave the crew today off."

How odd. I had only worked for him for two weeks but even I knew he didn't believe in days off. Work was everything to him. He always had to keep moving forward. Like a shark.

"Oh," I said.

"I needed to sort out this mess with Henry," he said.

"You mean Evan?" I had stepped farther into the room now, but I still kept my distance. Memories of the party floated around me like a warning. As did everything Dot had told me. *He made a monster, Rose. He made a monster.*

Joey fixed me with a look. After a moment he said, "Did your brother like the show?"

My stomach twisted but I maintained my composure. "Oh yes, he did. Very much."

"And the glasses. How did he like those?"

I felt almost sick, like I could throw up if I opened my mouth again. I swallowed hard, my throat dry. "Amazing. A truly life-changing experience."

"I missed it live. But I came back here and watched it too. I watched it all night. Over and over. I went on such adventures . . ." He was lost in some kind of reverie even as he was still looking at and talking to me. "But we need more space. We need the world of the studio, you understand? It's more than just cartoon Bendy. It's an immersive experience. Like you said."

So he still saw me here. I was still a part of this conversation.

"Oh." Because I had nothing to say, nothing I wanted to say, and nothing I felt safe to say.

"Come here," he said, motioning to me. He smiled but it didn't reach his eyes. Something was still off about all of it. But I didn't dare disobey him.

I walked slowly through the jungle of twisted cables on the ground and he helped me up the small step onto the set itself. His hand was sweaty. He released mine and placed his on my back, gently but firmly guiding me over to the fake artist's table. There was one image on it, an illustration of a piece of paper on which there was a drawing of Bendy as a cowboy grinning up at us. It had always been a part of the set, since at least the first day Joey had shown it to me, but for some reason it made me uncomfortable now. Maybe because of my new personal relationship with the character.

Joey moved his hand to the back of my neck and squeezed just a bit. I didn't like that, I didn't like it at all, but at the same time I didn't think he meant it as anything threatening, more as something enthusiastic. He pushed at the base of my head on the left side, turning my attention right as he pointed at the table. "You see this? This is a version of the Music Department. How it looked at Joey Drew Studios. That's the little stage. And that's the Projector Booth. It's not entirely accurate because for whatever reason Henry is insisting on taking creative license, aren't you?"

My head was firmly under his control but I flicked my eyes down at the empty chair and then back at the nothing on the desk he was showing me. Just Bendy. Just Bendy grinning.

"I think sometimes creative license is good," I replied. "Sometimes accuracy can be a little dry."

Why I felt a need to defend an invisible person, I had no idea. I didn't want to anger Joey, so why was I taking the side of his traitorous imaginary friend? But somehow I knew it was the right thing to say anyway. It was perhaps the only true skill I had. Saying the right thing at the right time.

"Maybe. I suppose." He pressed on the right side of my neck now and I dutifully turned my head left. I felt like a marionette without the strings. He pointed again at nothing. "This is Heavenly Toys. This is where we made all the toys for all the girls and boys. Before we had to work with an outside company. That's why that Bendy toy I gave you is such crap."

I inwardly gasped. I'd never heard him swear before.

"It's really keen," I said.

Another push. Another invisible drawing. "The screening room. I could watch these cartoons all day and all night if I could. If they would let me." He raised his voice now and I could sense him turning his attention back to the empty chair with a snap of his head. He shouted at it right by my ear, "If they would only do their jobs!"

I couldn't help it, I flinched. It was too loud, too sudden, too scary. I felt him release the back of my neck and I took a step away, turning to look at him. "Oh my dear, was that a little much? I'm so sorry." He looked pitifully so. "I shouldn't yell at them, I know. They can only do so much. It's all on me. I'm the genius and that means I have to take on all the responsibility."

Maybe it was the attempt at an apology that gave me the confidence to do it, but I decided to try to bring up Archie. It felt like it might be a safe moment. And I feared I might not get another chance. "I heard you worked with Gent." Joey didn't change his expression at all. So I continued, "Evan told me."

"Evan doesn't exist anymore, Rose. Let's not mention his name ever again, understand?"

I nodded. "Oh yes, I understand, I just wanted to mention that's how I knew. I suppose it doesn't really matter."

"No, it doesn't."

"Well, anyway, I met a man who also seems to have worked for Gent. I think. Or rather I don't know actually, but he's very keen to meet you, and maybe he could be helpful in some way." I doubted that all very much, but at this point I really wanted the meeting to happen.

Joey shook his head. "I don't want to meet with anyone involved in that company. Rose, you are a sweet girl, so I'm sure you don't understand professional sabotage."

"I understand the concept," I said.

Suddenly Joey was leaning in so close to me I could smell the coffee on his breath. "It was my idea, it was all my idea. I told them what to do and how to do it. But where was the loyalty when the studio closed, eh? Where was it? Did they help me, invite me to work with them, to show them everything I know?"

"I assume not," I said so quietly I wasn't sure if he could hear me. I could see every line on his face, his bloodshot eyes, the veins in the whites. It looked like he hadn't slept in months. Years maybe.

"No, they did not. They kept on with my ideas, using *my* ideas. Such a pity they shut down last year. Such a terrible pity."

Clearly he didn't think so.

"So, you don't want to talk with the man."

"No, Rose. I don't want to talk with the man." He said it kind of snidely, almost mocking. It made me feel so small, so stupid. Even in all this strange madness, he had the ability to utterly disarm me. He pulled back and I let out a breath I hadn't realized I was holding. "Come on, let's leave Henry to it. I have something I need to show you."

The desire not to follow Joey was great, but the desire to know as much as I possibly could about my current situation as well as Ollie's was greater. So I followed him as I always did, next to him, but one step behind. He led us to the elevators, and then when we were inside; he hit "B." The button after the lobby button.

My heart started racing.

He didn't say anything to me, and I didn't say anything to him. We stood there in that small confined space, staring at the doors in front of us. I could see a hazy matte metal reflection of our two figures. It reminded me so much of the reflections in the puddles that had started my whole fantasy as a child. And now, here we were, entering the depths of this building.

How a weekend could change one's perspective so entirely. Last Monday this would have been a thrill, an adventure. Today, well, today it just felt downright ominous.

The bell dinged and the doors opened onto a cement wall. I followed him out into the narrow space and turned to look down what was a very uninspiring and poorly lit cement hallway. Floor, ceiling, walls. All terribly purpose-built. Or, alternatively, built for a terrible purpose. No. No, of course not. I pushed that thought out of my head as I followed him down the dim hall.

We arrived at a nondescript door and he pulled out a key ring. Unlocking it, he held it open for me to pass through before him. I shook my head. He laughed. And then entered first.

"Nothing to be scared of, Rose," he said.

I wasn't so sure about that. I stepped in behind him and the door slammed shut. We were there, trapped together in the pitch dark. Beads of sweat formed on my forehead even though it was icy cold down here. My palms itched. My breath got shallow. I was living my absolute nightmare. I had fallen into an actual puddle, and I wasn't sure how to escape. I reached out behind me, feeling for the door, an escape, anything.

Suddenly a row of fluorescent lights buzzed to life, turning on one after the other overhead. I watched them travel into the room, lighting a pathway, leading my gaze to a large machine. It was one huge square with tubes coming off it, and a giant curved tube opening up at the front.

"What is that?" I asked.

"That's my Ink Machine," replied Joey. He lightly skipped down the stairs from the platform we stood on and made his way over to it while I stayed rooted in place, holding tightly to the cold metal railing in front of me.

The Ink Machine. The very thing Dot had told me about only yesterday and here it was, before me, just like that. As easy as that. No fuss, no bother. No mystery. Joey seemed perfectly happy with sharing it with me. For my part, I felt my breathing get thin and quick, a little bit like I'd just finished running a race.

"Come on, Rose!" he said, turning and waving me over.

I felt very strongly I shouldn't go over. I rubbed the back of my neck with my hand.

"I'm okay here," I said.

"You need to see it, up close," he said.

"I can see it from here."

"Come here now, Rose." There it was again. That sudden shift in tone. The coldness, the anger. I was in full self-preservation mode now, not that I knew what I was preserving myself from. I shook my head but said nothing.

Joey sighed and walked farther so he was standing right by the machine. "It's a thing of beauty. You should really see it up close."

"What does it do?" I called out, trying to still be personable in spite of my stubborn refusal.

"What doesn't it do . . ." replied Joey almost too quietly, placing a hand on the beast and petting it like it was actually alive. He raised his voice again so I could hear him properly across the room. "This is where my ink is made, but so much more. Let's just say it's responsible for bringing my cartoons to life."

"The ink for Sillyvision?" I asked.

"Yes! Indeed."

"For the show?" I asked.

Joey finally looked away from the machine back up at me standing on the platform at the top of the stairs. I wondered what I looked like to him. Probably very small and very insignificant.

"Absolutely for the show. This week, Rose, this week's show it's going to be magnificent. I feel confident I finally figured it out. All thanks to this incredible machine," he said. Then he started making his way back toward me. Just like that, right for me. I felt almost like I was tied to the tracks with a train coming right for me the way he was walking with such purpose. He just looked at me the whole time, even as he was marching up the stairs. Until there we stood practically nose to nose. "You should see it up close."

"Maybe another day," I stuttered back.

He gave me that scrutinizing stare. I worried that if he could read my thoughts right now, he would not be happy with what he saw. If my meeting with Dot hadn't convinced me to be wary, his behavior today didn't change my mind in the least. To be honest, I was starting to feel genuinely scared of him. Even though the worst thing I'd seen him do so far was fire Evan. *But that was a pretty bad thing*, I thought.

He pushed his way past me to the door and opened it, flicking off the lights as he did so. He stood now, silhouetted like he sometimes liked to be, in the light from the hallway.

"Let's go," he said and I nodded. I made to join him but then he slammed the door shut in my face.

Once again I was surrounded by that complete inky blackness. But this time true panic set in. It was not just the fear of the darkness that consumed me, but fear of the man who would trap me in it as well. Why on earth would he do such a thing?

"Joey!" I called out. I reached for the door, trying to pull it open, but it was shut firmly tight. "Joey!" my voice cracked. I banged my fists on the door.

In a rush I felt around for the light switch panel somewhere on the wall. My hands were shaking. "Joey, please open the door!"

Something grabbed my ankle from below the platform, making me whip around, pushing my back flat against the door, even as my foot slipped out from under me. I screamed, full out lungs-filled-with-air screamed. It felt like a cold wet hand, and the grip was strong. I shook my foot but I couldn't seem to dislodge whatever it was, and then, somewhere deep into the room, I heard a roar. It sounded like an animal and like a human, part guttural, part cry. "Joey!"

I reached out behind me to the side where I knew the panel for the light switch had to be. I ran my fingers quickly over every space they could find. Another roar. The hand around my ankle pulled hard now, making me collapse at the knees. My hand slipped on the wall, suddenly finding the switch. In an instant I turned on the lights.

I stared down at my foot, my heart still pounding in my chest.

Nothing.

Absolutely nothing. As the lights flickered their way on down toward the machine, I gazed out to find the source of the roar.

Nothing.

Oh god. Oh god. I was losing my mind. That was all there was to it. I was certifiably insane. I felt all strength evaporate from my body and I slid down the wall. My hand found the doorknob above me and held on. It wouldn't turn but I tried nonetheless.

Then the door burst open, yanking my arm with it, and I heard Joey laughing heartily. I didn't turn to look; I didn't even release the doorknob. I sat there on the ground, my arm aloft, my body weak and numb.

"Just a silly prank, Rose. Nothing to be scared of," he said, still laughing.

"Oh," I said. I stared at the Ink Machine. It was just a metal box with some tubes. It wasn't threatening, it wasn't scary. It was just an object used to make ink. And yet.

I bowed my head, closing my eyes. I felt so tired. These waves upon waves of exhaustion that found me of late, that was a new thing. I didn't like it much.

"Rose?" Joey was right beside me. He had lowered himself down to talk to me. "Are you okay?"

His concern seemed sincere.

"Yes," I said, eyes still closed.

"Then get up, we have work to do." He stood briskly and walked away. *So changeable*, I thought to myself. Always changing.

I pulled myself up to standing using the doorknob. The door swayed as I did and I lost my balance slightly but managed to stay upright. I slipped out through the doorway into the hall just in time to see Joey's retreating back.

I closed the door behind me and bent down to massage my ankle. It hurt even though the attack hadn't been real. Why did it hurt? It made no sense. I saw something then and leaned over more. A smudge. Of black ink. On my stocking. I reached out and touched it. It felt wet. I glanced at my finger. Black there too. I didn't want to rub it, I didn't want the skin to pull away, to open a wound, to bleed out black ooze.

I told myself it wasn't real. None of it was real. What I was seeing was a lie. Anyone else would say there was nothing there.

I stood upright so quickly it made my head spin, or maybe I was already light-headed. I didn't know what to do anymore, my mind was racing and my thoughts were a sandstorm, stinging me from inside. No, wait, I did know what to do. I had to call Dot. I had to tell her about the machine.

Yes. Yes, that calmed me down a little. It was exactly right. I had to tell her.

I had to tell her about me.

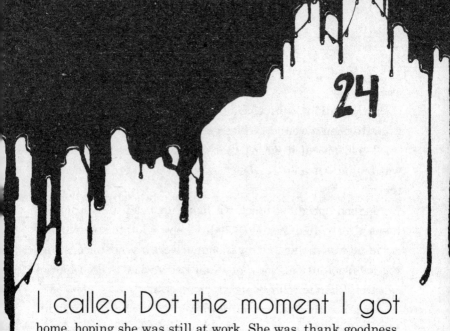

24

I called Dot the moment I got home, hoping she was still at work. She was, thank goodness, and agreed to meet me and Archie at 5:00 p.m. the next day. I spent an anxious evening afterward trying to play a game with Ollie, but he was so distracted, so disheartened. "He's right there," he whispered in my ear, indicating an empty space next to us on the floor where we had set up the board.

"No, he's not," I replied, exhausted. "I promise you he's not."

Just like there was no monster in the basement.

And no ink on my ankle.

I was terrified of going to work the next day. My stomach was in knots and I didn't think I would be able to handle any more of Joey's strangeness on my own. But miraculously the crew was back. There was the regular preparing and planning for the show this week. It was almost too normal, but I welcomed the activity around me. The other people. It was so good to see other people.

I tried to avoid Joey as much as possible and focused on everyone else. I got coffee and took complicated lunch orders that I knew would take me at least an hour to fill outside the office. I stayed in the shadows and out of Joey's line of vision, and he for his part was so focused on this week's show he seemed to have completely forgotten about me. With all this combined, I managed somehow to make it through the day without once having any kind of conversation with him. And when I left at the end of it all, I didn't even bother saying good-bye.

I rushed over to the diner as quickly as I could. When I entered, there he was, Archie, at his spot by the counter. He was already looking at me even as I spotted him almost immediately. He must have been watching me since I left the studio and crossed the street. He stood up and we met in the middle, not quite at the counter, not quite by the hostess stand, awkwardly in the way of Delores, who sighed hard as she pushed past us with her coffee pot.

"He's not coming, but I have someone else I need to introduce you to."

"What do you mean he's not coming?" I could see the worry even behind the sunglasses.

"Trust me, you don't want him to. I don't think he'll have anything nice to say," I replied. I indicated a booth in the far corner. The same booth, in fact, that Evan and I had sat in just last week. Why did it feel like years ago now? How I wished he was here now. I could have used his help.

Archie followed me to the booth and slid in opposite me, still looking furtively around. He was a nervous mess, but I didn't blame him. I wasn't exactly all that calm myself. The little bell at the door rang and I leaned over to the side to see around the opposite banquette, and sure enough it was Dot. She was wearing an overcoat and winter hat pulled low over her ears, hiding most of her hair. And sunglasses. Everyone wanted to be invisible. I was starting to think I wasn't taking any of this seriously enough.

She took off the glasses and replaced them with her regular ones, looking around the diner with her usual serious intensity. Finally she spotted me waving at her. She gave a sharp nod and made a beeline for us, sliding into the booth beside Archie. I admired her for that. There had been a reason I had decided to sit opposite him and not next to him. He still gave me the willies.

"Dot," she said, extending her hand to him in the tiny space between them.

Archie stared at the hand for a moment and then took it, looking up at her. "Archie," he replied.

"You're the one who worked for Gent?" she asked, unbuttoning her coat and untying her scarf.

"No," he replied.

Dot turned to me. "I thought he worked for Gent."

"I . . . thought he did," I replied. I looked at Archie. I didn't really know what to say now. "You *had* mentioned Gent, didn't you?" Was I remembering incorrectly?

"Yes, I did. I didn't really work there though, miss. That's not why . . ." He stopped talking and he fiddled with the brim of his hat. "I need to tell Joey Drew what they were doing."

Dot turned to face him again. She was looking at him closely now. She must have noticed the yellowing, sickly skin at least. He was otherwise still quite hidden under his coat and hat and glasses. She looked at me and I glanced at his hands. Then she did too. The black nails.

"What were they doing?" she asked after she looked back up at me again.

"Joey Drew really isn't coming, then?" he asked me.

I shook my head but Dot spoke sternly, "Of course he isn't. He hates Gent."

"Yes," I said, speaking up. "I can't say for sure, but he said something the other day that makes me think he might have had a hand in them shutting down."

Archie shook his head vigorously now, so much so that a loose strand of that strange inky hair slipped out from under his hat and across his forehead. Dot noticed. "They ain't shut down, they'll never shut down. They'll find a way to get things going again, mark my words."

Dot reached out then and grabbed his hand. This startled him and he looked up at her. "Tell us what you wanted to tell Joey Drew. I promise you you're better off for it."

"I don't know."

"Well, tell me why you think Joey Drew can help, then," she said. Her voice was warming up. There was a little kindness to it that I hadn't heard before. She either genuinely cared about Archie and could see his struggle, or she genuinely cared about the information he had.

"Well, the Ink Machine, I guess," he said carefully.

I watched Dot closely. I knew her feelings on this subject. It's what I needed to talk to her about myself, but this was not the time for me to interrupt.

"Go on," she said, betraying no emotions on her face.

"I don't rightly know much about it. I know it was his idea, and I know that because folks at Gent would talk about it, about how they took it all from him. Some said it was okay 'cause it was Gent that built the thing. Made it okay that they used it for the experiments."

"What experiments?" I asked.

He looked at me now, still holding on to Dot's hand. "They advertised for folks, they paid. Someone like me, with my history, well, no one would hire me, see? We needed the money and that's why we did it."

"No one blames you for anything," said Dot.

"Of course not," I added.

"I didn't know what they got up to with everyone else, they split us up. But I heard the screams. And I saw the body bags. By then it was too late for me. By then I was . . . well, this."

"What did they do to you?" asked Dot.

"I'm not a scientist, I'm just some bloke who was down on his luck, so I can't tell you the why or even the how, just the what."

"That's okay," she said.

Archie paused and then exhaled a long slow breath. "They gave us injections, they put us in these sealed-off rooms sometimes and filled the bottom with this terrible black ink stuff."

"Do you know why?" I asked, horrified.

"They ain't never spoke to us about it. They was paying us, and that's all that mattered. But I did hear conversations sometimes. I remember a pair of them talking. Something about wanting to bridge some kind of divide. I don't rightly remember it all. My mind isn't that sharp anymore, never was much to begin with, but now . . . I think they wanted to use the ink to help people, heal them maybe?"

Dot looked angry, absolutely seething. She shook her head fiercely. "No, it's the opposite. The ink kills people, it destroys them."

"I know. I seen it. But they just kept trying. They kept looking for the answer. When lads started getting suspicious, that's when they started locking us up at night. The dorms turned into a prison, and I would know what that feels like. We ain't done nothing wrong. But they wouldn't let us go."

"Oh my god," I said.

"I escaped. I swam through the pipes. I made it out to the sewer. But the rest of them. I rightly don't know what happened to them. That's why I need Joey Drew. He has to help them."

I felt sick to my stomach.

"He'd never do that," said Dot. "Gent started all this because of him. And if he did shut them down, then it's not because he had any problems with what they were doing, but rather he was mad they were doing it without him."

"No, that's not true," said Archie.

But it was. I knew it was. Because I'd seen it. "He has the Ink Machine," I said.

"What?" asked Dot. She turned to look at me again with that fierce stare of hers.

"I saw it yesterday. He has it. It's in the basement across the street. He's using it for the show. I think Dot's right, Archie. I don't think he's your savior."

I thought about it for a moment longer. No one broke the silence; it seemed they were all waiting on me. "You talked about a divide," I finally said. "I think . . . I think . . . the

Sillyvision and the glasses. Archie, Joey Drew has created this new kind of 3-D where you enter the world so completely it feels real. And he's been putting the film through the Ink Machine, and I don't know. But I think there's something deeply wrong about crossing that divide you were talking about, Archie. I think it does something to a person. I think it makes that line between reality and fiction very hazy." The more I tried to make sense of it the crazier I felt, and yet at the same time the more right I felt.

"So he did it, what Gent was trying to do?" asked Archie quietly.

"I don't know what Gent was trying to do, and I don't even think Joey knows what he's doing. I'm not entirely sure he knows what he's done." I thought some more. Now the thoughts were a whirling tornado. "I watched it for a moment. Ollie watched two whole shows. If I'm seeing what I'm seeing . . ." I placed my hand over my mouth to hold in the sob bubbling in my throat.

"When I dream, I think I'm awake. When I'm awake, I think I'm dreaming," said Archie quietly. "When I close my eyes, I see shadows of men, I see creatures in the dark, hands reaching out for me. Like they want my help, like they want to destroy me. When I open my eyes, sometimes . . . sometimes they're still there." He was staring at his own hands, now turning them over and back again. He looked up at me. "What do you see, miss?"

I stared at him, my mouth trapped shut. I couldn't speak.

"We need to destroy it," said Dot decisively.

I nodded, still trying to swallow my fear. I didn't know if destroying it would fix me or Ollie, but I did know we could stop anyone else from suffering like us. Like Archie. Like so many other people I had no idea had been hurt.

"He has it," said Archie, almost more to himself. "And it's right across the street." He looked out the window at the glowing lights of the studio building. The building that never slept in the city that never slept.

"Do you know how to do such a thing?" I asked Dot, finally finding my voice again.

"I think it's easier to break something than to make it, so I'm sure I can figure something out." She looked almost excited.

"I'll help," said Archie, still sounding meek but determined now as well.

"No, Archie, that's okay," I said.

"Why not? What else am I good for? You don't know what it's like in here." He poked at his own chest with his finger. "Inside here. It's a mess. I hear my thoughts like voices next to me, but then sometimes I hear the voices, I think, of my mates, from the testing. I hear them crying and screaming. And sometimes I see them too. I ain't living, I ain't real."

"You are," I said. How could I explain to him that I did know a little bit about what he was saying.

"I can't work, I can't sleep, I can't eat. I don't even know if I can die. I *can* do this though. I can help you." I looked at my own reflection once more in his glasses and felt somehow his desperation to help.

"Okay," I said. "But how on earth do we do this?"

"We need to get into the building and destroy it, simple enough," said Dot.

"In theory, yes," I said. I thought carefully. "Joey is unpredictable, especially now. I think the ink might be making him a bit mad too. I think out of everyone, he's the one spending the most time with it. I can't say when he'll suddenly decide to go downstairs to work with it."

Dot was thinking about it carefully. "When is he not at the studio, then?"

When was he not indeed. I couldn't say. Maybe he went home at night, but then again. . . I couldn't say. It seemed like he pretty much lived there these days. Wait. "Saturday night."

"Saturday night?" asked Dot.

"The show. He needs to watch the show. Even if he's in the studio he will have to watch the show somewhere that isn't the basement, like the lab or something. I'd say we have half an hour starting at eight. It isn't much," I added.

"It's enough," said Dot. "We'll need a key, preferably a master key."

"He won't give me that."

"Does anyone else in the building have one? A janitor maybe or someone?"

I leaned back in my seat and stared out once again at the building. I could see our own faces reflected back in the darkness. We all looked so out of our depths. But I admired both Dot's and Archie's determination. They made me want to help as best I could. To just do it, just get the job done. No matter what.

Then I knew the answer. "Yes," I said. "I believe I know just the person."

25

It took two days before I was finally afforded an opportunity to slip away. It was as if Joey realized how unavailable I'd been to him the previous day and the next morning suddenly became incredibly clingy. So much more than anything I'd seen of him before. He made me sit in the lab with him as he engaged in full-on conversations now with Henry, just so that every once in a while he could turn to me and ask if I agreed. I always said yes. But it felt very much like being trapped in a room with a madman. Because, well, that's exactly what it was. Coaxing him out of there to get on set for rehearsals was like getting blood from a stone, and again it was all down to me because for whatever reason I was the only person Joey seemed to listen to. The tension in the air was palpable, everyone was exhausted, and there was general unease. Joey would snap at the slightest thing and then reference people we'd never heard of. "Talk to Cohen about the numbers!" or "Tell Abby I need her immediately!" And so on.

But finally after lunch on Thursday Joey completely lost it on the crew, threw his coffee at Steve the second cameraman, and stormed out. I followed close behind him, and then he whipped around and pointed at me: "I'm going to the machine. I don't want to be disturbed." I nodded as he marched onto the elevator, and I breathed a sigh of relief as the doors closed.

And that's when I took my moment. As soon as the elevator returned, I went up to nine and stepped out into a familiar and friendly lobby.

"Rose! It's so lovely to see you!" Gladys was as harried as ever and yet she smiled warmly at me. She was surrounded by even more scripts if that was possible, practically a fort of them around her desk.

"Hi, Gladys!" I said, approaching her.

"Oh dear, you look even worse than me," she said, and she stood up to give me an actual genuine hug. I stood there for a moment in shock and then hugged her back.

"The TV business," I said.

She released me and looked at me carefully. "The TV business." Then she leaned against the desk. "So, what can I help you with?"

Here we go. "I'm in a bit of a desperate way. Joey's managed to lock the film reels for the cartoons in the wrong closet and we don't have the key for it."

Gladys furrowed her brow. "Oh."

"Yes, and I was thinking maybe someone here did. Or maybe they knew of who might in the building. Everyone on seven is stumped, I have to say."

Gladys nodded carefully. "Well, that's tricky."

"Maybe Papa D?" I asked.

It seemed quite obvious now that she saw through my lie,

though of course she couldn't know the truth of it all either. But she nodded again and stood upright. "Never hurts to ask, does it?"

"Well . . . with Papa D . . ."

"Maybe a little," she acknowledged. And we exchanged small smiles.

She led me down to his office and knocked on his door. "Stephen, you have a visitor!"

"Tell them to get stuffed!"

"Stephen!"

"Fine, let them in, let them in."

Gladys opened the door and gestured for me to go inside. "Good luck," she whispered. And she closed it gently behind me once I was in the office.

"Hi, Papa D," I said carefully.

Papa D looked up and stared at me. I smiled. He stared. "What?"

"How are you?"

"What is wrong with you, Rose, truly? I feel as if you're just getting more and more pathetic every time I see you."

"That's not very nice," I replied.

"I'm not trying to be nice. Why are you being so meek all of a sudden?"

"I just asked how you were."

"And do you really care? No. No, you don't. I despise small talk, you know that." He pushed the pile of papers he had in front of him off the desk and onto the floor. They floated down softly as he crossed his arms and continued his withering stare.

"I need the master key for the building," I said.

"Why?"

"I can't tell you."

I bit the insides of my cheeks to keep steady and to prevent myself from looking away. Papa D slowly leaned forward and turned his head slightly so he was examining me through mostly his right eye. Then, while staying otherwise still, he opened a drawer, rummaged around enough to make some noise, and then produced a key ring over the top of the desk. Suddenly it was flying right for my head and I ducked.

"You were supposed to catch it," he said with a heavy sigh and a shake of his head.

"I didn't know that," I replied. I turned and bent over to pick it up as quickly as possible. I turned back to him but he was already scribbling again into his notebook. "Thank you, thank you so much," I said.

Without looking up he replied, "Get it back to me within the hour or you're fired."

I nodded enthusiastically and quickly exited his office. I practically skipped back to Gladys's desk. "I'll be back in an hour!" I announced.

"Good to know," she replied. As I pushed the button for the elevator, she said, "Rose?"

I turned to look at her.

"Are you okay?"

I didn't know what to say. I barely knew the woman. I had worked with her for all of one full day. But she seemed to notice something in me that no one on seven had seen. Or maybe she hadn't. Maybe it was all just my mind, again, lying to me. "Yes," I said. "Yes, I'm just fine."

With the keys copied, I felt like finally we were properly on track with our plan, so I returned home that evening more happy than I had been all week. Hope can have that effect, I suppose. Even in the darkest times, hope can, well, give you hope. When I stepped into our dark and silent foyer, however, I could tell that something was wrong.

"He didn't do it again?" I asked as I entered the kitchen. Both Mother and Father were sitting at the table while the meat loaf cooked in the oven and they looked so much more severe than usual. And with Ollie nowhere to be seen, I had to assume he was upstairs, yet again in trouble. My heart sank.

"He got in trouble today, for pushing a boy off the jungle gym," said Mother.

"What?" I said, astonished. "No, he'd never do that."

"He claimed that Bendy was going to catch him at the bottom. That it would be a fun game. The boy agreed, evidently." Mother looked worn to the bone. Father just sat there staring at his own hands.

"I'll go talk with him," I said.

"Rose, there's nothing you can say."

"There is!" I snapped back. Mother recoiled in her seat and gave me a look of complete disappointment. "I'm sorry, Mother, I'm sorry. But there is, you just don't understand."

"Why don't you explain it to me, then?" she said, still upset even as her voice was measured and calm.

I glanced at Father. No, I couldn't talk about this. Not in front of him. And I certainly couldn't add to the weight of Mother's responsibilities. She didn't need three family members trapped in the puddles. I could handle it.

"I can't," I replied. And I turned and made my way to his room.

I opened the door to a disturbing sight: Bendy's torso, fluff coming out of his neck, the head nowhere to be found. And Ollie, sitting in the far corner on the ground beside the window. I slowly walked over and picked up the Bendy body.

"What is this?" I asked, turning to Ollie.

"He deserved it," Ollie replied.

"He's a toy, he doesn't deserve or not deserve anything." I walked over to him. My foot kicked something soft. I looked down in time to see Bendy's head roll away toward the closet. I sat down next to my brother and picked at the fluff falling out of Bendy. "I thought we talked about doing the opposite of what Bendy tells you to do."

"I can't, Rose. If I don't do what he says, he says he'll do it. And if he does it, I think it'll be even worse."

"It doesn't matter what Bendy says he'll do, he's not real. That's the point."

"I know."

"You have to stop. You're hurting yourself, and now you're hurting other people."

Ollie nodded. "I know. I will. I hate him."

"Bendy?"

"Yes."

I leaned my head back against the wall.

"I didn't want to hurt Timmy."

"I know you didn't, kiddo."

He leaned his head against my shoulder. "I won't let Bendy hurt anyone ever again," he said.

"Is that why you did this?" I held up the Bendy torso. I could feel Ollie nod against my shoulder. "Well, that's a nice gesture. But even nicer is for you to just ignore him, okay? Just pretend he doesn't exist."

"Because he doesn't," said Ollie.

I leaned my head against his. "Because he doesn't."

26

Friday was more of the same

stress and insanity at the studio. Joey kept changing the script for the show, and there were these uncomfortably long periods where we all just waited for him as he rewrote the scene over and over at the desk on the set. There was nothing we could do or say to convince him to get back to rehearsal, and if anyone dared speak up, he'd yell at them for not knocking before coming into his office. I could sense the whole crew was on tenterhooks just like me, so when I was able to, I slipped out and got doughnuts for everyone. It's all I could think of doing. But otherwise we finished on time and miraculously we had made it to the weekend.

Saturday was an overcast day; not too cold, and the kids in the neighborhood were trying to build a fort in the street. Ollie wasn't with them. He watched them instead from his window, the one Father had carefully nailed shut just in case. We didn't need a repeat of last Sunday. He looked so low as I peeked into his room, his chin on the sill staring out at the street. But I didn't think he wanted to play with them even if he hadn't been grounded. I think he was scared, and confused.

"You want to play a board game?" I asked, softly.

But he just shook his head.

I didn't do much that day. I helped out around the house, did some dusting. But my stomach was in knots the whole day and I could hardly eat come mealtimes. I still hadn't planned what I was going to say to my parents about why I needed to go out this evening. Something about meeting up with friends to watch the show, but I hadn't fully figured it out yet. Both Mother and Father looked so tired I wasn't sure whether or not they'd even care that much. Perhaps me out of the house would be helpful, one less thing to worry about. I helped Mother make an early dinner for all of us, and then excused myself after only a few bites. The clock was ticking and my body was buzzing and I could barely keep anything down at this point.

I went into my room and lay on my bed. I closed my eyes. How would we do this? I had no idea what the plan actually was aside from some nebulous idea of "destroy." I had to hold fast to the hope that Dot at least had some kind of idea about what to do. She seemed the most ready and the most competent of the three of us.

I rolled onto my side and reached for *The Illusion of Living* sitting on my bedside table. Rolling back onto my back, I opened it. It fell open to the chapter about Joey somehow being a part of a murder mystery, and I thought to myself how ridiculous he was. I marveled how one could go so quickly from pure admiration of someone to utter disdain. Three weeks was all it had taken. I wondered about the people who had worked for him in his studio. He hadn't been crazy then, that might have helped. And more people worked there than on his show, so they probably had far less one-on-one time with him.

And maybe it was the studio closing down in the first place that had caused him to be this way. But as I flipped through the book, I thought that couldn't be the case. This was a man who always had blinders on, could only see from his point of view. His version of reality was sorely distorted. Which is what allowed him to utterly push the concept of reality aside, it seemed.

There was a bloodcurdling scream from downstairs.

Mother.

I threw down the book and was up in a flash, charging down the stairs and into the kitchen. It was my turn to scream as Father quickly pushed me back several steps and turned so that he was standing in front of me. Protecting me.

I put my hand to my mouth. Mother was cornered against the fridge, a deep gash in her arm, her dress torn and bloody. She was shaking all over, not crying, but I could see she was in terrible shock and pain. And standing there, his back to us, was Ollie in front of her with one of the butcher knives.

"Ollie!" yelled Father. Ollie whirled around to face us. His face was red and utterly rage filled. He stared at us and then lashed out. Father pushed me behind him again even as I tried to rush forward, keeping me at bay as Ollie swiped at the air furiously with the knife.

"Stay away from them!" Ollie cried out.

Father held me back with one hand as he reached out for his son with the other. "It's okay, son." Ollie sliced the air with the knife, nicking the palm of Father's hand. Father pulled away and looked down at it. I could see from my vantage point the cut and the blood. Not deep, but the knife was sharp. I looked at Father's face for a change, but his expression was stern and strong.

Ollie spun around, waving the knife as if he was chasing something. He slashed the air as he turned in a full circle. "Stay away!" he screamed.

He was facing us again, and again he came right for us, thrusting the knife straight out, trying to stab at Father's middle. We both jumped back.

"Ollie, stop this now!" ordered my Father, his voice strained.

"No, no, no!" On each word Ollie advanced, and then suddenly in the quickest movement he dove to the ground just at Father's feet. He sat high on his knees and started to stab at the tile kitchen floor. Over and over. The knife bounced off each time, and now I had a great panic it would fly back into Ollie's face.

Suddenly I understood. "Is it Bendy?" I asked from behind Father's shoulder. I tried to move closer, but Father was strong, stronger than I knew him to be usually. He was like a brick wall. Even when I pushed on his arm, it didn't move an inch.

"I won't let him hurt you!" said Ollie, still desperately trying to stab the floor.

"Ollie, he's not real!" I said, tears in my eyes.

"Yes, he is, Rose. He is." He dropped the knife suddenly. It skidded to Mother's feet, and in a flash she had grabbed it and put it up on top of the fridge, too high for Ollie to reach. But Ollie had forgotten about the knife. He balled up his little fists and punched hard onto the ground. So hard I heard a sickening crunch. I gasped as he pulled back the fist, bloody from the floor. He punched with the other hand.

"I can't see him, Ollie. Remember what I said! Mother, can you see him?"

Mother was just staring at her little boy, her face as white as a sheet. Still not crying, not reacting at all to the wound that was now bleeding onto the floor.

"Mother!" I cried.

"No, I don't see anything," she said softly.

"Father? Do you see Bendy?"

"No," he replied. And then, so swiftly, so quickly that it took my breath away, Father had scooped up Ollie into his arms and off the floor. Ollie was kicking and screaming as I flattened myself against the wall and Father carried him out of the kitchen. I watched them leave and then I turned and rushed over to Mother.

"Sit down," I said and pulled out a chair for her. She nodded numbly and sat, blinking very slowly. "Let me look." I gently held on to her arm, my fingers quickly getting slick with blood, to examine the wound. It was a deep cut. I'd never seen anything like it. I felt a little nauseous but I quickly went to grab a clean kitchen towel. I could hear the sounds of struggle upstairs. I returned to her with the towel. I didn't want to push down too hard, so I gently pressed it against the wound. Mother cried out. "I'm sorry!" I said.

"It's okay. Call an ambulance, Rose," she said. Still level-headed, even now when it seemed she was about to pass out.

"I don't want to leave you."

"Don't be silly, you can see me from the phone. Just do it."

I nodded and stood upright. As I got on the phone, Father came slowly down the stairs, gripping the railing with his hand so tight. That strength I had seen was fading, I could see the puddles returning. But he looked so determined to keep them at bay.

"Father?" I asked as the phone on the other end of the line rang. "I'm calling the ambulance for Mother," I explained.

He placed a finger on the cradle and hung up. "I'll take her. They will take forever in the snow getting here." He spoke as if in a daze.

"No, Father, let me."

"No!" he snapped. I staggered backward. "This is my wife, this is my house, I will protect it. I can protect it. You need to hide all the cutlery, anything that might hurt him or anyone else. He's locked in his room. Protect your brother, Rose."

I didn't agree with any of this. I didn't think Father could handle taking Mother to the hospital. But I also didn't know how to fight him. I'd never seen him like this before, severe, angry, determined.

So I let him. I let him take her and I stayed behind. When they were gone, I walked carefully and slowly upstairs to Ollie's room. I knocked on the door.

"Ollie?" I asked quietly.

"Rose," he said back. I put my ear to the door. "Let me out, please." He was right there suddenly, right on the other side of the door.

I placed my hand to it. "Hey, kiddo, are you okay?"

"Please," he pleaded. He was crying. I could hear it in his voice. It was desperate and scared.

"I can't, kiddo. I'm so sorry."

"Rose, please . . . he's in here with me."

I felt the wave of fear wash over me. It was ice-cold. "He's not. He's not real. Just remember that, he's not real."

"He's going to hurt you, Rose."

I closed my eyes and took in a deep breath. I opened them again. "He's not. He's not real."

There was silence. It was too long, too quiet. I pressed my ear hard against the door to hear something, anything, him walking across the floor, him breathing, anything.

A whisper suddenly. "He's going to hurt you."

I pulled myself away from the door in a cold sweat. I wanted to hold him so badly, but I was also petrified to the bone. I didn't dare unlock it and go inside. I knew I wasn't strong enough to catch him if he tried to run away.

I placed my hand against the door and quietly said, "I'm sorry."

Then I backed away, tears forming in my eyes. No. No, I didn't have time to wallow or feel sorry for myself. I set to work instead.

I removed all the knives and the fire poker, and the forks as well, even. And I put them all out back in the alley. I didn't care if someone mistook it all for trash and stole it. Let them take it, let them! I came back inside but it still didn't feel good enough. So I took the iron. I took books off the shelf. I took the drinking glasses because if they broke into pieces . . . I took the little statuettes Mother collected, and I took the candle-holders. I took everything outside and I kept taking more and more. Until the house was quite empty.

And then I started to clean up the blood. The blood pooling where Mother had stood. The blood that had dripped along the hallway from Father's hand. The blood in the middle of the kitchen where Ollie had attacked the floor.

I cleaned it all until my hands were red and raw.

And then I cleaned some more.

I couldn't stop scrubbing. I just kept going in little circles over and over. I had to get it all clean, and it just wasn't getting clean. Why couldn't I get it clean?

Suddenly I stopped. I looked up. What time was it?

In all the chaos and madness I had completely forgot about the Ink Machine.

Six thirty.

I stood up in another wave of panic. I had the keys. I had to be there, I couldn't abandon them. This might be our only chance. Or even if we had another, who knew what would happen after the show aired tonight with the latest pass the film had made through the ink. But I also couldn't leave Ollie alone. I was stuck, I was completely stuck.

I flew out of the kitchen and out the front door into the snow. I ran up the steps to the Martin house and banged hard on their door.

"My heavens, Rose, are you okay?"

"I am, yes," I said, but of course I was freezing so I was shaking like crazy.

"Come in, come in," said Mrs. Martin.

"No, I can't. Can you come over and watch Ollie?" I asked.

"What's happened?" She stepped out onto the stoop to join me, wrapping her arms around her torso.

"Mother has had an accident. She's okay," I added when Mrs. Martin gasped. Though of course I didn't actually know if that was true. "Father had to take her to the hospital, but I have to go to work and there are people depending on me . . ."

Mrs. Martin nodded. "Of course, I'll stay until your parents get back."

"Thank you so much," I replied. I could cry from the relief.

"I'll just get my sewing, be over in a jiff," she said. I nodded and ran back to our house.

I grabbed all my things and then, standing in the foyer, took stock of the house. It looked absurd, cleared of all the little odds and ends. Cleared of everything except one object. My eyes fell on the glasses sitting on top of the television. I grabbed them and stormed upstairs, whipping open my bedroom door and then the top drawer of my dresser. I shoved the glasses underneath a pile of socks and pushed them as far back as I could. I wanted to break them like Evan had, or toss them out into the alley, but I couldn't get past how rare they were. How expensive too. If Joey ever asked for them back . . . I just didn't think I could destroy them, not yet. But I could hide them.

There was a knock on the door and once more I flew down the stairs to open it.

"Hi, Mrs. Martin," I said, breathless.

She smiled and came in the house with her little tote bag of fabric scraps. She looked around, confused.

"Mother is doing some early spring cleaning," I explained as she stared at the empty shelves. I hoped she wouldn't look out the back window but comforted myself that it was so dark outside she probably wouldn't be able to see the pile of household items anyway.

"Very early," she replied.

"Yes. Okay, so Ollie is grounded in his room, so he should be pretty easy, really," I said.

"Of course. Rose, are you sure you're okay?" She looked genuinely concerned.

"I am. I just need to go, and it's been scary, with Mother. I didn't know what to do. So thank you."

"It's no bother," replied Mrs. Martin, sitting herself down in Father's chair. "Oh, the television. I had forgot."

"Yes, don't watch it," I said.

She looked at me, a little affronted.

"Oh, it's just Father is trying to save on electricity."

"Well, I wasn't planning to anyway. I don't love television. I find it all a little boring." I didn't know what to say to that. I wished I could find it boring right about now. "You go on now, Rose. Don't you worry about us."

I nodded and went back out into the foyer to grab my coat. After I put it on, I stopped and looked up the stairs. I wanted so badly for him to be okay. Maybe I shouldn't leave. But no. No, this was the best thing I could do for him. Destroying that machine once and for all. It was the only solution.

"Okay, I'm off. Thank you, Mrs. Martin," I called out. Then I slipped out through the door and into the cold dark night.

27

We met in the dank alley beside

the diner in the freezing cold, a trio of not very intimidating individuals, determined but also visibly nervous. Hardly an inspiring group. Archie looked even more sickly than usual if that was possible, and I had never noticed just how small Dot really was. Then there was me. The girl with all the trauma, who had just seen her mother bleeding onto the kitchen tiles and her brother having some kind of psychotic break. The girl who just went along to get along. The girl who was losing her mind.

"Do you have the keys?" asked Dot, blowing warm air into her hands and rubbing them together.

The girl with the keys.

"I do."

Archie stared at me from behind those glasses. I couldn't read his expression at all. "We should do it," he said.

Dot pulled up the sleeve of her coat and looked at her watch. "It's almost eight. I think we should. Rose?"

We were all scared, I knew that, and somehow I had become the decision-maker? But it was only right—it was my idea to do it during the show, and I was the only one who knew

252

where the Ink Machine was in the building. And yet, I felt quite the opposite of a leader in the moment.

"Yes, let's go."

Getting into the building was surprisingly easy with the master key. Almost too easy. I expected someone to come up on us from behind as I hastily tried to fit the key in the lock, to grab me and yank me away, or hit me over the head with a brick. I felt sweat on my brow as I rushed, and the key shook in my mittened hand. But no one came to stop us. No one walked by. The streets seemed deserted tonight. Too deserted for a Saturday. Maybe it was the cold. Or maybe the rest of the world felt as ill at ease as we did, even if they didn't know why, and decided to stay home.

The door opened with a clang and echoed through the lobby. We stepped inside and I went to lock it behind us. "No," said Archie.

I looked at him.

"We might need a quick escape," he explained. Then he stepped into the large vaulted room, his footsteps sharp and precise. I looked to Dot. She nodded. I agreed. But I hated that I agreed. The thought of having to escape someone or something . . . well, it was a horror I couldn't bear at the moment. Not with all we still had to face.

I led Archie and Rose to the elevators and rode in silence down to the basement. When the doors opened, we stood for a brief moment, then I said, "This way." And I led them along the cold cement hallway. I felt a chill when we arrived at the door. I remembered Joey's prank, the terrifying darkness and the hand around my ankle. I knew it was just my mind playing tricks on me again, but I still feared what was on the other side.

"Did you hear that?" asked Dot in a whisper. She had placed her ear to the door immediately upon our arrival and was now furrowing her eyebrows in deep concentration.

"What?" I asked.

"I heard a bang." She listened closely, squinting. "I don't know. He might be in there."

"That's not possible, I promise you." I clearly didn't know nearly half as much as I thought I did about Joey, but I did know one thing: He would watch the show. There wasn't a fancy party tonight to distract him. It's all he'd been talking about all week. The show and the new processed film reels. All week. Of course there was the potential that something else was making noise behind that door, but again, I had to insist, for my own sanity, that that something else had been entirely of my own mind's invention.

"It's getting late," said Archie. He was right. We didn't have the time to stand outside doors and wonder what was on the other side. Either we did this or we didn't.

Dot pulled herself away from the door and nodded.

And I unlocked it.

I took in a deep breath. *There is no monster*, I told myself. Then I opened the door quickly and stood there, shocked. All the lights were on, and as we stared down to the far side of the giant room, I could see a figure at the other end. By the machine.

"Joey Drew," said Archie softly.

"No, I don't think so," I replied. We stepped inside and watched as the figure attacked the machine with something metal, something that made a loud clang that filled the empty space. "Evan?" I called out.

The figure stopped, froze mid-swing, and turned to look at us.

"It's Evan. Oh my goodness, this is a good thing," I said. My heart swelled, and without taking a moment, I dashed down the steps and raced across the room.

There he stood, a large pipe held up high in his hand. Not moving, utterly stunned, he just stared at me as I made my way over to him. I didn't blame him. I was quite surprised to see him too but more elated than anything. It was so good to see that annoyed face of his again!

"Evan!" I ran right for him and grabbed him into a hug, his arm still up over his head. He placed the other hand on my back and patted it a couple times.

"Rose, what on earth?" he said.

I released him and couldn't stop smiling. "I'm so happy to see you!"

"What are you doing here? Who are they?" He lowered the pipe and then carefully placed it on the floor beside him. It was a hefty thing, made up of two pieces attached at the middle by a metal connector with the word "Gent" inscribed on it. He rolled his shoulder; I could hear a small crack.

"We're here to destroy the machine. I take it you had the same idea."

"Rose . . ." he said. But then stopped as Archie and Dot approached.

"This is Dot. She worked at Joey Drew Studios," I said. Dot nodded but still looked at him with deep suspicion. "And this is Archie. He . . ." I didn't know what to say, I couldn't just tell his personal traumatic story by way of a casual introduction. And then, suddenly, I remembered. It hit me like a ton of bricks. That as much as Evan hated Joey Drew and hated working on the show, and that even though he had saved me with the glasses and destroyed them himself, and even though he had been fired and had every right to seek revenge, Evan had worked for Gent.

I took a little step back from him. And then I looked at the machine. Several gears that had once been attached to it were lying in a pile to its side. The pipe that Evan had been holding that now lay on the ground seemed to have come from somewhere inside. He was taking the machine apart, that was certain, but he was doing it awfully neat and tidy like.

"Evan, what are you doing?" I asked.

He just stared at me. I'd never seen him at a loss for words before.

"I don't think he's here to destroy it, Rose," said Dot quietly.

"No, I'm not," he replied, finally finding his voice. He kept looking at me in a way I just didn't understand. Like I was meant to read his mind or something. "I'm stealing it."

"We can't let you do that," said Dot. Her voice was stronger now, commanding.

Finally he looked at her. "Who are you?"

"I told you who she was," I said quietly.

"Look," said Evan, turning back to me, "it's simple. Joey Drew has lost his mind, and he is woefully misusing this machine. It's Gent property; I'm taking it back."

"You don't work for Gent anymore though," I said.

"You worked for Gent?" said Archie. His voice was hard now, not at all the quiet timid one I had gotten used to.

"I can get the place back up and running. I can do it, Rose. Forget Joey Drew, forget all this cartoon nonsense. Do you not understand what he's done? He's created this world, this whole other world. The glasses, they pull your mind in. It's unlike anything anyone has ever done. And yet all he cares about are the stupid cartoons! He doesn't deserve this technology. But I know what it can do. I can bring Gent back."

"No," said Dot. "That can't happen."

Evan turned to her. "Try to stop me."

And then Archie bashed him over the head with the Gent pipe.

Evan fell hard to the ground in a heap. I gasped and bent over quickly to see if he was still breathing. He was, thank goodness, and I stared at his unconscious face, his body twisted awkwardly on the ground. Like in my vision except not. Blood pooled out from under him and I quickly took off my scarf to wrap it around the gash on his head. So much blood tonight. So much blood. It was unbearable. I wanted to scream out, but I also knew that Archie was just trying to do the right thing. Even if it was oh so wrong.

Meanwhile, Dot and Archie were working quickly behind me, I heard them drag the parts of the machine Evan had already collected and move them to the side. Then a loud clang and another and another. I looked up at Archie bashing the Gent pipe against the machine over and over again. I didn't think this would break it. It didn't even seem to make a dent, but Archie needed to take out his anger on something and it was better the machine than another human head.

Dot was on the ground working with a wrench left behind by Evan, following his plan and taking the machine apart piece by piece. "We need to take it all with us. We need to make sure that all the parts are thrown away where they can never find them." She was so focused and so determined. And still I sat there with Evan.

I looked at him again. I was clearly in a daze. The world around me seemed to dim. Was I about to pass out? Possibly, the strain of the day was maybe just a little too much. But I didn't feel light-headed. That was the weird part. I felt sad and I felt scared but I felt alert too. I looked up. It did seem like the room had got a little darker somehow, but all the lights were on. No, no, no, I didn't have time for another vision. I had no time for make-believe.

"Did a light just go out?" asked Dot, pulling herself out from under the machine and looking around.

"You see it too?" I asked. I felt relieved but then dread. If it was real, if it was happening, then what on earth was going on?

There was a clang as Archie dropped the Gent pipe hard onto the floor. He stopped moving entirely and just stood there. He was shaking. I could see that now even as the dark crept in more and more. Like shadows suffocating a lit candle.

"We have to leave," he said, but he didn't move. He seemed rooted to the spot.

"We can't leave, we have to finish what we started," said Dot.

Archie seemed to find his footing again and backed away slowly from the machine. "No, we have to leave now. You don't understand."

"Why, Archie, what's happening?" I asked, standing up.

"The monster," he said.

"The monster?" asked Dot. She sounded suddenly terrified. She pulled herself up to standing along the side of the machine. "No, it can't be."

"I can feel him, he's out there, he's hunting us. I can hear his thoughts." Archie's voice was so quiet but I could hear every word. "He's laughing at us."

It was so dark now you couldn't see to the exit. We were in

the last small pool of light. I remembered Dot's story. "What do we do?"

"He's connected to me. I can't hide and I'm leading him right for you both. You have to run for it. You have to run. I'll keep him away."

"No, Archie," I said.

"I'll keep him away. I'll keep him away." And suddenly, just like that, Archie bolted. He just ran. He ran off left into the darkness, toward the far recesses of the room. "Archie, no!" called out Dot, but then I heard a roar. That same roar from before. That animalistic scream. And then another scream, this time human, this time Archie. In the dark blackness before us. Then a horrific crunch. Like when you step on a beetle. Crisp, precise. Sickening.

There was a horrible stillness in the air and the sound of heavy breathing and a limp walking-away somewhere off to the left. We listened as it got quieter and quieter. Until we were surrounded by a threatening silence.

"What happened, what's happening?" I asked in a panicked whisper. "Is this real? Dot, is this real?"

I turned to her and she just nodded, staring out at the black. "It lives in the darkness. We need to stay in the light." But even as she said it, the pool of light we were in dimmed further.

"No, I think we need to run. We have no choice," I said. "We have to do it now while it's gone."

"I don't know," she stammered, but she sounded so unsure and scared.

I wasn't going to just wait to be killed by a monster. "Come on, help me with Evan," I said, leaning down. I couldn't carry him, but I was pretty sure that together we could drag him, one arm for each of us to pull.

"Rose, you can't be serious," she said.

"I'm not leaving him to die. I know he's not a saint, but this is just not something I can do, okay?" I said. Tears were forming in my eyes, not that Dot could see them, it was so dim now. She looked almost like a shadow to me. I could barely register her expression anymore.

"Fine, okay, yes." She marched over and leaned down to grab his left arm. I did the same with the right. "Ready?" she said.

"Wait." I saw the Gent pipe Archie had dropped. I picked it up. "Okay. Let's go."

We pulled hard on Evan's arms and he was so much heavier than I anticipated. But once we started moving toward the dark, we picked up some momentum. I held the pipe out in front of me and steadied my breathing as best I could as the dark engulfed us. I knew the stairs were ahead, I knew the beast was somewhere to our left. There wasn't anything to see or hear except our footsteps and the sound of Evan's body on the ground, dragging along like a sack of potatoes.

We just had to keep moving forward. Just keep moving forward.

There was a loud crash from behind and we both jumped. My heart was pounding fast and I couldn't help but look back. I stared at the machine, the only thing lit now in the room. I saw a huge figure lunge at it and the flash of a giant grin and sickeningly huge sharp teeth. I was overwhelmed with the terror, feeling both light-headed and heavy as cement at the same time. I couldn't breathe. I couldn't swallow. Evan's arm slipped out of my sweaty palm.

I felt a tug on my sleeve. It sent a jolt through me like an electric shock. Dot, insistent even when I couldn't see her. I had stopped walking. We had to keep going. I grabbed Evan's arm again and turned and started moving again.

The beast behind us terrified me to the core, but hearing it attack the machine over and over helped to keep track of it. And in some small corner of my mind I was grateful for its help. If we humans couldn't destroy it, then maybe it would.

Caught up in my thoughts and panic, I bumped into the stairs hard, the pipe clanging against it. Instantly, the sound from behind us went silent.

It had heard us.

I looked again and saw the silhouette, now just enough light to create almost an illusion of an image. It stood staring at us in the distance. Round huge head with horns shaped on top. A long, lean figure with too-long arms and too-long legs. Perfectly still.

And we were perfectly still too. I could hear Dot take in a sharp breath and hold it. I bit the inside of my cheeks so hard I could taste blood.

Silence.

And then that scream. That horrifying wail of a scream.

"Come on!" said Dot. There was no point in staying silent now. A rush of adrenaline flowed through me as I felt my way around the wall to the base of the stairs, pulling Evan along the side. I was certain he would be bloody and bruised from it all, but it didn't matter right now.

We found the stairs and together took the first step. I had to drop the pipe; I needed both my hands. "On three," instructed Dot. "One, two, three."

We hoisted Evan's torso up the first step, his legs dangling down. We were now holding almost his entire body weight. It strained against my hands, pulling at my shoulders.

"Again," said Dot. "Ready?"

And again she counted to three and again we got him up the next step.

"Only a couple more to go," I said, to encourage myself more than anyone.

"One, two . . ." Suddenly it felt as if Evan was falling away from us. We pulled back hard. My hands were raw from the effort but he wasn't going to slip, we had him, we had him.

Another roar. So loud it shook me to my core and pierced my skull. I gasped. It was right there. Right at the base of the stairs. And it had grabbed tight onto Evan.

We pulled back. I could hear the effort in Dot's straining, and I full on cried out from the pain. We were playing tug-of-war with Evan's body and I feared it would rip in two.

"Stop," he said, suddenly. So quietly I almost missed it in the chaos.

"Evan, thank goodness, you're awake."

"Stop, Rose. Please, save yourselves." His voice was strange; there was a gurgling in his throat. I didn't know if it was saliva, bile, or blood. But it sent terror down into my very marrow.

"Evan, no," I said.

"Don't die because you couldn't let go of an unpleasant work colleague."

I couldn't help but laugh wryly at that even as the tears stung my face. If only he knew how wrong he was about that.

Another roar and another pull. Dot and I pulled back in

unison, yelling out together as we did. We were a team, we would save him. Evan screamed then, a bloodcurdling scream. I could hear the sound of something tearing in the dark. Something ripping.

"Rose!" he cried out.

"I can save you!" I yelled it above the struggle, above the pain, above my own fear. I would not let him go, not even if my own life was in the balance.

"You can't be a Pollyanna about this one! I need you to not die!" He screamed again so that the words barely sounded like words, more like just one horrifying anguished noise.

"He's right!" Dot shouted. She sounded strained. She didn't let go, but I could hear her panting, I could hear the terror in her voice.

He screamed again, and I knew he was right. We were tearing him in two. He was suffering. Tears stung my eyes. My fingers twisted into his shirt to find a tighter grip but even as they did, he slipped farther away with another wail. But how did you just let someone go? How did you just stop helping?

Evan was suddenly twice as heavy in my grip and I felt Dot's hand on mine. She had released his arm. "I know what it's like to lose someone when they are right there. Please," she spoke in a panicked whisper. "You have to let him go. This is torturing him."

"Rose!" Evan screamed one more time.

I closed my eyes and I opened my hand. I felt him slip away. I heard the sickening crunch as his head hit the cement stairs. The tears streamed down my face as I opened my eyes again to the ever present darkness. Evan stopped making any sound. There were no more screams of pain or strained breathing. Even as the monster dragged him away from us somewhere deeper into the dark, all I could hear was his silence. A kind of silence I had never heard before.

And I felt a hollow emptiness inside me unlike anything I had ever felt before. A space of such grief and sadness I thought I might die.

"Come on," said Dot, touching my shoulder.

"I can't," I said in shaky sobs. But somehow she found my hand and she pulled me up toward the exit. And somehow I managed to follow her, stumbling as we went, but I followed.

We burst out into the hallway, into what felt like an unbearable brightness. Dot grabbed the keys from my pocket as I lay there on the cold floor. I started to sob uncontrollably. Just crying as if I had never cried before in my entire life when I had cried more than ever during the last few weeks. Once she locked the door she was at my side.

"It's okay," she said.

"It's not okay." I could barely say the words. I heaved them out of me along with another sob.

"I know," she said. "I know it's not. I'm so sorry."

"He wasn't evil, you know," I said. "Just because he wasn't good didn't make him evil. He saved me."

"I know," Dot repeated.

"He knew how dangerous the glasses were. He would have been convinced how bad Gent was in time. I know it."

"I know."

But I didn't think she believed me. I didn't know what she thought. We stayed there for a moment, a long moment. Me on the floor curled on my side, her, a gentle hand on my shoulder. I couldn't speak. I couldn't think. I just stared down the long, narrow, cement hallway. And then, slowly, after several minutes of stillness had passed, the tears started to slow, my breathing started to even out. My mind was clearer even though the fog remained.

"Do you think the machine is destroyed?" I asked quietly, finally looking up at her. She looked so tired and worn thin.

"I don't know. I think strangely the monster helped the most. But I don't think it's gone forever." She sighed and closed her eyes. "I don't know if there's any way to stop it. Maybe it's all just too late. Maybe there's no getting the ink back into the pen."

I pushed myself onto my elbows. I felt so heavy, like my body was made of clay. "No, it has to be. Archie's sacrifice can't have been in vain," I said. The pang in my middle. The guilt, the grief. "Poor Archie."

"Poor Archie."

We looked at each other. I don't know what Dot thought of me, if she saw some child who didn't understand, but I had to convince her, I had to convince myself, that it had been worth all this.

"It'll definitely put a wrench in the works for him for next week," I said. I sent the words over to her, to try to cheer her even in this bleak moment. "And I promise you, Dot, I'm going to find every single test family and I'm going to destroy their televisions and glasses. I'm done with being any kind of guinea pig for Joey Drew."

Dot was quiet for a moment as I wiped the tears off my face with determination. "I don't know you very well, but I think you're very impressive," she said quietly.

I shook my head. "No, I'm not. I've just always been the girl who does what needs to get done. No matter what." I reached out for her hand and she grabbed mine tight. "And I am very done with all of this."

28

I returned home in a daze. The salt of tears still caked to my face, eyes swollen, and nose red. Every step of the journey was like a waking nightmare. I just needed to be home, with my family, to hold Ollie. I didn't care if he was swept up in any kind of madness, I would nurse him back to health if it was the last thing I did.

I climbed up the stairs and went to open the door but it was flung open before I could touch it. Mrs. Martin stared at me wildly, holding her tote bag. "Rose!" she said in surprise.

"What's going on?" I replied.

"I don't . . . I'm sorry . . ." She dashed out past me, her voice caught in her throat. I watched her race up her own steps and escape into her home.

I slowly walked across the dark threshold of my own.

"Hello?" I called out.

"Rose!" Father turned the corner, pale as a ghost. He clutched at my hand and drew me inside, slamming the door behind me.

"What is it? How's Mother?" I could barely get the words out; they stuck and clawed at the inside of my throat.

"She's fine, she's still in the hospital. She lost a lot of blood so they are keeping her overnight. I came home for some of her things. Rose, it's Ollie."

I could hardly breathe.

He pulled me along the foyer into the living room.

The television was on.

Static on the screen and a soft white noise. Quiet and not full volume, but present.

And there he was, just sitting there.

Ollie watching the television.

Wearing the glasses.

No. No, this was a vision, this wasn't real. This was all in my mind, my worst nightmare realized. And yet. I approached him carefully with Father standing behind me. I reached out with a shaking hand and touched his shoulder. He was there. He was real. "Mrs. Martin said she felt sorry for him." Father's voice sounded far away. "She said he promised he would only watch *The Joey Drew Show* and then go back to bed. He was scared about his mother."

"I told her not to turn on the television." I backed away. "This can't be happening," I said, my breath quickening.

I turned on my heel and quickly ran upstairs and was greeted by the sight of my door, wide open.

"No."

I stared inside. It was a mess, sheets on the floor, clothes everywhere. My drawers pulled out, dangling precariously as far out as they could go.

I charged back down the stairs. I couldn't stop myself, I was barely in control. I bolted into the living room, past Father, and tore the glasses off Ollie's face. "Ollie!" I shouted. "Ollie!"

I crouched down and grabbed him by the shoulders and shook. "Ollie, snap out of it!" I shook harder. Nothing. No reaction, he didn't turn his head, he didn't acknowledge me. He didn't blink. Why wasn't he blinking?

I was in a full-on panic now, tears streaming down my face, I had no idea what to do. I pulled him in close to me. It was like he was a deadweight. Alive somehow, but not here. Like in some kind of a coma except not asleep.

Like he was in a waking nightmare.

Everything Evan said came flooding back to me now. Was my little brother trapped in that world? That wasn't possible. And yet. Why shouldn't I trust him? I remembered how he'd whipped the glasses off my face at the party, destroyed them underfoot.

I carefully laid Ollie on the ground on his side. He stared still, his eyes hollow and lifeless even as they stayed perfectly open. I touched his hair for a moment. And then I turned and reached for the glasses.

I picked them up.

"We need to take him to the hospital," said Father. Father. I had forgotten he was even here.

"No, that won't help him," I replied.

"Rose, we need to do something, I don't think I have the strength . . ." He stopped talking, just faded away.

I looked at the television.

It was just static. No Bendy. No studio. It didn't make any sense. The show had finished ages ago, but still he had been watching. Watching nothing? No, I had to stop thinking like that. Right now sense was the least sensible thing. So I put the glasses on and looked at the static.

I was standing on the set again. I was right where I had been two weeks ago when I had tried the glasses. I took them off. Again just static. Just a television with whirling white in a dark room with empty shelves. If I put these back on, I risked long-term damage to my mind, I knew it. But I felt deep down in the fiber of my being that the only way I could pull Ollie out of this deranged coma was to go into the parallel world and find a way to shut it down or something. Something to break whatever connection he had to it. Whatever was holding him hostage.

I had to go into the puddles.

I had to rescue Ollie.

29

"I don't understand," said Father.

I had tried to explain it all to him as quickly as possible. I needed someone else to know, in case, well, in case I never came back. In case we both ended up trapped somewhere between the real world and the not. "It's unbelievable, but it's true. You know better than anyone how the mind can warp our perception of things."

"I do." He was sitting in his chair, hunched over, staring at Ollie lying on the carpet, a frozen statue.

"He's trapped in there, but I think I can get him out. Just like I've done with you in the past. When you've disappeared."

"No, it's not the same. You know it's not the same," he said.

"I can do it. I can."

Father shook his head and then he reached out a hand to me. "Rose, you've always been so optimistic."

I took his hand; it was cold. "I know. But I believe I can do this. I know a lot now. I'm an expert."

Father squeezed my hand tight. "You shouldn't be."

"Maybe that's the point. Maybe I was supposed to learn all this just for this moment."

"Or maybe you've had too much put on your shoulders. I should do this. I should take care of my son." He looked so sad and so lost.

"Father, if something happens to me, then you will come for both of us, but right now it's absurd for you to say such things. He's my brother, I love him like you do. And I know what I'm doing." I didn't know where the lies began because I didn't know what was true. I didn't really know what I was doing but I knew more than he did. More than anyone did at this point.

"Okay. It's time," I said. Father didn't exactly release my hand but he didn't fight back when I pulled away.

I sat myself cross-legged on the floor and took in a deep breath. I reached out with my left hand and placed it on Ollie's arm, I wanted him to know I was here. "I'm going to help you," I said softly and looked at his lifeless body. "I promise."

I turned back to the screen and then, like jumping into a cold pool, I just did it. I just put on the glasses and did it.

There I was, back in Joey's artificial studio. The only difference being that Joey himself wasn't there. It was just me. All by myself. Like before it was like walking around a drawing come to life. Every edge had a black border to it, wood grain was drawn on with pen scratches, even the view out the window of the city had that cartoon appearance of an exaggerated approximation of reality. And of course it all looked yellow. I was in a black-and-white illustration, but tinted by the color of the glasses. I felt afraid, I felt very alone. But I also felt determined.

I gathered myself and turned to face the door, that door that didn't exist in our set and that had made me curious for that brief moment I had worn these glasses two weeks ago. I took in a deep breath, or at least the version of myself in this strange world did. And I reached out for the door.

I saw my hand. I gasped and stumbled backward.

What in the world.

I held up my hands in front of my face, looking at my own body for the first time. I hadn't even thought to before. But here was my hand. And it was different. Was it even mine? I wiggled my fingers and they responded as if mine. I couldn't quite believe what I was seeing but I supposed it made sense. I was now a cartoon version of myself in this cartoon version of the world. My hands looked like a drawing come to life, three-dimensional yes, but once again with everything drawn on: the lines on my knuckles, the edges of my fingers delineated with a black line of ink. I hoped there were no mirrors in this world because I was certain I might faint to see all of me. I looked down farther though. I couldn't resist. My legs, my shoes. The little tear in my stockings. It was all very accurate and deeply disturbing.

Ollie. Would Ollie be a cartoon of himself? I wasn't sure I could bear to see him like that. No. I didn't have time to analyze or question, I had to find him, and I had to get us out of here. I didn't have time for fear or for awe. Or to ask questions. I had to accept the reality I was in, and work by its rules.

And save my little brother.

I reached out again for the door and grabbed the knob. I could hold it in my hand, I could feel cool metal against my palm, I could turn it. I could hear an actual click as the latch released and the yawning sound as I opened the door slowly. So evidently I could interact with my environment after all.

I had no idea what would greet me on the other side, if it

would be another room or a great black void. But I inched my way close and opened the door farther, pulling it toward me.

There was a hallway. An actual hallway. It was drawn, just like the office, and like the office, had a wooden ceiling and floor. It ran directly from the door as if we were at the very end and opened up farther in the distance. I could see a flickering light at the far end. It scared me but I knew that I had no choice but to investigate it. The wall to my left had a Bendy poster: "The Devil's Treasure." I took a step forward, and another one, and finally I committed to the moment and stepped into the hallway. There were long tube lights running along the baseboards, illuminating the space and making it feel higher. I reached out to touch the wall to my left. It was solid. Very real. Very wall-like. I looked at my cartoon fingers as I traced my hand along the wall. So strange.

The hallway opened up onto a large space. A giant cardboard cutout of Bendy stood in the far corner, and the flickering I had seen turned out to belong to a projector, empty, playing nothing, just flickering a bright white rectangle on the wall. Before it was the most staggering thing, a giant moving sign made of slowly spinning wooden film reels that read "Joey Drew Studios."

So I had started in his office, and now I was in the studio itself, I supposed.

But where was Ollie?

I turned a full circle. He was nowhere to be found. I did notice then the few upturned chairs and scattered pages on the floor as if maybe a gust of wind had passed through. I wondered if Ollie had done that, if he had been running or even playing. He was known to knock things over once in a while when he was full of energy. But the mess was significant. Far more damage than I thought he alone could make.

Well, one thing was for certain: He wasn't in this room.

There was another hallway off the room on the other side, so that was where I went. I walked carefully, certain at any moment this strange reality would have me slip right through the floor like a ghost. I had never paid more attention to my feet taking each step: heel, toe, heel, toe.

I reached the entrance to the hall and stood staring, not sure what to do now. It fell away into a black void and only continued about twenty feet across. I could see more floor and more walls and even posters on the walls. But for those twenty feet it was pure black, like an unfinished picture. I looked back over my shoulder, but all that lay behind me was the room and the hallway back to Joey's office. This was the only way forward. I turned and crouched. I reached out to touch the black on the "ground." After all, none of this was real, so even considering the lack of floor, possibly there was one? My hand dipped into something wet and thick. I pulled it back and it was covered in black ooze. I looked closer. No, ink. Black ink.

Like the smudge on my face.

On my ankle.

On my finger.

I got down on my stomach to look flat across the wet and could now see glints of light reflected in it. The darkness on either side that extended up and around—well, that seemed intangible, like a room with a light turned off. But the floor did seem real. Or as real as anything in this world. It was a pool.

No.

I shuddered.

It was a puddle.

How deep was it? Had Ollie fallen in and drowned? Somehow I doubted it because the hallway on the other side almost seemed to beckon me like it had something to show me. And yet . . .

I returned into the room and picked up a chair. I dragged it over to the blackness and then, as gently as I could, I lowered the chair into the ink. The legs descended about halfway down and then stopped. I'd hit something hard. The bottom? I certainly hoped so.

I reminded myself that none of this was actually real, even my own body, so walking through thick black ink wasn't about to stain my clothes or skin in actuality. And then I took a deep breath and stepped into the ooze.

It was thicker than water but not quite as thick as mud, and the ink seeped up around my calves. I tried to walk as quickly as I could without falling over. I didn't think I'd get stuck in here, but I wondered what might happen if I did. If I drowned. Would I wake up at home in my living room, or would that be it. Could you die in here?

I wasn't about to test the theory.

"What was that?" I said out loud as something brushed by my ankle. My voice echoed into the black void.

My heart started racing fast. It hadn't occurred to me that there might be something in the ink, creatures swimming about like in a muddy pond. I looked over my shoulder. I was halfway there; it made no sense to turn around. So I continued, picking up my pace.

There it was again. Another brush along the other side. I told myself to think of it as a little fish or guppies even. An innocent creature trapped down here just like I was, just like Ollie was.

I took another step, and another. The ink around me rippled with each movement, out into the endless black on each side. I was almost there as another something brushed against my leg. I picked up speed. I wasn't running, but I was splashing through the ink now, droplets rising up and hitting my blouse. I could feel some on my face. I was there. I stepped onto the wooden floor with a great relief and looked down at my ink-black feet now. They shone in the light, the wet reflecting back that yellow light. That yellow everything.

Suddenly there was a hand wrapped around my ankle. I saw it for just a brief second before my leg was pulled out from under me and I fell hard, my chin knocking into the wooden floor and my teeth crashing together, sending a sharp pain up through my head. An inky hand, a hand made of ink, it was pulling me backward. I had a vision then, of Archie pulling me back from the edge of the subway platform, but this was quite literally the opposite situation. I kicked back with my other leg and squirmed, flailing, and managed to turn myself over onto my back.

I screamed. There was a figure there, a gaunt, inky figure. It was half out of the black pool, reaching and pulling for me. It was dripping black with glowing yellow eyes, hollow in the same way as Archie's, but I could see a deep anger in the burning brightness. It hated me. It held my leg fast, tight in its grip. It reached out with its other arm, clawing at me, dragging me along the floor back toward the puddle. I kicked at it, batting away its arm, but it kept coming for me. I screamed as it yanked on my leg hard, and I kicked at the same time, managing to get the corner of what appeared to be its head. It cried out, an otherworldly sound, both animal and human. And then immediately it started clawing at me again.

That was it. The head. The head. I had to take a risk. I had to let it pull me close. I stopped fighting back and I flew across the floor into the puddle, the wet rising up my neck. I pressed my lips together hard as the ink splashed onto my face. I wasn't going to swallow that toxic goop. And then I sat up and punched the thing in the face. I'd never punched anyone before in my life, but I did it, just like in the movies. I punched it with everything I could give it from my position. It released its grip and I scrambled to standing, and just as it launched for me again I kicked it in the head. Another howl and it raised its hands to hold its head, shutting its eyes in pain. I kicked it again. And again. I felt an incredible energy rushing through me, and the more I kicked the more I felt it. It wailed and flailed, the bottom half of its body submerged in the ink, its torso twisting about. I gave it another kick, right to the side where its temple would be, and it fell hard into the ink. Sinking below the surface. As if it had never been.

I turned and ran. I ran as fast as I could out of the ooze it had dragged me back into, and when I hit the wooden floor, I ran even faster. I didn't turn around, I didn't stop running. I kept on down the hall, and when it turned, I went with it. And when it suddenly ended in a black void I took in a deep breath and ran right into that ink again.

Except it wasn't ink, it was a void, like the edge of a picture. I flailed in the air as I fell down, my skirt rising, my hair in my face. Then I landed hard, on my back, onto another wooden floor. My head bounced up and then slammed into the ground. My whole body cried out in pain.

I lay there for a moment, winded, trying to catch my breath, my legs twisted beneath me. I stared up at the blackness above me. Like a starless night sky. Everything hurt and I feared my body was broken. I saw myself as if from above. I saw a twisted, mangled body at the bottom of an elevator shaft. Was I paralyzed? Was I dead? I wondered then. I raised my hand to my face to remove the glasses, but no, I couldn't seem to do that. I swiped at my ear, but grabbing the arms of the glasses seemed out of reach for me. I wasn't surprised by this—if I could do that, then Ollie could as well and none of this would be happening. Whatever the rules were, it felt like the only place I had control over the glasses would be in Joey Drew's office, my only connection to the real world.

I dropped my arm to my side. My breathing was more regular now, and I tried to wiggle my toes. They moved. So I slowly pushed myself up, propping myself onto my elbows. My head ached, and my body still sent shooting pain up my back and down my arm, but I was okay. I looked around. I was on a kind of floating platform, just the wooden floor of the studio. Otherwise I was surrounded by black above and around me.

I looked over my shoulder and saw a door standing there, no wall, just more blackness surrounding it. I stood up and walked tentatively to the edge of the floor. I leaned out just a little, just enough to see more blackness beneath me. No, it did seem that the mystery door was my only way out of this mess. Or, worse, there was no way out. I would be doomed to stay here until my actual body starved and withered away in the real world. A prison in my own mind. A death sentence.

I felt dizzy, and I stepped back from the edge. I didn't have time to waste on this kind of thinking. Either the door would somehow lead somewhere or it wouldn't, but how would I know unless I tried?

I crossed the floor, my footsteps echoing out into the darkness. And I stared at the door. I shook my head and then opened it with great gusto and determination.

"Oh, thank goodness," I said, and I actually smiled. There was a large room on the other side. No black void, no inky puddles.

I quickly stepped in and closed the door behind me for good measure. I felt weirdly safe, even though of course there was nowhere safe in here. But it was nice to have the illusion of solid floors and walls to contend with and not the illusion of an infinite darkness.

I was in some kind of music room, with a stage to my left, and to my right up on a second level was a projection booth. Like with the first room, the projector was on, lighting the space with that large flickering white rectangle on the far wall behind the stage. I remembered then that description Joey had made that day. Of this very room. His hand holding the back of my neck. No, I shook the thought away.

"Ollie?" I called out. I listened for him and heard nothing but a strange static-like noise. I turned around and looked into the shadows and then saw a record player, in the corner, spinning a record around and around. I walked over to it and habit, I suppose, had me place the needle down.

A little friendly tune started to play. Something possibly Bendy and his friends had danced to. The warmth of the music felt almost eerie in the present situation, and it echoed in the vast room, setting me on edge.

Suddenly I was bathed in a bright light. I could see my shadow on the wall, a sharply defined black silhouette, and the record player itself was so well lit I could see each single groove on the disk. I turned and held my hand up to shade my eyes. The light was coming from the booth. From the projector itself. Someone had moved it. Someone had aimed it on me. Fear was coursing through my veins, but I also knew I had to run toward the danger. It was the first sign beyond that ink creature that I wasn't alone, and I needed answers. Maybe there was someone else, someone who knew where Ollie was.

I ran toward the stairs to the booth along the opposite wall and the light moved with me like a spotlight. I dashed up them, taking them two at a time. And I burst into the projection room. Then I stumbled backward, back out through the door I had flung open, tripping down the stairs and barely catching myself with the railing. Now standing framed in the door was another creature. This one inky black as well but instead of a head, even one with glowing eyes, it had the projector. Cables attached to it fell down its back like long ropes of hair. Embedded in its chest was something metal and round. I couldn't make it out as the creature looked at me as if through the lens itself, the light blinding me even as I raised my hand to block it. It cocked its head slightly. Appraising me.

We stood there, each staring, the creature in the doorway at the top of the stairs, me halfway down clutching to the railing. It didn't do anything. It wasn't trying to chase me. I had to try; I had to try something. "Have you seen a little boy around?" I called out. It wasn't doing anything but staring. Maybe it was good. Or at the least, not evil.

Suddenly it let forth a mechanical roar that emanated from that round metal in the creature's chest. It was a speaker, that's what it was. I understood in a flash just as it lunged for me. But I didn't need to understand anything, I just needed to run again. I had no idea where to go this time, I simply charged out into the room, its light heating up my back, but also showing me the way, for any direction I turned it did too. And so I stumbled after my own shadow in front of me, running in a wide circle, past a recording booth with a microphone dangling from the ceiling until I found another door and burst through it. I kept going and saw at the end of my new hallway another black void. I skidded to a stop. The light was getting brighter behind me and only made the darkness in front of me darker. There was nothing out there. I took a step closer to the edge. There was nothing down there either, not that I could see. And even if there was, if I fell that far down, to a level that you couldn't even see, I was certain I would die.

I turned to see the projector creature barreling toward me, screaming that metallic scream from the speaker in its chest. Perhaps I could dive low, between its legs, or maybe I could hit it like the ink creature. It seemed too large and impossible, but I raised my fists like I'd seen boxers do. I wasn't falling to my doom and I wasn't going to let it get me this easily.

There was a clang as something hit the projector creature's head from behind, making the creature stop in its tracks. It turned around slowly to see what had done that. Then it started to move in the opposite direction, walking at first and then picking up speed.

"Run to the booth, Rose!"

It was Ollie's voice! "Ollie?"

"Run!"

30

"Ollie, are you okay?!" I called

out as I ran after the creature. Now it was my turn to chase, but it wasn't paying attention to me. No, now it was hunting my little brother. That certainly gave me enough fuel to propel me back into the Music Room. The beast charged up the stairs after a small figure who slammed the door in its face. I quickly darted across the room as the creature banged on the door to the booth, and up the stairs on the other side. Ollie was holding the second door open for me even as the projector creature battered the first. I dove inside and closed it behind me.

"I need a chair," I said instantly, and together we pushed a chair to the door and up against it. Ollie had already put one against the other door and we each sat on the floor, barricading ourselves inside, leaning against the legs of our respective chairs.

"Are you okay?" I asked.

Ollie nodded. "It goes away; it gets frustrated. Just wait."

My turn to nod. Light flashed in the room as the projection creature looked through the slats in the wood. Then there was a sudden silence. The screaming died away. And we heard heavy footfalls heading down the stairs behind Ollie. Slow, steady, calm. Ollie scrambled up to peer over the edge of the window of the booth. "See, it's leaving." And he pointed.

I got up from my spot and hunched next to him just in time to see the creature saunter off, leaving just a light getting dimmer and dimmer down the hallway.

I was finally able to breathe again and I slipped back down to sit on the floor. Ollie slid down beside me. I turned to look at him. With the projector creature gone, the room was now lit by a dim bulb in the ceiling, but it was enough to see. And I couldn't believe what I was seeing. There was my little brother, but like me he was a three-dimensional drawing of himself. Even the hairs that always stood up at the back of his head were each individually articulated by a black outline. I reached out to touch him and, as I did, he flung himself at me, grabbing me tight and giving me one of his signature hugs.

I fell back and held him, leaning against the table. I could feel the tears flowing down my cheeks and wondered if maybe they too were outlined. They must be.

"You came for me!" he said, muffled in my blouse.

"Of course I did! Are you okay?" I asked. I pulled his head away and looked closely into those cartoon eyes of his, big and glistening.

"Yes, but I want to go home. Rose, can we go home?"

"Of course. I just need to find the way out, kiddo," I said, my heart in my throat. Somehow I had to rescue us. "I think we need to go back to the start," I said. I didn't know why, but the deeper I made my way into this world, the more I knew the only way out was the way in. Like climbing into a cave. But I had no idea how to get us back to Joey's office. "We can't go back the way we came."

Ollie nodded, still looking up at me. "There's a door on the other side of the room, but it's locked."

"Well, that's something. Maybe together we can break it down," I said. "Come on!" He wriggled out of my lap and extended a small hand to help me up. I smiled as he did. "Thank you. Now, let's keep as quiet as we can. We don't know if that thing is nearby."

"Okay," he said.

"Hey, thanks for saving me by the way," I said.

He grinned a toothy cartoon grin. "Well, thanks for coming to save me!"

"I guess it's what siblings do, huh?" I gave him a friendly little punch in the shoulder and he laughed. "Okay, let's go. Quietly. You have to lead the way."

He nodded, now all seriousness. Together we moved the chair away from the door and opened it as softly as we could. Then we tiptoed down the stairs carefully. Thank goodness for the music still playing on the record player because it felt like every step now had its own unique creak to it. When we reached the bottom, Ollie pointed to the right, and what I had once thought was a wall I saw actually had a wide gap in it behind several music stands and a desk piled high with sheet music. I followed him down a short, dark hallway. There was almost no light, and we came to a door.

I tried to open it, just to check, but sure enough it was locked. I took a moment and stared at it hard. "So we need something to break down the door with, I think," I whispered.

Just as I said it, suddenly the door flew open. Instinctively I pushed Ollie backward. "Run!" I managed to say it under my breath but only just and turned to follow my brother's retreat.

"Rose?"

I turned.

I was stunned silent, staring at the figure in front of me. Then I remembered Ollie. I called out over my shoulder, not turning around, not breaking eye contact. "Ollie! Stop, come back!" I had to add volume to it. I heard the pitter-patter of his feet stop and then start up again.

"I can't believe this."

"Archie, is that you?" I asked.

Ollie returned then and drew up beside me. "Who's that?" he asked.

There was a sudden metallic clang and that awful synthetic-sounding roar behind us. "Quick, follow me," said Archie. He held the door wide for both of us as we dove past him and through it.

He slammed the door shut and locked it. Then he paused, grabbed a heavy-looking desk, and shoved it in front, barricading it. Then he turned once again to me.

"How are you here?" asked Archie.

It was Archie, it had to be. He was a creature entirely made of black ink, covered head to toe much like the one that had grabbed me. But he wasn't dripping, he was very solid. And he wore real clothes, that trench coat and that fedora, even the sunglasses. Or as real as they could be in a cartoon world. It was the voice though, that English accent of his.

"The glasses that I told you about. Whatever Joey did with the machine this week, it's clearly bridged the divide. I'm at home, sitting in front of the television, but I'm also here. With you." It didn't make any sense to say it out loud. I hoped it was enough of an explanation for him.

"I'm so sorry," he said.

"How are *you* here? I thought you were . . . dead." I glanced at Ollie. I didn't like saying such things in front of him. He was standing close to my side, holding on to my hand tightly.

"I thought I was too. Still think I maybe am," he replied.

"Rose," said Ollie. His little voice shaking now. "Are we dead?"

"No, kiddo, no, we're not." I gave him a little smile before turning back to Archie. "This is the world you step into when you put on Joey's 3-D glasses," I explained. "Wherever we are, it is entirely man-made."

"Well, then," said Archie. Though he had no discernable face, I could tell he was feeling overwhelmed by everything.

"Do you remember what happened to you?" I asked. There was a sudden bang on the other side of the door, making me jump. The projection creature roared at us.

"Come on, I'll take you to the others," said Archie.

"The others?"

"Follow me," he said and started to make his way through the small room we were in and out the door on the other side, where we were met with another hallway.

"What others?" I asked, holding tight to Ollie's hand and following him.

"Others that look like you," he said, moving quickly. "I don't rightly remember much. I'm sorry, Rose. I remember the dark. And I remember the monster attacking me. Everything got very black and then there was a bright light and I woke up here. Suppose that's why I thought I was dead." He stopped and opened a door to our right, another small office-like room, which we made our way through to another hallway.

"I can tell you it felt like I was melting away. I felt like all the voices I was hearing got louder, and I was surrounded by all these different people. Not just in my head anymore."

"I wonder if it has to do with the ink . . ." I said.

"And then I was here. And that was all. That's all it's been for a very long time, miss. I can't keep track. How long has it been? Has it been months? Has it been years?" he asked.

"It's been a couple hours," I replied. I was out of breath and couldn't say it with the carefulness it deserved.

Archie looked back at me. At least that's what it seemed he was doing. With no face and a strange melted form, it was hard to tell. "How is that possible? I've lived so many lives already. Born and died and born again."

"I'm so sorry," I said.

We burst out of the hallway into a giant two-story room with a huge sign hanging from the ceiling that read "Heavenly Toys." Behind it flowed a waterfall of ink down from the ceiling into the floor.

"Oh, wow," said Ollie.

He wasn't wrong. We were surrounded by shelves with Bendy and Alice and Boris toys. With the Butcher Gang. All stuffed toys staring down at us. I was so distracted by it all that at first I didn't notice the small huddle of people sitting on boxes or on the floor off to the side under a Bendy poster that read "Hell Firefighter."

"Who are they?" I asked.

"I don't know. They was scared of me at first, but I think they trust me now."

"Wait," I said as I approached. They were in a kind of circle and I could hear a voice telling a story, like they were sitting around a campfire. A very familiar voice. "Oh no."

"Rose, what is it?" asked Ollie.

My throat felt dry and I couldn't swallow. "It's Joey."

31

Archie rushed over to the group, and Ollie and I came up quickly from behind to join him. "What are you doing?" he demanded in an angry whisper.

"He's talking to us," replied a little girl, younger than Ollie even. She was wearing a nightgown and her hair fell long and lank down her back.

"I said no noise. I mean it." Archie didn't sound angry, he sounded terrified.

I pushed my way into the circle and saw a tape recorder lying on the ground in the center. Archie quickly picked it up and hit the stop button but not before I heard, "This studio is my dream come to life!"

"Joey?" I said to myself.

The little girl looked up at me. "Is that his name?"

I didn't know what to say.

"Where did you find this?" asked Archie. He crouched in front of the little girl and I saw her recoil in horror. She pressed her lips together and wouldn't answer. "Tell me!" He spoke in whispers, but with such passion it felt like a yell.

"Hey, man, stop. You're scaring the kid." I turned and saw a teen boy, maybe my age or just a little younger. He was in jeans and a checkered button-up shirt. Who was he? Who were any of them? I looked at each of them. There was another teen boy in boxer shorts and a white undershirt, and a couple, elderly, both in bathrobes. The man wore small spectacles, the woman's hair was in curlers.

"Who are you people?" I asked softly.

Archie slowly stood and came over to me, carrying the tape recorder in his inky hand. "They say Joey Drew gave them all televisions and glasses. Like you, Rose."

Of course. Of course. The other test families. Why wouldn't they all be trapped down here too, just like Ollie? Just like I now was. I wondered, and I looked around furtively then: Was Joey Drew himself here as well?

No. I realized as soon as I turned to examine the cavernous room, that that was absurd. If there was one thing I knew about Joey, it was that he knew better than to find himself trapped anywhere, especially here.

I turned back to Archie and looked at the tape recorder. "What is that?"

"I don't know."

"Penny found it on one of the shelves," said the teen boy in the button-up shirt. He had stood and come over to us. He spoke quietly as well. "It's a recording of Joey Drew talking about the studio."

I nodded. "Why are you worried about the noise, Archie?" I asked.

Archie shook his head at me and I seemed to somehow

understand that he didn't want to say right now, in front of the boy.

"Hey, man, we have a right to know," said the boy. "I'm Mike by the way." He stuck out a hand and I took it. Handshakes didn't seem all that appealing to me anymore. In fact, they felt downright silly in the circumstances.

"I'm Rose."

"That's Danny, and the old folks, that's Simon and Angela."

They were all staring at us, still sitting in their little circle. They looked worn to the bone and absolutely terrified.

"Hi," I said. I felt a tug on my sleeve and I turned to Ollie. "And this is my brother, Ollie. So now we're all friends. Archie, tell us the truth. Why do we have to stay quiet?" I asked because I dreaded the answer. I asked because somehow I knew the answer already.

"Rose. You know why."

I nodded. "The monster."

There was a sudden loud click and my heart jumped into my throat. I looked down to see the play button on the recorder had been pressed. There was a whirring then as the wheels of the tape inside started to spin.

"Did you do that?" I asked Archie.

He shook his head no. He immediately pressed the stop button. The whirring ceased. We stared at the recorder, me, Archie, Ollie, and Mike. We just stared at it, waiting for something. Anything.

Click.

Whirr.

And we kept staring as the white noise filled the room.

And then a tinny and artificial sound, along with an all-too-familiar voice: "You're late!" said Joey Drew with a laugh. He was so loud his voice echoed in the room.

I couldn't breathe. I tried, but I just couldn't. What was happening? I glanced at Archie. He was staring so intently at the tape recorder I thought he might burn a hole through it.

There was more white noise of the whirring and then, "I said, you're late!"

"Rose, is he talking to us?" asked Ollie in a whisper just meant for me.

I could barely speak but I had to reassure him. "No, it's just a recording, that's all."

"Rose, I *am* talking to you. Where were you?" asked Joey Drew, his voice spilling from the tape recorder.

I gasped and took a step back. I looked over at the small group. They were all watching us closely. The old man, Simon, he gave me a little nod. Like he was giving me permission to do something. He wanted me to talk back, But I couldn't, I just couldn't.

"Are you Joey Drew?" asked Ollie, leaning close to the recorder and speaking into it.

"Well, well, well, this must be Oliver! It's a pleasure to meet you, young man."

I rushed to Ollie and grabbed him, pulling him away. "Don't," I told him. "Don't talk to him."

"Now, Rose, you don't have to be scared. It really is me. Your old pal. What do you think of my studio, Rose?"

I didn't know what to say. I didn't know what any of this meant. I wanted to scream and yell at him, I wanted to throw the tape recorder across the room and dash it to pieces. But I also didn't know what he wanted, and how much he controlled. And what he could do to us all trapped in here.

"It's quite something," I said, using everything within me to sound harmless as ever. That high calm voice. "But I must admit I'm a bit confused," I said. "You know I don't understand your incredible technology. How are we here?"

There was a pause and I worried I'd scared him off. But then:

"To be perfectly honest with you, Rose, I don't fully understand what happened myself, but I do know something: It's marvelous seeing the old studio again. After the first show I thought to myself, I wonder if I can wander. Turns out I can! But wandering can be a terrible sin, and who knows what dangers lurk in the inky world, as I call it, so I thought, maybe there's another way I can interact with the environment at a safe distance. As you can see, I found one."

"But you let *us* just wander around," I said. I was seething with anger now. Keeping my voice and expression calm was a challenge.

"Well, I wanted to see what would happen. I am a scientist after all!"

"And we're your lab rats," said Mike, his voice tinged with bitterness.

"You've always had a dark sense of humor, Michael," said Joey.

"How big is this place?" I asked.

"Well," replied Joey, sounding very thoughtful on the other side of the recorder, "I started creating more rooms as the show went on. Not nearly enough of course, just a few rooms here and there. But I think I'll be able to make it big enough."

I furrowed my eyebrows. "Big enough for what?" I asked.

"Why, the whole studio, Rose. We need to rebuild it of course!"

By now the others had stood to join us. I looked at them all. I could see their fear, tangible in their faces. I assumed mine was now as well. If Joey could see us all, he would know how scared we all were. He just didn't seem to care. "But . . . why . . ."

"I haven't decided why yet, what purpose this place can serve. It's got to have its uses. More than just my own personal nostalgia."

"Ain't no purpose but suffering," said Archie. His voice was low but filled with emotion.

"Archie, shh," I said. I reached out and placed a gentle hand on his arm to try to calm him.

There was another pause. Then, "So you know this creature, do you?"

"Archie isn't a creature, he's a man. A man destroyed by your ink." I didn't feel a need to keep up appearances anymore. What was the point? He so clearly didn't care what we felt. "This is what he became after your monster killed him."

Penny gasped and I looked to see Angela draw her in to her side protectively.

"How interesting. You know, I have seen the creatures down here, such unexpected things . . . I think they are related to the ink. I think they too exist across the divide. Just like us. Me, at home in my office, and you at home in your living room. In two places at once. I think it has something to do with the Ink Machine. I think the souls in it might have found two homes."

"What souls, Joey? What are you talking about?" I asked.

"The experiments," said Archie, his voice wavering. "They wanted our souls. As if that was a real thing they could take from us."

"Ah! You're the man Rose wanted me to meet. You're the one from Gent," said Joey. "What a mess they made of my work. You can't create new life out of nothing. Believe me, I tried. It went horribly wrong. You need a life for a life." I felt a cold wash over me.

"What did you do?" I asked quietly.

"Uh, Mister Drew," said Simon then. He bent down and spoke with his mouth almost touching the tape recorder.

"Yes, Simon?" Joey said.

"I think we'd like to get home now. The wife is getting very tired." He held out his hand for Angela, who took it in hers.

"Ah, well," said Joey. Then nothing. Just whirring silence.

"How do we get out of here, Joey?" I asked. My insides twisted. I feared his answer more than asking the question.

The pause continued. "Don't you like it here, Rose? Don't you like my studio?"

I shook my head no. My throat was so tight, I couldn't speak.

"How disappointing," he said.

So he could see me somehow. He was watching.

"Joey, please answer the question," I finally managed to say.

"No."

"Joey." My voice was louder now. Firm. "Tell us now. We want to go home."

"Why? Why on earth would you want that?" Joey's voice was becoming irritated. I could hear some of that unhinged quality he had when talking with the imaginary Henry. "What's so special about home? You want to go back to being a PA in an office building when you could live this fantastical existence?"

"Joey, it's dangerous in here. You are putting our lives at risk!"

"Nonsense!" He laughed loudly and brightly. "You can't get hurt in there! None of it's real, my girl; it's all an illusion!"

But I still felt the sharp pain in my back from the fall, I still could feel the sting where the ink creature had clawed at me in the puddle, so I knew this to be untrue. Or a bald-faced lie. Either Joey was ignorant or he was cruel. Or, most likely, he was simply both.

"Oh no, Mister Drew, you're wrong there, like, it's very real," said Archie, speaking up. He sounded stronger now, more sure of himself. "I'm not one of them. And yet I'm here. Whatever you've made, you need to be prouder of it, Mister Drew, because you've managed to create an entire new world." He was speaking quickly and with so much anger just bursting out of him. I didn't fault him for it for an instant. "Maybe we can't die in here like they do out there, but we can suffer. It's only been hours since I was in that basement of yours, but time has no meaning here. I've died over and over since then, been pulled into the inky puddles by creatures, killed by other strange monsters. Each time after? I'm back again, here, always back. And they come for me again and again. And I die again. And wake up again. The pain is real, the terror is real, the cycle is real. You're right, you don't need to fear dying, you need to fear waking up here over and over again."

There was a heavy silence after that. Even Joey seemed to be processing the horror of what Archie had just told us. Then he said, almost more to himself than to us, "Never dying. Just living the same experience over and over."

I closed my eyes. I didn't even want to consider such a nightmare.

"A limbo. A perpetual loop. What an interesting idea," Joey said again to himself. Thoughtfully. Carefully.

I opened my eyes suddenly, feeling a white-hot rage. No, absolutely not, this wasn't a time for contemplation or philosophical conversations.

"Enough, we're all getting out of here. We're getting out of here now!" I announced loudly to the group.

As if on cue something roared. Something very familiar, something I had only just left behind in the dark in the basement of Kismet. It was off in the distance somewhere, but I knew the sound. I knew it so well. I turned to look around the room, searching for it. Archie did too.

"No," I said. "Not that."

"Oh my, Rose," said Joey, casually. "I think you woke the beast."

"We need to get out of here," I said to the others. I could see the terror in their eyes.

"Yes, we need to go now!" insisted Archie. I grabbed Ollie's hand.

"Good luck," said Joey with a laugh.

I couldn't stand it anymore. Why were we just listening to this evil man talk at us? I grabbed the recorder from Archie's grasp and threw it as hard as I could across the room. It crashed against the floor into a thousand pieces, the echo careening around the cavernous space.

Suddenly the roar was right above us and we all looked up. The monster from the basement had burst through the waterfall. I could see him this time, fully realized. He was Bendy. But not Bendy of course, not the little cartoon, but a stretched-out monstrous version with no eyes and a grin full of malicious teeth.

Angela screamed. So did Penny beside her. We were huddled all together as the light began to dim and the monster thrashed about in the falling ink as if it was disturbed by its presence.

"We have to go, now!" I cried out. "We have to get back to Joey's office!" It was the only plan I had, and since Joey hadn't seemed to have had a better one . . .

"I'll take you back," said Archie.

"Let's go!"

We ran for it with Archie leading the way, my heart pounding wildly in my chest. We ran back along the hallway and through the empty offices, the dark encroaching upon us. We made it to the door, and together Archie and I pulled the desk barricading it and flew into the Music Room with the others close at our heels.

They weren't the only ones.

There was a massive roar from behind and the light in the room all but vanished. I could barely see around me. I squeezed Ollie's hand tight.

"Archie! Can you see?" I called out into the darkness.

"Rose, I'm over here!" I could hear his voice but I felt turned around. I had no idea where he was, and the wails of the creature made it impossible to hear where Archie's voice was coming from.

There was a scream from behind. It was Simon, crying out in pain.

I couldn't see anything! I couldn't find the way!

There was a sudden burst of light that blinded me and a mechanical roar that seared me right to my core. But I felt a strange hopefulness then. I could see shadows in the room as the light focused its gaze not on me, not on any of our group, but up and behind us.

I looked over my shoulder and saw glinting teeth gnashing at the air, and then the light attacked the beast, launching itself at it.

It was the projector creature. It was fighting the monster, they were fighting each other. The light flashed in all directions as they twisted and turned, tearing at each other. It was enough for me to see the exit.

"Follow me!" I cried out over the sounds of battle happening around us. "Can you see the exit?"

"Go, Rose, we're behind you," said Danny.

I flew out of the Music Room, holding Ollie's hand tight. The space was dimly lit but so much better than the flashing lights or the pitch dark. I stopped to hold the door for everyone else as they ran right for it. One, two, three, four, five, six. They were all here. They had all made it. Simon was limping and being helped by Mike. But they were all here.

Archie slammed the door shut and the silence was all-encompassing. The light got a little brighter and I could see better now. And I was reminded suddenly of where we were.

We were back on that strange platform: a wooden floor, a single door, and darkness as far as the eye could see otherwise.

I looked above us, into the inky void.

How on earth would we manage to get back up there?

32

We had come so far but we were now standing in the spot where I had landed on my back. Just the thought of it reminded me of the pain, and I felt it again, searing through my body. I continued to stare up. And slowly my eyes adjusted to something. Far up above us I could see a platform. That was the way out.

"I don't know what to do," I said. From hope to utter defeat. This was it. This was where it all ended.

"This can't be it," said Mike. "There must be another way."

"This is it. This is the only way back to his office," replied Archie. The weight of that fact weighed heavy on all of us.

"What is wrong with the sort of mind that could invent a place like this?" said Angela. She spoke so quietly and so sadly. Simon went to her and held her close.

I thought about that for a moment. "Wait, the mind. This is all in the mind, isn't it?" I said. I had an absurd notion. But it just might work. "None of this is real. The floor we're standing on. The space around us. We can't seem to leave this reality without following certain rules. But what about altering it? Something small and simple . . ." I thought some more. I thought of the train, the wind I had felt in my hair. It had all been real in that moment. So why couldn't this be?

I looked at Ollie. "Do you want to try to walk on air with me?"

He nodded, he understood. "This time for real."

I couldn't say if it was real or not, that wasn't the point. I just nodded and looked up at the platform high in the distance. The darkness around us pooled like ink, and I could hear the battle raging still in the Music Department. I had no idea how much time we had left before one or both came after us.

I raised my foot as if I was going to walk up stairs. It landed hard, like a stomp, on the floor.

"Let me do it," said Ollie. "If I can show you, then you'll believe. And they'll all believe."

I looked back at our little ragtag group. They looked so scared and lost.

"Do it," I said.

Ollie closed his eyes. He was so still, so calm. I didn't rush him. I just watched, hopeful and terrified.

With his eyes still closed he raised his foot as I had done and took a step up. He didn't stomp down, he didn't fall. He stood on one foot in the dark, in the air. And then placed the other foot at its side.

"Is it working?" he asked, eyes still closed.

"Yes, yes, it is," I replied, trying not to sound too excited, trying to stay calm so that Ollie would stay calm.

He took another step, and another, and he walked with more confidence higher and higher up the invisible staircase. I held my breath, and my arms floated forward, ready to catch him if he fell. *Oh, please don't fall, Ollie, please don't fall.* He kept going, steady and true and then, just like that, he was at the top on the other platform. "You're there!" I called out. "Just take a step forward."

He followed my instructions and did it.

"You can open your eyes now!" I shouted.

He did. He looked down at me, far below him. He was so tiny up there. And yet he had never seemed as large. I was so proud.

"I'll help you now. You should close your eyes too!" he called out.

"Okay!"

I did so. I tried to steady my nerves and calm my breathing. I tried to visualize stairs. I knew I could do it. I had seen a ghost train and Bendy in the real world after all. I could see stairs in my own imagination. Somehow that thought gave me a confidence I needed and I could see our staircase from home now. Just the staircase surrounded by a black void. It floated there, welcoming me. Taking me upstairs to my room, and Ollie's room, and warmth and safety.

I raised my foot.

I took a step.

And I stepped into the sky.

I couldn't celebrate. I had to just keep going or I would lose the vision. I took another step and another. I extended my hand to grab the banister and felt the cool surface in my grip. It was so real. Because it was real. Right now everything and anything was real.

"You can take a step forward now." Ollie's voice, suddenly so close to me. It was a surprise. I took one more step and then opened my eyes. There he was and there I was up on the platform. "It worked!" said Ollie, beaming.

"It really did." I was stunned and oh so relieved. I was out of breath, like I had just raced a marathon, but I had done it. I had done it.

It was time for the others to join us, and one by one they did it too. Archie was first, running as if it was nothing for him. Penny was carried on Mike's shoulders, and Simon and Angela came up hand in hand. Danny cheered them on. And then he attempted to sprint, tumbling down to the ground in his excitement. He had to take four tries before he finally calmed himself enough to make the journey.

And then we were all together again.

We all took a moment, just to breathe. Just to live in the moment of what we'd all just done. I could tell they were all exhausted. The act of pretend had taken a great deal out of all of us. But we couldn't stop to rest. I didn't know if the monster would come back. Worse, I didn't know if Joey would do something. Was he watching us now? Was he laughing at us? Was he angry that we'd climbed the air? Maybe he wasn't paying any attention to us at all. Because we were nothing to him. There was no way to know. All we could do was get out of here as quickly as possible.

I turned to Archie. "Let's go."

I knew what was coming next. I knew the deep puddle with the creatures in it was waiting for us. One last test, it felt like, before we could go home. Before I hoped we could go home.

The vast black pool stretched out before us. It was still and quiet. But I knew what lurked in its depths.

"Maybe it's gone," said Penny, speaking what we were all thinking.

"No," replied Archie.

"Maybe we can climb over. Like the void," suggested Angela. She sounded so tired and frail.

"It's a possibility," I said. But I doubted myself. With all the strength and energy the stairs had taken, I wasn't sure I could do it again. I was pretty certain she wouldn't be able to at all.

"No, too big a risk," said Archie. "What happens if you're halfway across and can't hold it. No. There's an easy solution. We need a distraction." He took a step forward and I suddenly knew exactly what he was going to do. I grabbed his shoulder.

"I can't let you do this, not again," I said quietly, just to him, just for him to hear.

"Oh love, it's not the end, remember that. It's never the end for me. I'd never wish this on anyone, even my worst enemy. But this is my existence now. And it's a small sacrifice. I'll wake up again. Have no fear."

But I did. I had all the fear. "I don't want you to hurt."

"I'll be alright. Just you get yourselves out of this mess, promise me that," he said.

I didn't want to promise because I didn't want him to do it.

"Promise me, Rose."

I nodded. "I promise."

I let my hand slip from his shoulder as he stepped up to the edge. He turned and looked back at us. "When I go in, you run as quick as you can through this muck, got it?"

We all got it.

"Well, you all take care. I hope we never meet again," he said. Then he stepped into the blackness and waded into its middle.

I bit the inside of my cheeks and squeezed Ollie's hand hard.

The ink started to churn around Archie's legs, then suddenly arms burst out of the blackness and grabbed hold of him. He screamed out as more and more arms reached out, grabbing him, pulling him down into the puddle. They piled on top of him more and more until he sank under the surface, his scream silenced by the ooze.

"Now!" I ordered. While the ink was still churning and while the creatures were still occupied, I charged with Ollie into the puddle and kept my eye on the far side. I heard splashing behind me as everyone joined us and we pushed forward through the sticky thick liquid. A hand grazed against my ankle and I stomped down on it hard. I wasn't going to give them an inch, not one inch.

Ollie and I jumped for the other side and climbed into the light, quickly turning to help the others and they in turn doing the same. Simon and Angela were the last of them, the slowest moving, and we all offered our hands, extending them out over the black. A figure rose from behind them, an inky black creature reaching out for them just as we were doing the same.

"No!" Mike charged back out into the puddle. He grabbed both Simon and Angela and pulled them back toward us even as he launched himself at the creature. He attacked it, yelling loudly as he did. They twisted and turned together in the ink as Simon and Angela made it to us and climbed out of the ooze. Mike thrashed against the creature, wrestling it to the ground. Into the puddle. It grabbed him in a tight squeeze and pulled him down with it. They fell under and into the black ink.

And then he was gone.

Just like that.

Gone.

A victim of the puddles.

"Rose, we have to keep going," said Ollie, tugging on my hand.

I stared at the now still, calm black. I had failed Mike and my heart sank. I could hear Angela softly crying behind me.

"We have to keep going," said Ollie again. I looked down at him. He seemed somehow wan and pale even in his cartoon form. I remembered why I was here. I couldn't fail Ollie too.

I reached out and took his outstretched hand. It was time to go home.

And we made our way back to the beginning.

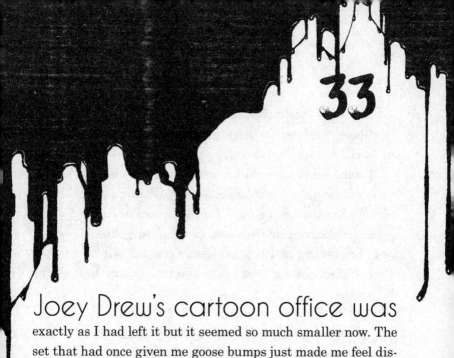

33

Joey Drew's cartoon office was exactly as I had left it but it seemed so much smaller now. The set that had once given me goose bumps just made me feel disgust. I hated everything about it.

"What should we do now?" asked Danny, his voice shaking.

"I don't know," I said, because I didn't. "I think try to take off the glasses?" It felt stupid and obvious. But what did I really know? I didn't even know if taking us all this way, if sacrificing Archie and Mike, if any of it had actually been worth it.

But Danny, who evidently just did things without thinking too hard about them, shrugged at the suggestion and reached his hands up to his face to touch something that wasn't there.

And then he was gone.

He had just disappeared. Not even a puff of smoke or anything.

"Did he do it? Did it work?" asked Simon.

"I think . . . I think yes. It did," I said. I was stunned.

Simon turned to his wife and reached out his hand for hers. They linked fingers and together, watching each other, slowly reached up in unison to their faces. Then they too were gone. I turned to Penny.

"Do you know what to do?" I asked her.

She nodded but still I held her hand and guided it up to her face. When she touched it, she smiled at me and she made a little fist, grabbing the air by her ear.

Poof. Just like that.

Then all that was left was me and Ollie.

Ollie reached up to his face and then brought his hand slowly down again. "I'm not wearing the glasses."

I realized he was right. Of course he was right. He wasn't wearing his glasses, I was.

He had this look on his face. It was sad but also brave. He looked determined. "It's okay, Rose. I'll find Archie. I'll make sure I'm not alone. I did okay by myself anyway before you showed up."

"No, no, don't you dare. Don't you dare give up, not now at the end. Your imagination is brighter than all of ours. You got us up the void, you can do this," I said, crouching in front of him and holding both his hands in mine.

He nodded.

"Ollie, I need you to close your eyes again. I need you to imagine you're back in our living room. Can you do that?" I had no idea if it would work but I had to try.

"Yes, Rose," he replied. He didn't sound too sure.

"Listen to me, Ollie. You can do this. You already have done this. Do you trust me?"

He looked at me and then nodded slowly. I saw the confidence grow in his face. "I do, I always trust you, Rose."

"Then trust me now, you can do this."

Ollie nodded. He looked determined. He was ready.

"Do it. Do it now," I told him.

He nodded.

He closed his eyes.

"Can you picture the living room?"

"I can," he said quietly.

"Can you feel the rug under you?"

Ollie nodded. "I can hear Father," he said softly.

"What?" That surprised me.

"He's telling me it'll be okay. He's telling me that my mind is stronger than my fear."

"Good." I couldn't hold back the tears anymore. I didn't know if it was true or not, I didn't know if he was actually hearing Father or imagining it, but something inside me told me it was real.

"Now imagine opening your eyes and seeing Father," I said, the voice catching in my throat. Ollie nodded and I stared at him, not sure what I was expecting or what I needed to see. I just stared so hard I didn't dare even blink.

And then he vanished. Just like that. He was there and then he was gone. I felt tears well in my eyes. I wasn't sad, it was pure joy and relief. I knew it. I just knew it. He was home.

I reached up now and felt my own face. I could feel the shape of the glasses again. I was almost there. It was time to finally go.

"Hey, Joey!" I called out. I didn't know if he could hear me; it wasn't about him anyway. "I quit."

And I pulled off my glasses.

I felt two sets of hands on my back as I collapsed onto the

floor. Father and Ollie slowed my fall and I lay there staring up at my own living room ceiling. A very real, very not-at-all-cartoonish living room ceiling.

"Rose, can you hear me?" asked Father, appearing in my line of vision.

"Yes, Father, I can." The tears were streaming down the sides of my cheeks toward the carpet.

"Oh, thank heavens." I could see the tears in his eyes too, but I didn't fear them. He was crying from relief. Just like I was.

I tried to push myself up to sitting but suddenly I was attacked by a little demon. Ollie. He threw himself on me and I was back on the ground, holding him tight in my arms.

"You're awake," I said into his hair.

"So are you!" he said.

"Don't you dare ever leave me like that again," I said.

"Never ever!"

"Ollie, be careful!" said Father, placing a hand on his back. "You both need to take it easy." I looked at him over Ollie's shoulder and nodded, releasing my little brother.

Ollie clambered off me as I lay there on the floor. I could feel every muscle in my body relaxing. I remembered then the glasses in my hand. I held them up above my head and I bent them hard, and harder still, until they broke in two and fell in pieces to the floor.

I closed my eyes and felt the carpet against my skin, smelled the familiar scent of my house. Heard a car trundle over that pothole in the street. My home. My senses. My reality.

Ollie took me by the hand and I smiled. I turned my head to look at him and opened my eyes.

Bendy smiled back.

ACKNOWLEDGMENTS

I want to thank my agent, Jess Regel, and my editor, Lori Wieczorek, along with everyone else at AFK Scholastic, for all the amazing help and support with this book. I also have to thank my parents who are always there for me (go Team Kress) and my guys: my husband, Scott, and my cat, Atticus, for being awesome. And of course the Meatly and Bookpast for allowing me to play in their world in the first place. I will always be so grateful for the opportunities you have given me!

Lastly, but certainly not least-ly, to all the Bendy fans who have been utterly amazing. I absolutely could not do this without you!

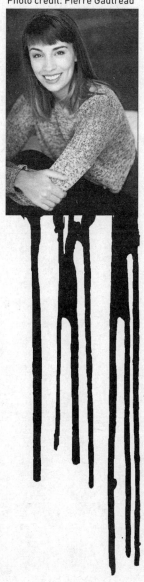

ADRiENNE KRESS is a Toronto-born actor and writer. Her books include the award-winning and internationally published novels *Alex and the Ironic Gentleman, Timothy and the Dragon's Gate,* and *Hatter Madigan: Ghost in the H.A.T.B.O.X.* (with bestselling author Frank Beddor), as well as Steampunk novel *The Friday Society* and the gothic *Outcast*. She is also the author of the quirky three-book series The Explorers.

Bendy and the Ink Machine: Dreams Come to Life was Adrienne's first foray into writing horror, but as an actor she has had the pleasure of being creepy in such horror films as *Devil's Mile* and *Wolves*. And she took great pleasure in getting to haunt teenagers in SyFy's *Neverknock*.

Find her at AdrienneKress.com.

Twitter/Instagram: @AdrienneKress